Unbound

R. C. Butler

Bulldog Press
Red Deer, AB

Copyright © 2015 by R. C. Butler
www.bulldogpress.ga
First Printing, 2015

Warning: This book contains graphic sexual material and is not intended for anyone present at the author's birth.

Published by:

Bulldog Press
Red Deer, AB

ISBN-13: 978-0-9879958-7-2
ISBN-10: 0-9879958-7-1

Submissive:: (n) /sub-mis-iv/:   One who finds empowerment through yielding to another.

"A submissive trusts that the dominant is out only to please them, to protect and care for them. They give themselves fully with the knowledge that doing so is not for the dominant's benefit but for their own."

Prologue

*T*he preparation, while half the fun, was now complete. It was time for the job to begin. Entering the hotel bar, a soft suede sports coat slung over his shoulder, Sebastian paused and leaned against the doorway to take in the room. It was a classy establishment with all the perks expected in a five-star resort destination. Dim lights shone down from the glacial chandeliers, casting a shimmer across the dark mahogany bar. The patrons? High-class executives sipping scotch and martinis. He let his gaze scan the crowd and settle on his prey. A stunning woman seated at the bar with a highball in hand. Her elegant black dress cascading off her shoulders in a deep v, showing just the right amount of cleavage for the status of the room.

Her demure eyes glanced his way, passing over him, recognition and interest not evident in the least. Her attention, instead, was captivated by the sleazy businessman in the thousand dollar suit seated next to her. Sebastian could hear the whispered giggles as he slid up to the bar. She shifted her back to him as if he barely existed.

He should have been angry, hurt, but instead he smiled

to himself. They'd played this game before and he knew the rules. He knew the tease and how much his effort would be rewarded. Ordering a gin and tonic, he relaxed, listening to the soft conversation.

The 'suit' was trying hard, complimenting her, flirting and attempting to be witty and charming. His attempts were rewarded but he suspected her attention was not entirely personal. An amazing woman such as her, dressed to the nines and relaxing, alone, in this locale? He was certain her company was going to cost him and, while he was more than willing to pay, he was unsure how to broach the subject. His eyes searched for the answer, for a way in.

"Such a good night, I'm glad I chose to start my evening here. It makes the job so much more enjoyable," she whispered and he saw his opening.

"The job, and just how well does it pay?" he asked coyly.

She smiled sheepishly, extending the act for both men's benefit. "Depends on how 'hard' the work is but I usually clear about three grand." She winked and the 'suit's' face tightened, trying to hide an involuntary reaction to the number while maintaining his calm composure.

"It just so happens I'm looking for an employee and that number fits the budget well," he responded.

"Sounds promising, let's finish these drinks and get to the contract, baby," she giggled, her eyes screaming out with passion and lust.

The 'suit' reached for her hand and Sebastian realized it was his turn, his move in their game. Reaching out he slid a hand gently up her forearm from behind and the 'suit's' eyes snapped to him in surprise. She put on a show of mock irritation but they could all sense her arousal growing.

The 'suit's' anger flared but before he could react Sebastian leaned in between the two of them, whispering softly.

"Sir, I'm sure you do not wish to make a scene. I happen to be a 'vice' detective," He gestured coyly to the badge strapped to his belt, "and while your exchange was fun to watch, I am afraid I can't let it slide. The hotel management has asked us to clean things up, so to speak. Now, I suggest you smile, pay for the lady's drink and make your way to the exit before things get embarrassing."

The 'suit's' eyes grew with anger and fear as he tossed a few bills on the bar and quickly retreated. Sebastian grasped the lady's wrist and walked her out of the lounge and into the lobby. Her eyes danced, not of fear but excitement as she tried to hide her smile. Entering the lobby, he slid her arms behind her back and quickly snapped on a pair of service issue cuffs. The tight metal grasped her wrists and lust flared in her eyes.

"Officer, surely there is some way we can work this out," she whisper breathlessly.

"Really?" he asked, unimpressed. "Do you honestly think you can flirt your way out, my dear? No, you are a whore. Perhaps a high class whore, working the rich and immoral, but a whore none the less and you need to be punished." Sebastian's voice was firm and commanding, it's what she needed, what she wanted.

"Please, I can't be arrested, my husband would never understand. There must be something else I can do, some other way I can make restitution. I'll do anything." Her begging had certainly improved since last they played. A tear slid down her cheek. He was impressed that she could get there with her arousal and passion fighting to push out all other emotions.

"Oh, you will be punished whore and you will feel the

pain of retribution." He grabbed her arms, leading her towards the front doors. Her eyes dropped in fear but lit up instantly as they turned, quickly, into an elevator heading up. An elderly lady scrambled off the lift, giving them a glaringly judgmental stare.

"Police business, ma'am," Sebastian nearly snickered as he passed the woman and the elevator doors slid shut.

The elevator, now empty, was lined with mirrored glass and he could see her lust filled eyes staring him down in the reflection. He pressed the button for the top floor and the motors went to work, beginning their ascent. As they passed the second floor Sebastian quickly hit the emergency stop button, turning the woman to the wall and shoving her forward. He kicked her legs apart slightly and began to run his hands down her shoulders, around the sides of her chest and across her firm stomach. He felt her body respond, the goose-bumps forming as her heart-rate soared.

"I'm not about to leave myself in a position of vulnerability. Do you have anything concealed on you, whore?" he whispered, his hot breath caressing her neck while his hands slowly passed over her firm breasts. Her nipples tightened, straining in the confines of the soft fabric. With a smile, he pinched them lightly and watched the arousal flood her face. She struggled to maintain her composure, her breath coming in soft gasps as his body pressed against her, his hard cock just inches below the reach of her cuffed hands.

Sebastian bent to his knees and ran his hands over her hips, across her ass and slowly down the soft skin of her outer legs. Crossing his hands, he began to run them up the inside of her calves, past her knees, beneath her dress and up her inner thighs. She quivered and he could feel the moistness of her pussy emanating as he grew ever closer to the prize. Her lust was overpowering and he could see that it had taken over. He'd done as intended and took pride in the result. Standing quickly, he pulled her off the wall by her cuffed wrists, pressed the emergency stop once again to resume their ride, and smiled coyly.

"It appears you're clean, nothing concealed and nowhere to do so, but I'll do a more thorough search in a moment," his voice commanding and confident.

The shock of the abrupt stop left her in a state of confusion, her mind a mess. For a moment she forgot her part and dropped her guard.

"But... I thought... why did you...?" she stammered.

"Why did I what? Not trust you? Do my job? Listen, you don't question what I do. You simply obey, you do as you're told and you respond how and when I tell you to. Otherwise, we will deal with your punishment in a more formal setting." The tone of his voice snapped her back into her role, her eyes steeling over. The lust and passion not forgotten, but buried behind the persona she had taken on.

"Do you understand me?"

She shifted her gaze to the floor showing pure submission and Sebastian's heart fluttered. He knew what was coming and he knew he was powerless to stop it. It happened in every game.

"Yes, Sir," she whispered and his entire body flushed with passion. She owned him. The power shift was obvious. Two simple words and he was hers.

The elevator stopped abruptly and he struggled to regain his role. Grasping the back of her neck lightly, he pulled her into the hall. She smiled, knowing she had just taken him to a new high. Sebastian let the smirk slide, for now. Instead, pulling open the door to room 1422, he matched the smile and walked her through the threshold.

"Time for your punishment, my little whore. I hope you are prepared."

Her body tightened as they entered the room, not from fear so much as surprise at its transformation. She had not expected the room to be cleared of its mundane hotel furnishings nor was she prepared for the play room he had concocted in its place. The blackout shades were drawn, the lights dim with a fleck of candlelight shimmering across the walls. The hotel bed had been removed and in its place sat a large king+ four-poster adorned with her personal restraints. Beneath the window was a long, narrow oak table with a selection of plugs, gags, cuffs and crops laid out meticulously. Hanging in the center of the bed, suspended from the ceiling by a series of pulleys and nylon ropes, was a leather bodice style harness. Her lips curled into a slight smile but catching his stern gaze she averted her eyes back to the floor, biting her lower lip and knowing exactly what the look of submission would do to him.

Sebastian fought to contain his composure but the lust was taking over. He knew what she needed and his entire being was pushing him to give it to her. Knowing that the game still needed to be played did little to control his impulses. She giggled softly and he realized she had done this on purpose. Her ace in the hole.

"What's so funny whore? Are you amused by my play-room. I dare you to laugh again!"

Her face flushed, the mischief draining away as his stern voice echoed throughout the room. He reached behind her and snapped the metal cuffs free, rubbing her wrists gently to help reduce the sting left behind.

"Time for your strip search, lose the clothing, NOW!"

She slowly removed her dress, mocking a look of panic and embarrassment.

"Oh, don't even pretend, slut. Modesty doesn't suit you."

The black fabric fell to her ankles and his blood began to boil, admiring her form in nothing but black stockings, a silk garter and four-inch stilettos. Her body, beautiful and begging to be taken. He stammered momentarily, catching his breath.

"Open your mouth!"

She followed the order and he gently rubbed a finger around her soft lips and across her tongue. The tenderness and passion of the moment lost on neither of them.

"Nothing hidden there," he commented, "but there are other places of concealment, aren't there, baby? Kneel on the bed facing the wall. I need to know if you're hiding anything."

"You'd better search deep," she whispered, breathlessly. "You can't be too careful, can you?"

Without hesitation she assumed the position, she played the game well but knew his orders were to be followed. She knew the pleasure it gave him. He ran a finger gently across the smooth lips of her pussy. She couldn't hide the moistness, the want, the need. Inserting it gently, mocking a search, he felt her body respond. Every nerve in overdrive. Every other thought pushed away as lust took over. She clenched against his finger as he slid it deeper and gasped when he abruptly removed it leaving her void and yearning.

"Nothing there either, but I do believe you are enjoying the search just a bit too much my little whore. I'm positive a high class lady such as yourself would not be out propositioning without some form of protection. I suppose there is only one more place to check."

Instinctively and without order she reached back and spread herself wide for him. Her heart raced, her body tingled and she waited in anticipation. He pulled a bottle of lube from the oak table, placed a small amount in his hand and warmed it seductively with his breath. Her body flushed in anticipation as he gently circled her ass with the warm lube and began to slide a finger inside. She clenched only momentarily before relaxing and savoring the feeling.

"Interesting. You appear to have nothing concealed but just to be safe let's make sure that anything you have hidden stays that way"

Sebastian pulled a two-inch, glass anal plug from the table, coated it in lube and gently coaxed it inside her, watching her shiver as her body accepted it.

"Beautiful! A whore should never be without her jewelry. Oh, but it appears I have forgotten some."

He picked up two emerald encrusted nipple clamps and walked beside the bed for better access to her beautiful tits.

"If you move you will be restrained, if you so much as moan you will be gagged. Do you understand me, my whore?"

"Yes, sir."

He shuddered at the response before reaching down and gently applying the clamps to her swollen nipples. She flinched and let out a soft "ooooh" in response.

He nearly laughed, knowing she was playing him, knowing how much she enjoyed the clamps and how easy it was for her to take them.

"Sorry sir, please don't restrain and gag me," she whispered innocently.

What could he do? She played his own words against him, and, as much as he wanted to prolong the game, the anticipation, he knew what she need. She had forced his hand and, as with all things, he was powerless to resist. Reaching up, he pulled her arms out, spread-eagle, towards the bedposts. He could see her smiling, knowing that she had won this round and bent him to her will. He slid the suede cuffs around her wrists, the softness of the material tender yet perfect as the ropes were pulled tight, stretching her arms just enough to make her feel helpless and happy.

Sebastian grabbed a black riding crop from the table and positioned himself at her side, gently caressing her exposed ass with the soft luxurious leather.

"We will forgo the gag for a moment. Time for your payment, my dear, how many do you think you deserve for your transgressions this evening?"

She paused as if thinking. "Umm... five, sir?" It was not a question, despite the tone.

His blood tingled as he raised the crop, watching her body relax in eager anticipation. The leather stung slightly as it connected with her flesh and a soft moan of pleasure escaped her lips. She was lost in the moment. The role she'd been playing, behind her. The game, forgotten as her body reacted on pure instinct.

Her lust grew with each stroke, the juices running softly down her legs, her mind a mixture of pleasure of the pain.

On the fifth stroke her body bucked and thrashed in a long, deep orgasm bringing a tight smile to Sebastian's face.

"Please, I need you, sir."

He required no further encouragement as he knelt in front of her restrained body and watched her luscious lips slide around his engorged cock. Her mouth, so soft and wet, slid across his length. The image sent him to new heights.

Sebastian could feel his cock pulsing, begging for more as she slowly devoured him. Reaching back, he quickly removed the cuffs from the ropes they were attached to, slid her wrists behind her back and fastened them together. He pulled the leather harness from above her and strapped it across her chest and shoulders for support while she worked him deeper into her throat. He was building towards a powerful orgasm but wanted more, needed more.

He pulled himself from her mouth and rolled beneath her, pulling a rope attached to the harness to lift her chest and balance her above him. She adjusted off her knees, squatting above his hard cock and slowly lowered herself onto him. He couldn't help but moan as her pussy encased him. The sight one of dreams, cuffed and harnessed for balance, she rode him, her beautiful tits bouncing with every stroke.

Her body begged for release as he reached up and pulled lightly on the nipple clamps. Her mind, so in the throes of passion, interpreted the pain as pleasure, tossing her over the edge into a long hard climax. She collapsed on top of him, taking him deep.

Her face filled with lust and satisfaction, her gorgeous body convulsing and sending him over the edge. He came hard, relief and pleasure pulsing through his body. They laid there, unable to move, for what felt like an eternity and only a second all in one. He gently removed her cuffs and harness, slid her down beside him on the black satin sheets and pulled her close. Holding her, caressing her hair and tracing soft kisses across her neck.

"So perfect," he whispered.

"Yes, it was. Thank you for setting this up. I needed it."

Chapter One

A cell phone chirped, indicating an incoming message and stirring Ell Frost from her slumber. Her mind was foggy. She reeled for a second, unsure of her location, before the events of the previous night came rushing back. The hotel bar, the elevator and of course the improvised playroom she had awoken in. She could feel Sebastian's strong arms still wrapped around her, holding her close. She'd never experienced a feeling as safe and satisfying as waking in his arms. How she wished it could always be that way. A ping of regret crept up before she could raise her guard, knowing it could never be.

The cell phone chirped again and Ell glanced around the room in search of the source. She knew it was hers as Sebastian refused to turn his on when they were together. A professional courtesy, perhaps, but she found it romantic.

She arrived the night before with nothing, but Sebastian always took care of the details, it was one of the things she enjoyed about him. She knew he would not forget anything she needed. Rolling to her back to help in her survey of the room, she felt him shift and begin to wake.

"It's in the top dresser drawer along with your clothes for the day," he murmured peacefully, in a state of near sleep.

Ell gave him a soft, gentle kiss and extracted herself from his arms. She strolled across the room, her naked, toned body just visible in the low light. She could feel his eyes on her, making her shiver as she pulled open the drawer and grabbed her iPhone. 'Fully charged', she thought, why was she not surprised?

There were three texts, each more urgent than the last and all of them from her partner Enrique Shaw.

"Shit," she mumbled, "Looks like Rique's got a live one. I've got to get dressed and hit the station or I'll never hear the end of it."

"Do what you need, Ellison, I'll take care of this," he said, circling a finger around the room. She smiled at the use of her full name, only Sebastian used it.

She flopped down on the bed again, her auburn hair flowing around her face, encasing her beautiful smile. "Thanks again for last night. You have no idea how much I needed a little stress relief. Things have been too hectic lately."

He smiled up at her, pulling her down into a long deep kiss. "You know I'm here for you. Always."

'If only that were true,' she thought but quickly brushed it off. "Thanks," she said, slipping into her jeans and button down grey dress shirt. She circled the bed and grabbed the police shield from his belt, securing it to her own. "I'm probably going to need this," she laughed, bringing a smile to his face.

"A little bit ironic, but so much fun," he responded.

Grabbing her purse she pulled out two hundred in cash and laid it on the oak table on top of the black leather crop. 'So worth it,' she thought with a sly grin.

"A little something extra," she winked.

He frowned up at her, "Ellison, don't. You know the agency takes care of that."

She leaned in for one last kiss before heading for the door, whispering, "But it was worth so much more."

Without glancing back, she strode from the room, a renewed confidence in her gate as she put the evening behind her and summoned up the cold, dispassionate persona of Lieutenant Ell Frost. She knew the persona was a falsehood but it was a required one when dealing with the stress of the job.

Exiting the elevator on the main floor, she headed for the concierge desk before noticing her Mercedes S550 conveniently situated at the front doors, a valet ready to hand her the keys. Smiling, she shook her head knowing Sebastian had taken the liberty of calling down as soon as she left the room. What she wouldn't give to have a man like that in her life. If only things were different.

She flipped the valet a twenty, grabbed her keys and settled into the soft leather driver's seat. The S550 wasn't exactly department issue, but it was reliable, comfortable and so sexy. Ell couldn't resist it. Activating the Bluetooth link, she made a quick call to her partner as she pulled out of the parking lot, the purr of the engine barely noticeable in the background.

"About time, LT. Out on a hot date or something?" barked Rique as the call connected. *If only he knew.*

"Yeah, and your dad says hi," she smirked in return.

"Like he could land a fine piece like you," laughed her partner in retort.

"So what's the emergency, Rique? And it better be good, I'm supposed to be on the first eight hours of a seventy-two hour leave."

"Yeah, but you know how much we miss that pretty face. Place just ain't the same without it, LT."

Ell smiled and rolled her eyes. "Less sucking up and more information, Shaw."

"Not much information to give, I'm on my way to midtown on a possible one-eight-seven. Dispatch came down straight from the Commander which means the mayor's pulling strings again and the vic's either a VIP or a known associate. Either way, it's high profile, which means I have to call in the big guns. Can't let us lowly detectives handle the important ones on our own."

"Well, don't I feel special," she replied with mock enthusiasm. "Text me the location and make sure the scene's still fresh when I get there."

She disconnected abruptly, pulled up her messages on the window display and up shifted as she merged onto the freeway. From fun and fantasy to death and decay in less than ten minutes, and she thought the S550 moved quick!

Running a search on her way, Ell discovered that the penthouse apartment belonged to Ms. Deedrie Bouton which explained the mayor's involvement. The Bouton family was one of his honor's largest benefactors. With holdings in real estate, telecommunications, and pharmaceuticals they had the money to sway his interest. If the Bouton family was involved the press would be as well. Slowing the Mercedes and pulling to the curb, she could see that the circus had already begun. The uniforms were doing a decent job keeping the paparazzi behind the yellow tape and away from the building, but the crowd was growing and it would only be minutes before the major networks had vans on-site.

"Bloody lovely," she muttered stepping out of the car and heading for the door. She badged her way past a couple uniforms who barley looked at her credentials reminding her of the night before and how easy it was for someone else to assume her role, temporarily. 'Just takes confidence and little swagger,' she mused.

Rique was waiting for her inside the apartment lobby and he appeared stressed and unhappy.

"God damn press, they're like vultures waiting for the next juicy meal."

"And who's on the menu this morning?" she asked, fearing the worst.

"None other than the tabloid queen herself, of course, and the scene's not pretty, LT. Not sure what this girl was into, but that room is like nothing I've ever seen.

"Well aren't you the little daffodil, Rique. Let's see what we've got."

They stepped into the luxurious elevator and waited as it whisked them towards the twenty-sixth storey penthouse. Ell looked over at her partner. His Latin decent and muscular physique were nice, not her style, but nice. He was dressed in the typical detective suit, stylish but practical, and it hung well on him. As her eyes crossed over the shield clipped to his belt her mind began to wander to a similar elevator ride the night before. She could almost feel the passion, the anticipation. It was so close to the surface but now buried beneath the job. How quickly the situation can shift and yet never truly disappear.

The doors opened to a luxurious foyer filled with uniformed

police officers and crime scene techs. The energy of the scene was typical for a high profile case. All hands on deck and everyone on their best behavior. Rique led the way past the uniforms, down a large hallway towards the master bedroom. The scene had been preserved, the techs concentrating on the points of access until the primary investigator gave the all clear on the bedroom.

Rique watched her closely as she entered the room and took in the scene. The look of shock and awe he expected was nowhere to be seen. Ell scanned the room casually, a large master suite with dark redwood furnishings and high end art adorning the walls, a peaceful and serene retreat if not for the bed and the area around it. The bed, a large king, was the focus of her attention. To its left was a small wooden table, its surface cluttered with bottles of lube, ropes, dildos, floggers and crops. The items scattered the surface with no care to organization as if discarded in haste. In the center of the bed lay Deedrie Bouton, the black sheep of the Bouton family. Identification had not been formally confirmed but Ell knew it was her. Half the free world could have identified her after her fall from grace. The tabloids had covered Deedrie's drug addicted, party fuelled, self-implosion for the past six months. How crazy would the stories be if they could see her now? Hogtied with soft leather cuffs, she was face down in the center of the elegant bed, an anal ball-hook inserted and fasten to a leather collar by a black nylon rope. Her mouth was propped open with the help of a ring gag and her knees held apart by a two foot metal spreader bar.

Under more relaxed circumstances Ell would have been aroused. As it was, she felt that side of her pushing to escape, but it was restrained by a deep sense of pity. She understood the fear of being discovered this way and how it would be handled by the press. She felt Rique's eyes on her, examining her reaction as she stepped over a discarded whip and approached the body.

Deedrie had been a beautiful woman, athletic and toned in her youth, but the last six months of partying had taken its toll. Her body now showed signs of abuse and malnutrition. Her muscle tone had begun to fade and her recent breast augmentation seemed unnatural and awkward on her slender frame. Through it all, however, her eyes were what captivated the public. They shone with a passion for life and even as her body faded away, those eyes remained bright. Until now. Lying there dead, in what should have been a highly passionate moment, the spark had disappeared completely. Ell felt for the woman, through all her troubles, she didn't deserve this.

"I don't know how you do it, LT. A scene like this and yet not even a modicum of shock on your face," quipped Rique as he joined her beside the bed.

"I've seen worse," she responded adding a silent self thought to the end. *'I've done worse.'*

"Initial M.E. report indicates strangulation, Sanders is thinking a garrote of some type. Possibly some of the rope based on the ligature marks on the neck."

Ell glanced at the woman's neck, careful not to touch the body as she bent for a closer look. As reported, a deep red ligature mark could be seen peeking out from beneath the collar.

"Did Sanders move anything?"

"Says no. You know the drill, L.T. Initial on-site, visual only. Once you clear it he'll do a more thorough and mold the marks for analysis. He should be able to get a more definitive

C.O.D. Based on lividity, he has an initial time of death between ten p.m. and two a.m. but figures he can tighten it up at the morgue."

Ell gave the body a quick once over, trying not to let the visual affect her. She'd been in similar positions and though the feeling was one of high restraint she absolutely adored it. Yearned for it. Did Deedrie feel that lust or was her experience purely fear?

Ell took a quick, rudimentary look around. "Have the techs pack up all her personal files, purse, etc and tell them I want the report by end of day. Who found the body?"

"S.O.P, gotcha," Rique flipped through his notebook. "Body was found at 5:43 a.m. by a member of the cleaning service. Debbie Flanto. Arrived at 5:30 a.m. to start her day. She passed by the open door shortly after. Says she was shocked at the site and screamed. When Ms. Bouton didn't respond she ran to the kitchen and called nine-one-one. Emergency call was logged and recorded at 5:44 a.m. I'm having the file sent to the precinct for review."

"So, she didn't enter the scene?"

Rique shrugged, holding his hands palms up. "Says she didn't but... you know."

"Yeah, I know. Witnesses lie. And doesn't that make our life so much more exciting? Not much we can do here except dodge the press and get in the way. Let's head back to the precinct and see what we can work up."

On the way back to the elevator Ell glanced at her partner. "You bring your personal or do you need a lift?"

"Caught a ride over in a squad."

"Then I suppose you're with me," she said entering the elevator.

"As always, LT... and I adore every moment of it," Rique responded with a large sarcastic grin. "Can I drive?"

Ell laughed as the elevator doors closed in front of her.

Chapter Two

*T*he press had swarmed the eleventh precinct before they could arrive. Word had spread and every reporter in the city was scrambling to be the first to garner the gruesome details of the debutante's final fall from grace. Based on the questions yelled, incoherently, from behind the recently erected police barrier in front of the main doors, Ell knew they had a leak somewhere at the scene. She had not yet released any details yet the victim's identity was out as were far too many details about the scene. It was concerning. Everyone at the victim's apartment, with the exception of Debbie Flanto, was on her payroll. 'Please let her be the leak', she muttered to herself but knew it was unlikely.

Slightly pissed by the unneeded commotion, she threw open the doors and stormed down the hall to her office, leaving Rique to give the standard 'no comment' and 'active investigation' brush off. Glancing quickly at the robbery/homicide bullpen on her way, she noticed it was nearly deserted. A few of her detectives were still at the Bouton scene, being high profile and all, but the serene quiet of the room was odd. Stopping short, she leaned against the doorway.

"Baker, where the hell is everyone?"

The tall redheaded detective snapped her head around with a surprised smile. "Lieutenant. I... I didn't expect to see you today. I thought you were on leave?"

Ell's composure softened at the sweet smile as she gave the young woman a quick once over. The twenty four year old, Jamie Baker, had been on her detail for a little over a year and the sight of her tight body, cute smile and luscious full lips still made Ell's mind wander. With every glance she could feel her lust rising, thoughts of the young redhead, wrapped in black leather, standing over her with a soft riding crop started to push through her composure. It was a reoccurring fantasy but one her professional ethics stopped her from pursuing.

"Deedrie Bouton," she responded, shaking off the thought.

Baker flashed a knowing look. "Let me guess, his honor's worried about optics."

"Goes with the rank. We can't let the press realize that the detectives actually solve these things. They need us paper pushers leading the charge." Ell gave her a quick wink. "So what's with the ghost town?"

"Donnely and Sharp are down in interrogation one wrapping up the Costigan double. Slick and Rook just caught a domestic gone bad and Jones is down in requisitions."

Ell rolled her eyes and Baker laughed. "Yeah, she's still trying to get that p.o.s. department issue transpo upgraded. She said you signed off on it but req's been giving her the paper shuffle run around. Haven't seen Rique yet, but I think he's with the rest of the crew on Bouton."

"I left him out front with the vultures," smiled Ell. "Tell Jones I'll deal with req, I don't want you two riding around in that death trap."

"We're willing to trade if you're feeling that bad about it." Baker gave her a wink, her cute smile throwing Ell off balance again. 'What is it about redheads?' she wondered.

"I'd hate to spoil you," she laughed flirtatiously, knowing it was a lie. How she wanted to spoil this girl, in so many ways.

Turning on her heels, Ell headed across the hall, closing her office door behind her and reprimanding herself for losing her composure. Ell's office was little more than a closet with a locking door, an old army surplus metal desk and the world's most uncomfortable guest chair. After two weeks of physiotherapy she had finally been able to convince requisitions to provide her with an ergonomic Aeron desk chair. It was her one solace in her own private cell. Well, that and her computer. A little flirting with that sexy young man, Rob, in I.T. had paid off in full. For the last year and half her computer was never lacking. She had dual monitors being powered by some geek speak mega graphics card that meant nothing to her. The machine was one of the quickest she'd ever used. She was at the top of the list for upgrades and she always made sure she was there to receive them. It was the least she could do for the personal service. Besides, he was great company and she rarely turned that down.

She settled in behind her desk, entered her password twice before getting the cryptic connection of random numbers and letters correct and was immediately greeted with a blank screen and security alert.

"Due to new departmental regulations and the nature of ongoing investigations, the files held by all ranking officers must now be fully encrypted. Please contact Information Services at ext 190 to schedule the required maintenance."

'Bloody bureaucrats,' she thought, grabbing for the handset

to her phone. She ignored the number listed in the alert and immediately dialed extension 1911.

"Long distance emergency, you've got Rob."

Ell groaned at the running joke about his random phone extension.

"Not yet but if you play your cards right I may," she replied in a flirty tone.

"Be careful Lieutenant, I'm holding a 'pair' of eyes for you and you're likely to lose this hand."

"Awe, but you just made me 'flush' so I suppose I clean up."

Rob let out a quick laugh and turned things back to business. "Let me guess, ranking officer encryption yadda yadda."

"Yeah, and no I haven't got a clue what that means other than I'm stuck here twiddling my thumbs waiting for my ever efficient I.T. slave boy to come work his wonders," she replied.

"Unfortunately, you're going to be waiting longer than you want. They've got me doing the rounds on this. Normally I'd have slated you in this morning but, since you're on leave, I booked you for first thing Wednesday. I assume you got pulled in on Bouton?"

"You know how it is. Money gets rank. So I'm dead in the water for the next seventy-two? Not going to work, Rob. The mayor's pushing and I need my station. Rique's antique would still be booting up by the time we have this thing solved."

"Tell you what, since I'm itching to see this 'flush', I'll bump Santinger's upgrade to lunch and be there in about thirty. Just don't tell him. The guy's a bit of a prick."

"Your secret's safe with me, thanks."

'Thirty minutes?' thought Ell. 'That should be plenty of time to rattle some chains and get things moving in the right direction.'

She quickly dialed ext 201. On the fourth ring a high pitched unhappy voice answered. "Requisitions, hold please."

"No," responded Ell.

The voice on the other end stumbled, having not expected a response. "Uhh, pardon? I need to put you on hold."

"No you don't and I wouldn't recommend doing so. You just put someone on hold in order to answer my call. In doing so, you have impressed upon that person that an unknown caller held more importance than they did. Are you about to tell me that I am now being delegated to a position of importance lower than that of an unknown caller as well?"

"But... I... who is this?"

"Seriously? If you take a moment to look at the display on your phone you will see ext 921- Lt. Ell Frost. Had you done so before answering, you'd have known if my call rated high enough importance to place your previous call on hold. For future record, unless the chief is on your other line, it does."

"What can I help you with, Lieutenant Frost?" the voice had gone from flustered to cold.

"I authorized a transpo upgrade for Detectives Baker and Jones over two weeks ago and it seems your department can't manage to find or deliver them their new keys."

"As I just explained to Ms. Jones..."

"Detective Jones," interrupted Ell.

"Yes," snapped the lady in a frustrated tone. "As I explained to 'Detective' Jones, the upgrade is being processed and they will be notified as soon as the new vehicle is prepared."

"Prepared? Do we have a crew of mechanics assembling this vehicle from spare parts? Listen, ma'am, there are over ten unmarked cars sitting in the parkade for random rotation. Each of them is in fine condition and fully outfitted for the detective's requirements. I expect the keys to one of these delivered to Robbery/Homicide, by end of shift."

"Lieutenant, there are procedures that need to be followed."

"Then follow them quickly. I have two detectives riding around in a deathtrap that is likely uninsurable. They've been stranded on duty five times in the last three months. Either the keys are in my department by end of shift or I'll be in yours."

Without waiting for a response Ell hung up and dialed ext 301 for Crime Scene.

"Lieutenant Frost," answered the stern but polite voice of James Lund, head of CSI. "Bouton scene evidence is just rolling in now. Materials are being catalogued and will be delivered to you within the hour. I expect to have a preliminary report to you by end of day but it may depend on this damn I.T. encryption upgrade. We're all hands on deck down here, and thanks to 'his honor' you just became our top priority."

Ell smiled to herself. "It's a relief to work with a professional for once. Thanks James, let me know if there is anything you guys need down there. These high profiles are a bitch but our job relies on yours."

"Don't I know it. Some doughnuts and a thirty hour day may help but we'll get you what you need, Ell."

"I'll see what I can do about that thirty hour day but no promises, my time machine's been really glitchy this week," laughed Ell. "Thanks again James, I won't keep you."

As soon as she hung up, the phone began to ring. Glancing at the display she smiled and picked up.

"Sanders, you beat me to the punch, I was just about to call you."

"I just got back to the morgue. It was a bloody nightmare

getting her out of there. The vultures are already circling."

"I'll do what I can to keep the press fed but I need something to give them. What can you tell me?"

"Nothing yet other than what I gave Rique on-site. Swing by here in about three hours and I'll give you a full run down. I should have a definite C.O.D and much tighter timeline."

"Sounds good. Text me if anything revealing comes up. Brass is pushing on this one and we need to hit it hard."

"Will do, now go harass Lund and stay off my ass."

Ell laughed, "Already ahead of you, see you in three."

With the preliminaries out of the way and the troops all on board, Ell headed across the hall to the bullpen. Jones and Baker were flipping through Rique's notes as he assembled the timeline, victim and witnesses on the "Kill" board. Ell took a moment to watch Jones and Baker together, bantering back and forth over the details and relevance. They made a great pair. Jones, a heavier set, Latin woman in her mid thirties, offset the youth and exuberance of Baker well. The two had closed some big cases in the year they'd been partnered and Ell had never heard about so much as a minor squabble between them.

"Jones, what's your current active?" she asked from the doorway.

"We just cleared up the Donaldson case last night. D.A. figures it's a slam dunk with the roommate's confession. We've got the Brunsen break-in ongoing but it looks like a bullshit insurance fraud, and we pulled two cold cases earlier this week that appear to have some similarities. Thought we'd dig and look for a tie-in."

"How cold?"

"Nearly freezing, twenty-two years. Figured with the DNA

advances we might get a hit. Lab keeps the samples active for twenty-five so it's something, but it's slim."

"Ok, work it in when you can but it's not a priority, and see if you can't pawn off the Brunsen case on Fraud. I want you and Baker on Bouton with us. It's going to be leg work but it needs to be discreet. I need you canvassing the building and talking to known associates both pre and post meltdown. Someone out there knows what Deedrie was into, and we need to determine if the body was staged and how the scene ties in. I don't buy the 'playtime got too kinky' angle here, there's something too obvious about it."

"I'll get Fraud on the line," said Baker, heading for her desk, "then we will coordinate with Detective Shaw. Anything else, Lieutenant?" Her smile and the possibilities embedded in the question brought back the familiar feelings of lust. Ell fought to remain in control.

"Yeah, get a couple dozen doughnuts sent down to Lund in CSI. Charge it to my personal."

Rique cleared his throat, a huge fake smile on his face.

"Fine, order two dozen for the bullpen as well." Staring Rique down, she said, "Save me a damn jelly this time or you'll be limping for a week."

"L.T., you wound me."

"If there's no jelly I will," she grinned, heading back to her office to wait for Rob.

Chapter Three

*H*e saw it on the news and immediately knew there'd be trouble. His name was bound to come up in the investigation and with Ellison Frost leading the charge, things were going to get tricky. He contemplated calling her but how exactly did he expect that call to go? First, would she even take it? And if she did, how much could he actually tell her? Most of what he knew fell under client confidentiality and while it may not be a legal stance, discretion was a must in his line of work. After a few moments of thought, he picked up his phone and hit her auto-dial number. The call went straight to voicemail. Either she was on another call or, more likely, at the precinct, a well known black hole for cell coverage.

Hanging up, he quickly googled the phone number for the eleventh precinct and dialed again.

"PD, eleventh precinct, how may I direct your call?"

"Lieutenant Ellison Frost, please."

"I'm sorry sir," his heart skipped for a moment, "Lieutenant Frost is currently on leave."

"I believe you'll find that her leave has been cancelled. Please transfer me to her extension."

"As you wish, sir," again his heart jumped and he held his breath as the phone rang. On the fourth ring he was directed to her voicemail.

"You've reached the personal and confidential voicemail of Lieutenant Ell Frost. If this is an emergency please dial nine to be redirected to the general switchboard. Otherwise, leave your name and number and I'll take care of the rest."

He quickly hung up. No matter how confidential she believed her voicemail, leaving his name and number would be too much of a risk.

Ell crossed the hallway and saw her personal I.T. slave, Rob, leaning nonchalantly on the door frame to her office. His soft brown hair was messed in a stylish wave. His ice blue eyes twinkling as she approached. She couldn't help but smile and he quickly returned the grin. He had a subtle air of playfulness mixed with professionalism that she adored. Plus, he wasn't hard on the eyes. She opened the door, leading him in while admiring the eye candy.

"Thanks for working this in," she said quietly.

"And how could I resist the opportunity to see that smile," replied Rob, looking into her eyes.

His gaze captivated her and she could feel her cheeks begin to burn.

"Ah, there's that flush you were talking about. I guess you do win."

Ell laughed and the joke broke the tension. Rob slid in behind her computer and inserted a USB drive.

"This should only take about 5 minutes to load and then

you'll be good as new. If you intend to transfer files to your home unit you will need the decryption key installed at that end. I'll leave the USB for you. Just insert it and reboot. The code should take care of itself."

"Sounds easy enough. I'll try not to screw it up," she laughed.

His eyes found hers and his look changed. His easy going nature disappeared as an unusual seriousness came over him.

"Lieutenant,"

"Please call me Ell. You're not officially PD so there's no reason to stand on formality."

"Ell, if the rumors about the Bouton scene are true, I believe I may have some insight for you."

"Pardon?" Ell's surprise was obvious.

"Word is she was found in a rather compromising position. One depicting a BDSM lifestyle or, at least, an encounter of that sort. I happen to have a fair bit of knowledge and experience on the subject, so if you need a reference please don't hesitate to ask."

Ell's heart rate soared at the thought. Her mind raced as she tried to process the information and calm her sudden arousal. She stared at him in complete disbelief, the mixture of emotions evident on her face.

"I'm sorry, I didn't mean to make you uncomfortable. I just thought I could offer something."

"No, it's not that," cut in Ell. "I suppose I'm just surprised at how easily you admit to this knowledge and experience."

"It's who I am. I am neither embarrassed by it nor concerned by what others may think. I live a particular lifestyle, sexually. I don't let it affect my job, my friendships, my day to day life but it is who I am and it does, on some level, define me. Do I need to flaunt it? No, nor do I feel I should hide it. Especially if that knowledge can be used for something positive. The lifestyle is not what many believe it is. It's not about control, anger and aggression like the media portrays."

"You don't need to convince me, trust me," Ell shifted her gaze to the floor, restraining from biting her lower lip. She wanted to tell him. Every bit of her wanted to tell him, to let him in, but she couldn't. Not here. Here she was in control. Here she was a leader and she couldn't risk letting her lives cross. Raising her head, she smiled and again reclaimed the poise of authority.

"Thanks, Rob. I appreciate your honesty and willingness. At this stage it is too early to determine if the scene was staged or if her sexual leanings have anything to do with her death. If something does come up, however, I'll be sure to call. It may help to get your insight."

Rob hit a series of keys and her machine booted back up. The annoying alert was gone and her standard login screen now visible. He placed the USB on her desk along with his personal business card and whispered, "I'm here for whatever you need, Ell."

Smiling, he walked out the door with a quick wave. Ell's thoughts were a mess as she struggled to articulate the words running through her mind.

'Thank you, sir.'

Chapter Four

*L*und was true to his word, and the crime scene materials were delivered to the Ell straight away. It took four techs two trips each to bring all the items into the bullpen. Rique immediately took charge, assigning review of all paperwork gathered from the crime scene to Baker and Jones while he started in on the electronics. Ell watched as her team dug in to the menial, unglamorous work that is the backbone of every investigation. Checking the time, she realized nearly three hours had passed since her arrival at the precinct.

"Shaw, we're supposed to go get an update from Sanders in about fifteen."

Rique looked up from the laptop with which he had been fighting to gain entry. A look of frustration and determination in his eyes.

"I'm knee deep in this thing, L.T. and I'd hate to pass it off now, why not take Baker. Jones and I can get through the grunt work while you two go have fun with the stiffs."

"What's the matter, Rique, stomach gone light on you already? Or maybe your I.T. skills are just not up to the task.

I've got Rob's personal number if you need some help," laughed Ell.

"Yeah, I don't think I'd get the service you do, Frost. My 'negotiating skills' seem to be lacking what he's looking for."

Ell smiled and shook her head, "Baker, you're with me."

The stunning redhead flashed a grin and turned to her partner.

"Enjoy the grunt work," she quipped.

"Enjoy the stiffs," laughed Jones.

Unlike the Central PD, the eleventh precinct did not have a morgue in the building. Sanders and his team of slightly creepy 'doctors for the dead' worked off-site and serviced five smaller precincts. Under most circumstances, it was a twenty-minute drive from the eleventh but, thanks to the S550 and some very aggressive driving, Ell made it in just less than twelve. The speed was a distraction and, with the stunning Detective Baker riding shotgun, Ell needed it. She could feel her skin tingling at the young woman's close proximity and funneled all the sexual tension into her driving.

She couldn't tell if the ride had frightened the detective but she rode in silence with a large heart stopping grin across her face. Ell looked over twice and had to fight back the urge to lean in and gently bite those beautiful soft lips. The girl had no idea how stunning she was, but, as always, Ell was taken by her.

The morgue itself was not what one would expect. The building was clean and bright with not a hint of the creepy macabre its use would suggest. A cheerful blonde assistant of no more than twenty greeted them as they entered.

"Let Sanders know we are here, please."

"Straight away, Detective Frost," replied the young girl, giving Detective Baker a, not so quick, look over, ending at the redhead's captivating gaze. Ell felt a pang of envy as the young girl stood there eye-fucking her detective, but quickly pushed it aside.

After a brief call they were sent back to examination two and informed that M.E. Sanders was expecting them. The young assistant followed them back, watching Bakers tight ass sway as she did.

"You have an admirer," whispered Ell.

"I'm open minded, L.T.," winked Baker, "but that one's a little too desperate for my tastes."

Rounding the corner, they were greeted by the never understated M.E. Davidson Sanders. His long silver hair was pulled back in a ponytail, exposing his slender face and wide grin. As was his custom, he was wearing tight fitting jeans and a stylish burnt orange, silk dress shirt. A pair of brown Italian leather Luisaviaroma boots completed the ensemble. If not for his lab coat Sanders would look more like a twenty five year old on his way to the club then a medical examiner in his late forties. Sure, his features had aged but his style and exuberance for life more than offset them.

"Thanks Mindy," he smiled at the young assistant, a slight spark in his eye.

"My pleasure," she responded, and with one last lingering look at Detective Baker she sauntered from the room.

"Such a lovely girl," commented the M.E.

Ell and Baker both laughed bringing a confused look to the man's face.

"I could be wrong, doc, but I don't think you're her type," quipped Ell.

Sanders raised his eyebrows, "And why's that? Too old for the lass?"

"You? Never. The hair may even work but I think your tits are too small for her."

The meaning hit him, "Oh? Mindy? Hmmm. Well I suppose that's for the best. It's getting harder and harder to find reliable help after all."

"Oh, the troubles of the handsome and horny," mocked Ell. "Speaking of horny, what's the word on my vic?"

Sanders smiled and shook his head, "Handsome? I didn't think you noticed, lieutenant."

"Get over yourself. I was just keen on the alliteration."

Sanders grabbed his chest in mock pain. "You wound me, Frost."

Baker barely suppressed a giggle at the exchange.

"You'll live, now what about my victim."

"Well, I'm afraid she won't." Both Baker and Frost rolled their eyes. "Sorry, gallows humor. A danger of the profession, I suppose." Sanders wandered over to the body of Deedrie Bouton and ran a gloved finger across the scarring on her neck. "Cause of death is confirmed as asphyxiation due to strangulation. Some form of garrote was used as evidenced by the bruising around her throat. The weapon left a distinct impression. I have sent photos and trace samples to Lund for analysis, but I believe they will come back a positive match to the nylon rope found on-site. No hesitation or adjustment marks so your killer was either experienced in taking a life, very determined or didn't mean to do so. I can't rule out airplay gone wrong."

"Airplay?" asked Baker.

"Sexual play," responded Ell. "Restricting air flow to increase the intensity of an orgasm."

"Does... Does that actually work?"

"Quite well," responded Ell without thinking.

Both Baker and Sanders raised their eyebrows but let it go.

"I can't say for certain if the scene was staged but the collar was either added or adjusted post mortem."

"I noticed that," commented the Lieutenant. "Any indication if the body was moved?"

Sanders pulled back the sheet to expose her arms. "If she was posed it was done before her heart stopped. As you can see by the discoloration on her forearms, the blood had settled to that point prior to death. There are similar marks on her knees. I'd say she died in the position she was found."

"What are the stripes on her chest?" asked Baker.

"Whip marks, likely soft leather. Not hard enough to visibly bruise but recent enough that rigor extenuated the damage. She has similar marks across her back and small square bruising on her buttocks."

"Riding crop?" asked Ell.

"Likely, but again I'll let Lund and the techs make the final determination."

Baker shook off the shock, choosing not to ask.

Ell noticed the girl's look of disbelief and stifled a laugh. How she'd love to introduce the sexy redhead to the pleasures of pain.

"Time of death?" asked Ell dismissing the thought.

"Somewhere between eleven and midnight, likely closer to the latter based on the air temp of the room."

"Anything else I need to know?"

"Possibly," replied Sanders, rolling Deedrie's body onto its left hip.

"What the fuck!" blurted the young detective in shock.

Ell bent down for a closer look. Tattooed on the right

shoulder blade was an image of Deedrie Bouton in the exact position she had been found murdered.

"How old?"

"Definitely pre-mortem but no more than six hours," responded Sanders, "and it's professionally done with a high end machine. Ink's barely set but it's quality product."

"What's the attraction?" asked Baker as they settled back into the Mercedes.

"The attraction?"

"Sorry, I didn't realize I said that aloud. I was just wondering what would draw a young, beautiful woman to that lifestyle. Pain, humiliation, subjugating herself to another's will. I don't see anything enjoyable in it."

Ell contemplated how much she wanted to reveal. She could certainly give this young woman some insight and god knows how much she'd love to give her some firsthand knowledge, but the duality of her life was always there. As she thought back to Rob's openness, his lack of concern for the shock and willingness to be honest, she envied him. 'To hell with it'.

"For some people it's just about the kink, doing something that is considered taboo and perhaps that's the case here, I don't know, but for those that are really involved in BDSM it's not about the pain or subjugation. It's about trust, pleasure, submission, care and protection."

Baker sat and thought for a moment, "How can the whips and ropes not be about pain? And isn't submission about allowing someone else to control you for their pleasure? Isn't that subjugation?"

"Don't get me wrong, there is pain involved but it's not 'about' the pain. How much do you know about neuroscience?"

Baker laughed, "I'm a cop. I barely know the word."

Ell smiled and was glad the mood had lightened some. "Let's try another angle, have you seen 9 ½ Weeks?"

"The movie? Yeah."

"Ok, then you know the famous ice cube scene, right?"

"What self respecting woman doesn't?" she giggled.

"Perfect, now the real question, have you tried it?"

"Can't say I've had the pleasure," she responded in a flirty tone that sent Ell's heart racing.

"Well, under normal circumstances ice freezes the nerve endings, the body interprets these signals as a danger and the mind then signals for the pain receptors to react. However, if the mind is in a state of arousal, complete arousal, it doesn't expect pain, it expects pleasure, so when the nerve endings react they misinterpret the signal and instead of firing off the pain receptors they trigger the pleasure center. Increase the pain, increase the pleasure. To an extent, of course. At some point each individual will hit a threshold where the pain/pleasure combination becomes too much."

"Ok, I think I understand that, I guess that's where a safe word comes in. I still couldn't see letting someone order me around for their pleasure. It just seems so old fashioned. Equal rights and all."

"I agree, but in a true submissive relationship, it's not like that. It's about trust and mutual pleasure. A submissive trusts that the dominant is out only to please them, to protect and care for them. They give themselves fully with the knowledge that doing so is not for the dominant's benefit but for their own. On the other hand a true dominant isn't out to get their rocks off. Their happiness and pleasure is derived from giving, from ensuring that they provide exactly what the submissive needs. Though the dominant 'controls' the situation, the roles are actually reversed from what most people believe. The submissive holds all the power. The problems arise when someone assumes the role of dominant without truly having the dominant mindset. Those people are out for control and power. They thrive on humiliating and degrading others. They're not dominant, they're abusive."

Baker sat in reflective silence and Ell could tell she was attempting to process the information.

"I suppose it's not as black and white as it seems. How do you know all this?"

And there it was, the question Ell had always feared and the reason she had never delved into discussions such as this in the past. She found herself at a crossroads and the real question was, how much does she trust the detective?

"I've read a lot on the subject and I have some experience."

Baker gave her a shy, flirty smile.

"Look, it's not something I usually get into and it's not something I like to publicize. Actually, it's not something I ever get into. I'm sure you understand."

"I do," she replied, "and thank you Lieutenant. I'm glad to know you trust me."

"You wouldn't be riding with me if I didn't."

"Yeah, but this is different, this isn't trusting the other cop to do what's right if the shit hits. This is personal."

Ell felt her face flush from embarrassment. "Ok, let's not get all mushy and start planning a slumber party."

Baker giggled to herself and winked, "I don't think I could survive one of your slumber parties."

Ell laughed and let the silence wash over them again.

Five minutes later, as they were pulling into the precinct parking lot, Baker finally broke the silence. "Our killer? Assuming the scene is what it appears, do you think they were a true dominant or an abusive?"

"Bouton's dead, no attempt at resuscitation, no nine-one-one call. Whoever did it just packed up and left. What do you think?"

Chapter Five

$\mathcal{F}$rost and Baker rolled back into the bullpen shortly after one o'clock to find Rique and Jones still buried in paperwork. They were sorting through the victim's financials and looked utterly confused.

"Do the fucking rich do anything simple?" commented Rique, running his hands through his hair.

"What's the issue?" asked Ell, surprising the two of them momentarily.

"It's the finances," responded Jones. "They're a bloody mess. It's a spider web of transactions, accounts and off-shore companies. Likely a pile of grey line tax and liability shelters, but it's making a solid picture of her finances nearly impossible. From what we can tell she was blowing through cash like a junkie with a briefcase full of coke but her income stream's next to impossible to trace."

"Daddy's a big wig. Is there a trust fund? Maybe an allowance?" inquired Baker.

"That's where we started," answered Rique, "but that well ran dry on her eighteenth. The old man funded until then and her trust fund was a little over five million when she cashed it in. You'd think that would last her, but we've nailed down over twenty million in expenses since then and we're not even sure that's all of it. There's gotta be another source but this shit's a mess."

"Give it up and call in Browne, if it's shell corps and tax shelters you two will never find it."

"Shit L.T., if we call Squirrelly you know what the response is going to be."

Andy 'Squirrelly' Browne was the best forensic accountant in the county but, like Rob, he was a civilian contractor which meant he was expensive, thorough, and brilliant but damn slow.

"Yeah, sometime next week. If we're lucky. Rique, get his ass on the phone. Tell him the mayor's overseeing this personally and we need it in the next twenty-four even if it means paying his dumbass overtime up charges. If that doesn't work get me on the line. In the meantime, Baker, I need you and Jones running down high end tattoo parlors uptown. I don't see her going out of her comfort zone to get the ink."

"Ink?" asked Jones.

Ell slipped her a photo Sanders had provided them and told Baker to fill her in on the way.

Taking a look around the room, Ell noticed the vic's laptop was nowhere to be seen.

"What happened to the laptop?"

Rique looked away and mumbled something.

"Pardon?"

She could see the anger and embarrassment in his eyes, "I said your fuckin' boyfriend's got it!"

Ell let out a loud laugh and headed back to her office.

She settled in and started to pull up the case file and sift through the data Jones and Rique had managed to assemble. Not five minutes later her phone rang, breaking her concentration. She glanced at the caller ID and rolled her eyes.

"Browne, I don't even want to hear it, this is Deedrie Bouton, a high profile dead girl and brass is crawling up my ass on it."

"Detective, you can't just expect me to drop everything and..."

"It's Lieutenant and that's exactly what I expect you to do. My partner's sending you the vic's financials now and if you want to keep your overpriced PD contract you'll have me a detailed breakdown in the next twenty-four hours."

"But..."

"But nothing, get it done!" she hung up without giving him a chance to argue.

She quickly texted Rique, "Send Squirrelly everything you've got and come see me. – E," then returned to her search of the files. Moments into the search her worlds abruptly collided. Jones had requested a copy of Deedric's cell phone records for the previous month. On the night in question the vic had made three calls to the same number. A number Ell knew by heart, Madame Angel's Escorts.

'Shit,' just what she needed.

Rique walked in, noticing the look on her face. "What is it?"

"Vic's cell records," she responded unenthusiastically.

"Right, Jones pulled them, but we haven't had a chance to run them yet. What did you find?"

"Only three calls made last night, all to the same number," she punched the number into Google for Rique's sake. "Madame Angel's Escorts, doesn't look like they open till six and off hours calls route to a third party booking service so we'll need to run this down after hours."

"No problem, I assumed we were working doubles till this one ran its course anyway."

Ell checked her watch, "Yeah, this may drag out. Tell you what, grab a few hours downtime. I'm gonna pack up and run through the rest of this shit at home and we'll meet back up at about six thirty to pay Madame Angel a visit."

"Sounds good, I could use some grub anyway. Oh, I almost forgot," he said, reaching into Ell's desk drawer. "Saved it for you like a good little soldier," he winked and handed her a frosted, jelly doughnut.

Ell laughed and flashed him a smile, "Ok, you just bought yourself one more wound free day. Now get the hell out of here."

Moments after settling into the S550 and hitting the freeway towards her two-storey brownstone, Ell engaged her Bluetooth.

"Call speed-dial eight."

The phone began to ring across the Mercedes sound system.

"Hello," said a smooth female voice on the other end.

"Angel?"

"Ell, I didn't expect to hear from you so soon. I trust everything went well with Sebastian?"

"Amazing as always, thanks. I'm actually calling for a bit of a favor," said Ell, still unsure what she was going to do. "Did you hear about Deedrie Bouton?"

"I did, such a tragedy. Since I'm getting this call I assume the rumors about how she was found are true. What do you need, Ell, a consult?"

"I wish that were it. Your service has come up in the course of the investigation. Deedrie called the booking line three times last night. My partner and I are going to have to come in tonight and ask some tough questions."

"Ell, you know I'll do anything I can but surely you don't think someone from my service did this?"

"Of course not. We go back, Angel, and I know the people you run, I know your screening process for both employees and clients, but I can't brush this off with the brass overseeing everything. I need to do the proper follow-up."

"I'll be in the office at six, drop by anytime after that and we'll give you anything we have. Our client records are confidential, as you know, but I can open them up for you."

"That's actually why I'm calling. I need you to fight that request?" Ell's voice trembled and she began to sweat, fighting to maintain a sense of calm and focus on the essentials.

"Pardon?"

"I'm going to be coming in with my partner and we will likely be demanding your client records. I need you to fight me on it. Agree to release anything on Deedrie but play every client confidentiality card you can on the full records. We both know that I'll eventually get a court order but I need you to delay it as much as possible."

"What's this about Ell?"

"Anything you hand over is going on the record in a high profile murder investigation and, odds are, it's going to get out."

"Jesus, Ell, I can wipe you from the database in a flash, it's nothing to worry about."

"I can't ask you to do that, it leaves you open to criminal charges, Angel, and I won't put you in that position. For now just do what you can to delay. I am sure I'm not your only client with something to lose. Do what's best for your company and let me try and solve this thing before it becomes an issue."

"And what about us, our past?"

"Fucked if I know, we can't hide it so we'll have to play it by ear. I'm sorry I have to drag you into this."

"I've had to deal with the cops before, Ell, it's just part of the business. I run a clean and discrete service and have the paperwork to back it up. No worries on my end."

"Thanks Angel, see you tonight."

"I'll be there."

'Fuck!' thought Ell as she disconnected the call, her heart-rate kicking up and her body tensing. Her hands trembled on the steering wheel and she gripped it tighter in an attempt to control the rising panic.

This is going to get sticky.

Chapter Six

*E*ll pulled into her suburban oasis, a two-storey Victorian brownstone which she had spent the last four years renovating and upgrading. Walking in, she tossed her leather coat on the chair in the foyer and immediately headed up the stairs two at a time. Settling into her home office, she fired up her computer and strolled over to the Keurig machine for a coffee while she waited. Her home computer was fine but it lacked Rob's touch. That thought sent her mind spinning, what she wouldn't give for a bit of that touch herself. The sudden fantasy surprised her. She had always found him attractive but now there was something else to it. Something more. She could not shake the thoughts of his soft caressing hands, chiseled chest and strong arms holding her down. She could feel the arousal growing with each thought. Her body reacting as she clenched her legs together.

Shaking herself out of the impromptu fantasy, she cursed her lack of control, 'Jesus, pull yourself together, Frost!'

She headed back to the desk, coffee in hand and clicked the icon for the P.D. remote connection. Seconds later an alert popped up on her screen.

"Due to new departmental regulations and the nature of ongoing investigations, the files held by all ranking officers must now be fully encrypted. Please contact Information Services at ext 190 to schedule the required maintenance."

"Fuck!" she cursed, realizing Rob's USB drive was still sitting on her desk at the precinct. Without thinking about the possible consequences she pulled out the card he had left her and dialed his cell number.

"Lieutenant Frost, to what do I owe the pleasure?"

Ell was a little shocked, "Do I want to know how you recognized my personal cell number?"

"I don't know, do you?" laughed Rob.

"I'm going to attribute it to tech genius instead of creepy stalker tendencies and let it go," she replied.

"Thank you for the vote of confidence. Now, what can I help you with?"

"I'm sitting in my home office and... files held by all ranking officials must now..." she quoted.

"You can't seriously be having issues with the USB decryption program? All you have to do is place it in the drive and hit 'OK' at the prompt. I wrote it to be idiot proof."

"I'm sure it's a masterpiece in technological programming, any way you can make it run from on top of my desk at the precinct?"

Rob broke out into laughter, "Seriously, Ell, I'm going to start thinking you can't get enough of me."

"Oooo Rob, I want you, I need you, I can't live without you," she replied in a deadbeat emotionless tone.

"That's what I like to hear," he laughed. "It's your lucky day, I happen to have a backup drive with me and can be there in under twenty minutes."

"Do you want the address?" asked Ell receiving nothing but laughter in return. "I should have known. But seriously, a little creepy, Rob," she smiled as she said it and hung up the phone. With little else to do and twenty minutes to spare she decided to grab the shower she missed that morning. She had just finished washing her hair, five minutes later, when her doorbell rang. Scrambling from the shower she threw on her silk robe and headed down to deal with whoever it was. She looked through the peephole and found Rob standing on her porch taking in the decor.

"Ell, are you in there?"

She gazed down at herself, dripping wet and wrapped in only thin silk. Frantically, she searched for something to cover up with, finally deciding on the only item in sight, her soft leather jacket. Shrugging in acceptance, she draped it around her shoulders and opened the door.

"Ell, you didn't need to get dressed up just for me," he chuckled surveying her wet hair and nearly naked form. Her jacket did nothing to conceal her tight body wrapped in wet, black silk.

Ell gave him a sarcastic, dirty look, "What happened to the twenty minutes?"

"I believe I said I would be here in 'under twenty minutes' and that statement would be accurate. What happened to 'I want you, I need you, I can't live without you'?"

"Oh for Christ sake just get your ass in here before the neighbors start talking." She grabbed his arm and pulled him into the foyer. Their bodies brushed up against each other as he entered. Ell looked up to see Rob's gorgeous eyes staring down at her with want.

He exhaled, breaking the tension. He was fighting the

urge to brush his fingers against her cheek. "Uh," he smiled, backing away just a little. Ell's face flushed as her arousal grew.

"Why don't you show me where the computer is so I can get you back to work," he said softly.

It was the last thing she wanted right now but she relented and led him up the stairs to the office.

"The computer's running, just let me throw some clothes on and I'll be right back."

He grabbed her wrist softly, pulling her to the desk, "Now why would I want to let you do that? I rarely get to work with such beautiful scenery."

Ell's initial instinct should have been to laugh and leave but his tone was so confident, almost demanding, and it melted her resolve. Her eyes dropped to the floor, goosebumps flared on her arms. "Thank you," she replied, her voice almost a whisper.

He settled into the desk chair, gave the mouse a wave and was greeted with her desktop photo of a naked blonde silhouette lying on a black background. Her arms were pulled behind her back and wrapped with black silk rope. It was a beautiful artistic image. Ell's eyes snapped open when she saw it, having momentarily forgotten the image was there. The implications hit her immediately.

To his credit, Rob did not comment. Instead, he pulled out a USB drive and watched as his program went to work. Ell stood beside the desk biting her lip and trying to avoid eye contact.

"This will be a few minutes, come, have a seat."

She looked around, knowing there was no additional chair in her home office, before noticing him tapping his lap.

Part of her wanted to resist, to maintain her professional resolve, but the lust, attraction and commanding tone in his voice were overpowering. She moved behind the desk and settled herself onto his lap, his left arm circling her and resting against her stomach as his right continued to work the mouse.

"It's a beautiful image," he said, motioning to the monitor.

"It's... uh... yes," she stammered.

"Relax, Ell. No one's judging you and you have nothing to be embarrassed about. Did you find it while researching the case?"

"The case? No." Her mind was a mess. She was approaching a line that part of her wanted to leap across, yet how could she do that? How could she let him in? "I... I suppose I just liked the image."

Rob could feel her tension and knew there was more to it than that. "The image or what it portrays?" he prodded.

This was it. Ell knew this was the moment. She either leapt in and let things fall where they may or she did what she always had and walked away. She gazed into his eyes and knew in that moment, she no longer wanted to run.

"Both, I suppose. The artist has a subtle, yet beautiful, eye for negative space and the pose is very provocative but, yes, it's the subject matter that attracted me most. You can see the pleasure on her face. The joy she feels from the restraint."

"I feel like quite the fool, Ell."

"What?" she asked beginning to settle her mind.

"I came to you this morning offering my insight. It appears that was a bit presumptuous of me."

"Oh," Instinctively, she thought of standing, of forcing some separation, but Rob's arm held her firm. "I'm sorry. I suppose I'm not as comfortable and forthcoming as you. I've found it necessary to hide my... desires."

"Are you new to the lifestyle?"

She contemplated the question. How open could she be? How much did she really want this?

"No, in fact it's almost all I've ever known though, for me, it can't be a 'lifestyle'. My position won't allow it. It's a sexual style, the only one I really know. Given my job, I have to be discreet."

"I understand the need for discretion but, with no long term partner, isn't that rather difficult? I assume you're not abstaining so how, exactly, do you manage that risk and not drive yourself insane with fear?"

"Carefully," responded Ell. "To be honest, I can't believe I'm having this conversation. It hasn't always been easy. I've had a few partners that didn't understand or respect my need to keep things private. My last break up was nearly three years ago and it wasn't cordial. I spent months in fear of him exposing me. That fear, the way it gripped me, made me realize that the only way to protect myself was to completely control all aspects of any partnership."

"I won't point out the logical flaw in that statement as I'm sure you're well aware, but how do you purpose to do so?"

"Agencies. One in particular, which I know to be extremely private and trustworthy."

Rob paused for a moment, gathering his thoughts. "Sexually, that's fine but there is so much more to a relationship than sex. It's companionship, connection, security. Anyone can have kinky sex, Ell. Don't you want more than that? Don't you deserve more?"

She glanced up at him, wanting all of it but afraid, deathly afraid, to take the risk.

"I do," she whispered almost to herself.

"So do I," he responded, making her heart skip. The joy was fleeting, however, as the fear rushed back.

Listen, Rob," she said reasserting herself and pulling to her feet. Her instincts to run were overriding her desires and will. "I want to explore this, I know you've picked up on that, but it can't happen. I know firsthand the problems it can cause when the lines between profession and pleasure are crossed. When I step foot in the precinct I have men and women that depend on me to lead them, to keep them safe. This," she waved her hand between them, "confuses the lines. I can't have that."

Rob rose in front of her and placed his hands on her wrists. Ell felt her resolve quickly melting. "I am aware of the boundaries required, Ell. I live them daily. If you can tell me you are promised to another or are not interested in pursuing something with me then I will walk away but, please, do not use boundaries as an excuse. I am not a horny child looking for some kink. I know what is required to make a relationship work."

"Rob..." she whispered, her breathless voice pulsing with lust. She stepped backwards but he matched her movement.

"Is there another?"

"No," 'sir', she added silently in her mind. Her heart raced as she stepped backwards again. He matched the step to stay with her. His eyes commanding and loving all at once. His grasp restraining but freeing as her will continued to melt.

"I want this, Ell, but you know that doesn't matter. You need to let me in."

She took one final step backwards and found herself against the office wall. Rob stepped in close, still grasping her wrists.

"Can you do that, Ell? Can you let me in?" his voice soft yet strong. The feeling of restraint coursed over her, her back, literally, against the wall. Her passion flared, feeling his warmth through the sheer silk of her robe. Her resolve was now gone, replaced by pure animalistic lust.

She cast her gaze to the floor, quirked her lip and responded, "Yes, sir!"

Rob raised her wrists above her head, pinning her arms against the wall and moved in closer. His body pressed against hers and Ell was overtaken with passion. His lips slowly brushed across her neck. She tipped her head to the side exposing it for him, her body yearning for more, begging for his hands, his touch. He traced her neck softly, running his mouth across her jaw before finally finding her lips. She parted them, taking him gently, the kiss sending sparks throughout her body, a rush like no other.

He released her wrists yet she remained in the pinned position, unwilling to move. His hands gently brushed across her shoulders spilling the leather jacket to the ground. The wet silk clung to her shoulders but fell open just enough to expose her breasts. Ell's chest heaved in anticipation as his mouth left hers, gliding slowly down her neck and surrounding her left nipple. His tongue flicked against the hardened flesh and she squirmed, struggling not to moan. Rob could feel her want, and sense her fight to remain in control. Biting down gently, the slight pain encompassed her, pushing out all other thoughts and breaking the final bit of resistance she had left.

"Fuck yes. Take me. Please."

She began to lower her arms but found them quickly pinned back to the wall as Rob's arm crashed across them with a surprising force. Strong yet painless. The restraint forcing her entire body to buck uncontrollably. Ell was lost, overcome with lust and on the brink of cumming without anything more than her left breast being touched. The confusion was there but it was inconsequential. All she could think of, all she wanted was the man forcing her against her office wall. They were both lost in a trance like state of want and desire, broken quickly and decisively by the chirp of Ell's cell phone.

Releasing her arms, Rob stepped back and laughed quietly, trying to settle his thoughts. He ran a finger gently across her cheek. "To be continued."

Ell stood there, lost in the rush of sudden emotions, staring at him with blank confusion.

"Get your phone, Ell, they'll be plenty of time to explore this again soon."

She shook off the trance, fighting to regain her composure, and stumbled across to the desk. Slightly confused, she grabbed her phone and looked down at the text message displayed.

"Ellison, please call. – S."

Sebastian? She felt an unexpected pang of guilt. Irrational and ridiculous, she chided herself. But why was he getting in touch? Had she forgotten something earlier? She brushed off the thought, resolving to call him later.

"Something important?" asked Rob seeing the confusion on her face.

"Sorry, no... just a friend. Rob, ... I... We," she stumbled over the words.

"Shh, we'll discuss it later, Ell. Right now, your plate is full and you've been placed under a microscope on this case."

"Ellison," she whispered, her eyes finding his.

"Pardon?"

"If we are going to explore this, please call me Ellison."

A beautiful smile crossed his face and Ell could not help but return it.

Rob stepped over to the computer, noticing his decryption program was completed. "It appears you're back online." Glancing up and down her beautiful body wrapped in thin silk, he added, "You may want to put those clothes on now. I love the view but I'm not sure how much of it I can take."

Ell winked as she turned and headed for the door. "If you play your cards right you'll be able to take all of it soon."

———

After finally getting her shower, Ell sauntered back into the office dressed in dark blue jeans and a white blouse. Rob was still there and had her computer in pieces strewn across her desk.

"Jesus Frost, how do you work on this thing? I'm guessing it hasn't been upgraded in years. Hell, you're still working on a CRT tube monitor. Why haven't you called me about this, or at least bought something from this decade?" He never looked up but, somehow, had known she was in the doorway.

"Department budget doesn't cover home equipment. It's still working so why would I shell out the dough for a new one?"

Rob laughed, "You ride around in that shiny wet dream parked out front and you're worried about the four hundred it would cost to make this thing usable?"

"The 'wet dream' is a necessity. It gets me out of a department issue beater and stops me from having to spend twenty years in federal lockup for killing the morons in requisitions."

"Right, and you couldn't have made due with a nice four door sedan for half the budget."

"But it's so shiny!" she replied in her best girlish tone.

Rob laughed and finally looked up at her. Her hair was wet and dripping slowly across the shoulders of her tight white blouse. The outfit showed every curve perfectly.

"Damn!" his jaw dropped.

Ell smiled and shook her head. "So, how long will it take to have this thing back up and running?"

"Properly? A couple hours with the right parts"

"Jesus Rob..."

"Which," he emphasized, "is why I swapped it out with a new unit from my truck." He gestured over to the far side of her desk. "Quad core processor, eighteen GB of RAM, dual LED displays with built in touch screen. The last of the software upgrades are just finishing now. You'll be up and running in about twenty seconds."

Ell settled in behind the machine as it finished the boot cycle. She clicked on the icon for the department remote connection and was greeted with a very familiar alert.

"Due to new departmental regulations and the nature of ongoing investigations, the files held by all ranking officers must now be fully encrypted. Please contact Information Services at ext 190 to schedule the required maintenance."

She smirked over at Rob who couldn't help but grin. "Sorry, I couldn't resist." He slipped the USB drive in, Ell clicked 'OK' and the decryption program went to work.

"See, idiot proof."

Ell gave him the finger. He leaned over and slowly took it

into his mouth, running his tongue down to the second knuckle. She shivered visibly.

"Ok, enough. I've got crimes to solve."

"Speaking of which, I sent Rique all the files off Bouton's laptop shortly before heading here but I have copies if you'd care to review them."

"Anything worthwhile?"

"It's hard to say without context. There was a bit of financial data, you're standard allotment of porn and illegal downloads and a ton of research into different escort services throughout the city."

"We figure she was looking for some kink for hire, she called the booking line for an S&M escort service three times on the night she died."

"Odd, I didn't get the impression she was vetting services, it looked more like research into the industry in general and spanned everything from low end call girls to bondage brothels. There was a lot of information on legality and legal loopholes for each model."

"So more than a passing interest," replied Ell. "I'll send Rique a note to dig into it and see if anything flags. If she was looking for more than a good time, she'd have had contact with some of the other agencies."

"I'll talk to some of my contacts as well. I don't use the services but I know quite a few people who have. It's possible they heard or saw something." He gathered up the loose components of her old computer. "I really should be going before I lose that overpriced P.D. contract."

Ell looked up into his soft captivating eyes, "Thanks, Rob... for everything."

"Always here to help, Lieutenant," he cupped her chin

with his free hand. "Please call me as soon as you have time, Ellison."

A shiver ran through her body at the use of her full name as she watched him head out the door.

Chapter Seven

She picked Rique up in front of the eleventh at just after six. The press had given up for the day and dispersed.

"You can finally see the pavement out here," commented her partner as he slid into the soft leather passenger's seat.

"Thank god, now we just need some politician to get caught with his pants down tonight so we can keep it that way."

"I doubt anything short of Armageddon will do it, L.T. This thing's really got legs. Every major network is reporting on the nature of Deedrie's life and death. With the amount of press she's had in the gossip rags lately, they have plenty of fodder to keep the fires burning."

"Fodder keeps fires burning? I think you're mixing your metaphors, Shaw."

"Oh gee, are they going to revoke my writer's credit?"

Ell chuckled, "Anything new pop while I was out?"

"Your boy toy cracked the uncrackable and sent me the files."

Ell cringed at the description, "Let me guess, all the

standard shit coupled with an assload of research into escort agencies."

Rique stared at her, dumbfounded.

"You don't get the stripes without some sources."

"We use stars, L.T. Stripes are for the military. If you ever put on a uniform you'd know that."

"I had it on last year for that bullshit 'Let's all get along' P.R. ceremony, could have sworn they were stripes."

"Wasn't that your promotion ceremony?"

Ell shrugged and Rique broke out into laughter.

"Ok, so the vic's got some unknown source of major cash and has been spending a lot of time looking for the right escort agency. She contacts one to book some slap and tickle, gets a freaked up tat and ends up strangled in her bedroom with all the fixings of kink gone bad," he summed up running through the basic timeline.

"We'll have a better grasp on the finances tomorrow," commented Ell. "It doesn't feel like she was looking for an agency, though, more like researching the industry as a whole."

"What the fuck? I held that bit of insight back to test you. Who the hell are your sources?"

"A lady never tells," laughed Ell.

They rode in silence for the next couple minutes until Ell pulled to a stop in front of a nice modern looking office space with a deep red neon sign glowing 'M.A.E.' with the slogan 'we find your pleasure' below in a smaller font.

"Cute," commented Rique.

Ell left the engine running and turned to face him.

"Rique, there's something you should know before we head in there."

"What? That you and Angel Demarco, proprietor of Madam Angel's Escorts, have some history?"

It was Ell's turn to be dumbfounded.

"Oh come on Ell, you knew I'd been looking into the company before we came out here. Didn't take much digging to find out it was formed fourteen years ago by Angel Demarco through a numbered corporation. Nor did it take long to determine that the original shareholders of that numbered company were Angel Demarco and Ellison Frost. You sold your shares about three months before she opened shop so I assume this," he gestured at the building, "had something to do with it."

"I knew there was a reason we kept you on the payroll. Angel and I met in high school and were roommates through college. We setup the numbered corp. as part of a business economics assignment. We had an online registry system developed to connect students with tutors. We made a couple grand over the course of the assignment with basically no day to day labor. The software ran us four hundred bucks and a party invite for a couple computer science students. When the class was over we decided to keep the company going. Two years later we were on the brink of graduation and clearing four thousand a piece monthly. It turns out the students had started using our service as a hookup tool. We turned a blind eye to it at the time. I was taking my crim degree and applying to the P.D. after graduation, Angel had a biz/com degree and no solid plans. She approached me about releasing the service to the public as a pure hookup app. I knew what my association with that could do to my career so I let her buy me out. You're looking at where she took it."

"Just think L.T., all this could have been yours," he winked pulling open the passenger door. "So how are things between the two of you now?"

"Friendly," responded Ell joining him at the front doors.

"Good, it should make this easier to deal with." He pulled open the doors and stood there shocked. The space before them was that of a typical corporate office.

Ell chuckled at the look of confusion on his face, "What did you expect whips, chains and dungeon racks? It's a company not a brothel."

Ell led him to the reception desk where a beautiful blonde in her late twenties greeted them.

"Welcome to Madame Angel's Escorts, how M.A.E we pleasure you today?"

"I think we'll skip the pleasure today," said Ell, flashing her badge. "Lieutenant Frost and Detective Shaw, we need to speak with Angel Demarco."

"Certainly, one moment please."

She pressed a button on her headset and waited a moment. "Ms. Demarco... Yes, there are two police officers here asking to see you... A Lieutenant Frost and Detective Shaw... Yes ma'am, right away."

She stood, her twelve-inch skirt and long smooth legs coming into site. "Follow me please."

"Damn," whispered Rique. "Do you see those legs?"

"Yup, they go all the way from her ankles to her hips," winked Ell.

"And they do it so well."

She led them to a large conference room and instructed them to take a seat. "Ms. Demarco will be with you shortly. Can I offer you anything to drink? Coffee? Soda?"

"I could use an ice water, thank you," said Rique and Ell rolled her eyes.

The assistant left and Ell leaned over to him. "You just wanted her to come back, didn't you?"

"Can you blame me? Did you see that ass? You could bounce quarters off it."

"If that's all you're going to do with it I would suggest you're wasting your time."

The receptionist returned with a bottle of water and a glass of ice. She was followed in by a petite, black haired woman no more than five foot four in height and likely under one hundred pounds. The woman's body was well proportioned for her size but her diminutive frame made her look much younger than her age. Her eyes were dark and her full lips blood red. If she were wrapped in latex instead of a tight fitting sundress she would appear to be the clichéd dominatrix.

"That will be all Janie, thank you for escorting the officers in."

Angel Demarco settled into a chair opposite the others and smiled across at Ell. "Lieutenant Frost, it's nice to see you. I assume, based on your company, that this is not a social call."

'Good,' thought Ell, 'she's playing dumb.'

"I am afraid not, though it is nice to see you again, Angel." Angel nodded, still smiling. "I assume by now that you have heard about Deedrie Bouton's death and the circumstances surrounding it?"

"Hard not to, every radio and T.V. station has been reporting it like she was the messiah. Sorry," she paused, "that was insensitive. I just don't understand why it needs to be so sensationalized. As you can imagine, in my line of work, this type of publicity can be quite negative."

"I would imagine it causes some problems when the negatives of this type of lifestyle are publicized," commented Rique.

Ell noticed Angel's demeanor change and steadied herself for the response.

"Rest assured, Detective, no matter what your preconceived ignorant notions of the 'lifestyle' may be, Ms. Bouton's death is not a result of it. Whoever did this is not a dominant, nor are they a member of our community. They are an abusive and do not have the slightest inclination as to the meaning, values or beliefs held within the world of BDSM. They couldn't begin to understand the pleasure that can be derived from a dom / sub relationship."

Rique could tell he started this on the wrong foot and decided silence was his best option. Ell let him stew for a moment, mostly for her own amusement.

"Angel, I am sure detective Shaw meant no offense. As you said he is merely ignorant to the lifestyle but I can assure you our investigation is not out to target or tarnish the reputations of those that participate in it."

"In that case how may I help you, Ell?"

"In the course of our investigation we have discovered that Ms. Bouton contacted your booking line three times on the night of her death."

"Yes, I am aware of this, one moment please." She hit the intercom button on the conference room phone. "Janie, can you please bring in three copies of the phone logs from last night along with any client records we have on Deedrie Bouton."

"I will have them there shortly."

"Ms. Bouton was not a regular client; however, she has used our services twice in the last month."

Janie arrived, much to Rique's delight, and set down a series of documents for each of them.

"As you can see, Ms. Bouton's first call arrived at four twenty two. She chose to use our automated booking service but failed to complete the booking and disconnected the call at four twenty seven. Her second call arrived at ten after five and she once again chose our automated service and again disconnected prior to finalizing the booking. Her third call arrived at five twenty four; she chose an assisted booking and was routed to operator 5348. Per the operator's notes Ms. Bouton was not satisfied with the available booking options and chose not to continue at that time."

"Operator 5384, how would we contact them?" asked Rique.

"I suppose you could call in and try to get lucky." Angel smiled sarcastically. "Sorry, I couldn't resist. Operator 5384 is Jane Smith."

Both Ell and Rique gave her a skeptical look.

"Seriously, Jane Smith, located out of our uptown call centre. We do thorough background checks on all employees from escorts to assistants. Ironic as it may seem, that's her real name."

"We'll need a copy of her employee file," he responded. "In fact, we will need access to all employee and client documents on file."

"Our employees are fully vetted, detective. They are also required to sign both confidentiality and disclosure paperwork so providing their files will not be an issue. Our client files, however, are fully confidential. I am sure you can understand the privacy concerns we are dealing with here."

"Angel, I assure you we will not break that confidentiality

unless it is directly related to this case," said Ell.

"I'm sorry, Ell, I need to do what's right to protect my clients. Without a court order there's nothing I can do."

"You know we'll have a warrant in the next forty-eight hours. Why not save all of us some time here, Angel. The quicker we can eliminate your clients from the suspect list the quicker we can move on."

"As much as I would like to do that, I have an obligation to provide discretion and confidentiality. I need to protect my business. If I am ordered by the courts to hand over those files then I will do so, but I cannot willingly break that confidentiality. My clients have placed their trust in me and I must do what I can to protect them. I will provide you all our information on Deedrie Bouton as I see no reason to withhold it, but that is the best I can do."

"Please have that information and the employee files sent to this email," Rique handed her a business card, "as soon as possible."

"You'll have them within the hour, if there is anything else I can do to help please let me know. I have a vested interest in seeing this solved quickly and, while my motives may be selfish, my offer to help is genuine."

Ell rose and reached to shake Angel's hand. "Thank you for your assistance." Angel bypassed the outstretched hand and pulled Ell into a hug.

"It's good to see you Ell, let's get together and catch up once all this is done," she whispered.

"I'll call," responded Ell.

Angel released Ell and saw Rique standing there with his arms parted and a big grin across his face. She laughed and hugged him as well.

"Sorry to come down on you so hard, detective, I'm a little passionate about my business."

"No harm done. Those of us with preconceived ignorant notions need a little verbal smack every now and again."

Angel giggled and turned to Ell, "I see why you like him."

<hr/>

They arrived back at the precinct shortly before seven and headed for the bullpen to regroup and coordinate with Jones and Baker before end of shift.

"Angel's files just came through. I'll run down the operator and give the employees a once over to see if anything pops. Do you want me to get Judge Horn on the line about the court order?"

"Let's give it twenty-four and see where we are. Right now all we have is a cancelled booking, not much to justify the client records. We could probably convince the judge to release the files based on that, the crime scene and Bouton's research, but I don't see what we'll get out of it other than some very embarrassed people."

"Is that the cop or the friend talking?"

Ell considered her response carefully, knowing she was walking a thin line.

"It's the cop's reasoning but the friend's concern, and I'm good with that."

Rounding the corner into the bullpen, they found Baker and Jones huddled around a computer rolling through some security footage.

"Damn, reality T.V. is getting worse by the day," snickered Rique as he walked up behind them.

"Yeah, rumor has it they are so hard up they're thinking about filming the life and times of Rique Shaw," quipped Jones.

"I thought that was already filmed as a pro abstinence movie for high school health classes?" laughed Ell, joining the ribbing.

"What the hell happened to my wound free day, L.T.?"

"Seven o two," said Ell gesturing to the clock. "New shift, new day. So what have you two found?"

"Turns out the vic live tweeted her tattoo appointment last night at seven forty," Jones handed her a print off of the twitter stream.

Ell looked down at the photo of Deedrie bent over the back of a tattoo chair, her new tat just being started, followed by the message. "New ink on the way, you'll be seeing it everywhere, D.B.E!"

"No mention of the location, but she's learnt to be discreet with the paparazzi constantly on her tail," continued Jones. "So, we took the photo and ran down all the premier shops uptown. Finally got a hit at Classic Ink on third. The owner was reluctant to admit she was there given all the press she's getting, but the photo's a dead match for his station. Baker ran him the standard obstructing justice spiel and he quickly became Mr. Cooperative. We received his security footage about ten minutes ago and just started to watch. Systems pretty antiquated so we've got picture but no sound."

"It's something, run it through and see if she was with anyone. Is Mr. Cooperative's statement filed?"

"I just finished typing it up but there's not much there. He was stuck in 'hot chick' fan-mode and didn't notice much other than her tits," responded Baker.

"Fire me a copy and keep on the video. Rique and I are pulling a double, if you want the O.T. it's available, otherwise get back on it first thing and we'll regroup to timeline and brainstorm in the morning."

"We're here for a few more anyway; we'll get this knocked off before we head out. Oh, and thanks for the assist, L.T." replied Jones dangling the new set of keys requisitions had dropped off earlier.

"Baker was threatening to make me trade. What choice did I have?"

Ell headed back to her office and noticed two new voicemails waiting for her. She hit the speaker phone and called up the messages. A familiar cold tone filled the air, "Lieutenant Frost, this is Donna Brennan in requisitions. I am calling to inform you that the new transportation for Detective Jones and Baker has now been processed. I trust this satisfies your request."

The line went dead and Ell smiled, 'Donna Brennan' just received a short reprieve from her wrath. She hit 'one' and was taken to the next message.

"Lieutenant," it was Commander Nuez's assistant, "the commander would like to speak to you as soon as possible. Please let me know when you will be available. Thank you."

She smiled again and shook her head, surprised it took twelve hours for brass to get involved. She knew the commander would be under plenty of pressure to micro-manage this one. Hitting extension 145, she waited for the call to connect.

"Commander Nuez's office. How may I help you?" It was the commander's assistant, the ever-formal Keith Dillon. His robotic, professional personality grated on her and she took every opportunity to point it out, but it was all in good fun.

On some level, Ell had an appreciation and fondness for the man. He was extremely loyal and she respected that.

"You can get him off my back and let me solve this damn thing," said Ell trying to act annoyed.

"Lieutenant Frost, a pleasure as always. The commander would like a moment of your time if you can spare it. He is aware that you are on an important case but would like to speak to you about its status as soon as you are available."

"Jesus Keith, 'The commander wants to see you' would have worked. Tell him I can be up there in ten."

"I will free his schedule as I know this is a priority and he does not want to keep you waiting."

"Next time go with 'Ten works', Keith. I'll be there."

"As always it has been a pleasure, Lieutenant."

Ell squeezed her temples and quickly compiled a brief report on the status of the case. Just as she was about to log off, an email arrived from Lund in crime scene.

"Ell, I've attached the CS preliminary report from the Bouton site. Details are uploading to the database now. We will let you know when we have more."

Ell grinned, looked at her clock and hit reply.

"Lund, you're slipping, you promised me this by end of day."

She closed out and headed for the elevator. While waiting for the lift to arrive, her phone chimed an incoming email.

"It's 7:18, Ell, get a new watch."

She laughed and hit reply as she stepped through the opening doors.

"As I tell my detectives, New shift, new day!"

The elevator arrived at the fifth floor and she was about to head into the commander's office when her phone chimed again.

"As I tell my detectives, even with empirical evidence... ah screw it. Fuck off, Frost. ;)"

She laughed and opened the door to Commander Nuez's office. The smiling, slightly creepy face of Keith Dillon was there to greet her.

"The commander is waiting and would like you to go in as soon as you arrive."

She headed across the reception area and called out to Keith before opening the door.

"He's waiting, would have worked."

———

"You need to get that robot out there a new personality chip," commented Ell, taking a seat across from Commander Nuez.

The commander grinned and ran a hand through his perfectly quaffed dark brown hair. For a man in his mid-forties with a desk job, Juan Nuez had aged well.

"I know a guy in I.T. that could probably hook that up for you," she continued.

"I doubt even Rob would have the abilities required there and I would hate to see his charge for it if he does."

Ell blushed slightly at the mention of Rob's name.

"Oh, come on Frost, everyone in the department knows about your personal I.T. slave."

'If only they knew the truth,' she thought, her heart beating faster at the mere thought of him.

"What can I say, Commander? It must be my charming personality."

"Let's go with that." His grin grew. "I think you know why I've called you in. I'm getting massive push on this Bouton case, Ell. I don't want to hold you up but I've got to ask you to keep me in the loop on this one. P.R. wants to get a press release out and the mayor's on my ass for updates."

"Lund pushed it hard and the preliminary crime scene came in about ten minutes ago. Sanders has COD as strangulation and TOD between elven and midnight. I've got Jones and Baker running down footage of the vic at a tattoo parlor about four hours prior to death. She had attempted to book an S&M escort earlier that evening but didn't follow through on it according to the agency. Rique is running that down and checking on the story. At first glance it appears to be sex play gone bad, but I'm not buying that she was with a pro. The scenes too sloppy and it doesn't feel like a professional dom. We are digging into the vic's last few weeks and I have Squirrelly, sorry, Browne trying to trace her income stream. I've given him twenty-four to get it done so you may want to prepare accounting for that bill."

"I'll give them a heads up. Where are we on motive and suspects?"

"Right now it's too early to say, I haven't had a chance to review the crime scene package yet, but if I'm right, there should be prints and possible DNA. I'm just starting on known associates but, with the life this girl's lived for the last six months, that list is long. I would like to interview the parents and siblings tomorrow and thought I should have you play point on that given the political ramifications."

"I'll organize it and let you know. They'll want their lawyer present. The mayor was grateful you didn't try and pull them in today."

"I could use the background but given the relationship reported in the media, I don't see them involved in this. We'll do the standard checks but, unless something jumps out in the financials, I don't see any reason to run them through the mud."

"Ok, keep on it Ell and if anything odd comes up, let me know. I have authorization to get you whatever you need on this one so pull in the troops for O.T. and push the consultants hard."

"Those are the things that keep me smiling, Commander. Maybe we can hide Keith's personality chip in the budget. Call it required tech upgrades. I can probably talk Rob into a discounted rate."

Nuez shook his head, smiling. "I'm sure you could. Get back to work, Lieutenant. Let's pin this one down fast."

Ell headed back to her office, giving Keith a quick nod on the way out. She settled back into her desk chair and pulled up the crime scene report. About thirty minutes and two aspirin into it, her office phone rang. She didn't recognize the number but decided to answer.

"Hello?"

"Hey beautiful," Rob's voice resonated in her mind, calming her almost instantly. "I'm just about done for the day and thought you might like to catch dinner."

Ell's heart rate rose, she could feel the tingle in her skin as the thought of seeing him again encompassed her. Her mind flashed to an image of her cooking in nothing but a short apron, him behind her running his hands across her body. His lips tracing across her neck and shoulders as he pinned her arms to the counter and bent her forward.

"Ell? You still there?"

"Sorry, just a little... distracted," she replied coming back to reality. "I'm sorry, Rob, I'm really tied up on this case. I'm pulling a double with little hope of getting out of here in time tonight."

"Ellison, you need to eat."

The use of her full name coupled with the strength of his tone melted her reserve.

"Rob..."

"I'm on my way to the eleventh now, I'll pick us up something on the way and give you a hand with the case when I get there. I'm sure you could use an extra set of eyes on it."

His tone left no room for argument but Ell didn't trust herself, she yearned to be alone with him, to give herself to him, and knew the distraction would be overwhelming.

"In that case pick up dinner for five and I'll expense it."

"Sounds good I'll be there in 'under twenty minutes'," he laughed and disconnected.

"Thank god," she muttered. In a group setting the likelihood for distraction would be mitigated. 'Oh, shit!' she thought. How could she explain the need to pull him in on this? She grabbed her phone and hit redial.

"Did you miss me already?"

"Oooo Rob, I want you, I need you, I can't live without you," she replied in a much more sultry and meaningful tone this time. He chuckled and she went on. "How comfortable are you discussing the lifestyle with my team?"

"Well, not as comfortable as I would be with you. Why?"

"Honestly?"

"Always the best policy, Ellison."

Her resolve weakened. "I need a valid reason to call you in on this. I don't really want to hit the bullpen and say, Rob wanted to take me out for supper but I've asked him to work with us instead."

"Are you embarrassed by me, Ms. Frost?" She could tell he is being facetious but the truth in the statement stung.

"I take enough flack about you already. I just don't want to put this out there prematurely."

"Rest your pretty head, Ellison. I'll be more than happy to share my kinky secrets to help save you the teasing. I can also bring you all up to speed on the additional data I found encrypted on a separate partition of Deedrie's laptop."

"What?" Ell's interest was piqued.

"You can wait in anticipation with the rest of your team. I'm just grabbing the food. See you soon."

Ell headed across the hall to the bullpen. "Jones, Baker, do you two have any immediate plans?"

"I've got a date with a glass of wine and a soft bed, but it can wait," replied Baker and Ell's mind temporarily slipped to an image of the beautiful redhead draped naked across rumpled, white silk sheets. She pushed the thoughts aside, hating to do so, and continued. "Jones?"

"Nothing I can't put off, L.T."

"Good, we're going to round table in about fifteen. Rob's on his way down with something he found on a hidden drive in Deedrie's laptop. I told him to bring food, though god knows what we'll end up with. He also, apparently, has some insight into the BDSM lifestyle that may come in handy, and I've asked him to reach out to his contacts for anything he can on Bouton."

"When you say insight, L.T. ..." Rique left the question hanging.

"Hell, I don't know Shaw, you ask him. Maybe he'll give you some tips."

The others laughed and Ell was relieved to have dodged a

bullet. She headed back to her office and refocused on the crime scene report. She was just getting back into it when a singular thought hit her.

'*Fuck!*' she just told her team about Rob's lifestyle, and he would likely be sharing a lot more detail on the subject. What the hell happens if and when their relationship comes out?

Chapter Eight

*C*rime scene had managed to locate nearly fifty different sets of prints from Deedrie's bedroom. It appeared the young lady entertained often. They were focusing on those lifted from the body and sex toys which reduced that number to three. These were being run through local, state and federal databases, but at the time of the report there had been no match. There was no DNA found on scene. The M.E report did indicate sexual penetration but no semen had been found on the body.

As suspected, the ligature marks were a positive match to the nylon rope found on scene. Sanders' team was also able to match the bruising on the victims back to a soft leather whip they had taken into evidence. The crop marks, however, could not be conclusively identified. There were two riding crops found amongst the toys inventoried, but neither matched the shape or size of the bruising on the body.

'A souvenir?' wondered Ell. 'Or perhaps something the killer brought with them?'

She was mulling over the possibilities when she heard a cough from her doorway. Her heart skipped when she saw him, his hair loose in a styled mess, his body rippling in tight jeans and a form fitting sweater. It was his eyes, however, that truly captivated her. Those deep blue eyes that seemed to pierce into her soul.

"Sorry, didn't mean to disturb you," said Rob, his voice quiet but strong. "I brought steaks," he continued, holding out a takeout bag from Dunn's Steakhouse.

Ell could not get over his calm confidence, it drew her to him. She felt safe in his presence.

"Buying my team's hearts with succulent beef and roast potatoes?"

"And homemade vanilla ice cream," he added with a smile.

"You don't play fair. Let's go feed the wildlife so we can get on with this."

He refused to move as she left the office, forcing her to squeeze past him, their bodies brushing together. Her breath caught as the electric spark between them attacked her pulse. She gazed up into his eyes, lost in the moment, yearning to press her lips to his. He leaned down, his lips brushing against her ear.

"Not the dessert I desire but it will have to do for now."

She shivered and slowly continued past him into the hall. She could feel his eyes on her ass as she headed to the bullpen, bringing a smile to her face.

"Hope you're all hungry, Rob is attempting to seduce us with food."

"My favorite type of seduction," responded Jones, eyeing up the takeout bag as Rob started handing out the portioned dinners to the thanks of all involved. Baker gave him a flirty smile and flicked her hair over her shoulder. If Ell were a jealous person she'd have reacted differently but as it were, the image of the two of them flirting and laughing brought her lust and passion to the forefront. Fighting off the mental image of the two of their beautiful bodies wrapped together, she began to question her plan. It was hard enough to concentrate with only Baker in the room.

"Jesus L.T., you need to invite him to more meetings." suggested Rique, salivating over the tender ribeye and garlic roasted potatoes.

"I agree," chimed in Baker who was salivating over something else entirely.

"Christ, Shaw, it's just a hunk of cow," said Ell. "A glorious, juicy, tasty hunk of cow," she added quietly after taking her first bite.

"Speaking of glorious, juicy and tasty," said Baker shamelessly, "Ell mentioned you may be able to enlighten us on the sexual aspects of this case, Rob."

For the first time, Ell saw Rob blush, a beautiful crimson glow filling his cheeks.

"I believe I can offer some insight," he responded. "My understanding is that the victim was found bound and gagged with no signs of struggle. Please understand, I have not seen the full report on this. Assuming the body wasn't staged..."

"It wasn't" said Ell.

"Then we can also assume the victim not only knew her partner, but trusted them. Our suspect will likely be someone she trusted, with knowledge of kink but not a dominant by nature."

"What makes you say that?" asked Jones.

"The position, rope work and accessories used suggest a certain level of experience in the basics of pleasure through restraint. I believe the toys were high end and the photos I have seen suggest decent knowledge in wrap and knot techniques."

"But not a dominant because of the lack of care and concern, right?" asked Baker smiling over at Ell.

"Very insightful," responded Rob. "The core beliefs of a true dominant would have been to protect. If something had gone wrong they would have done everything to save her. The crime scene suggests otherwise. It also suggests a lack of respect for the art of giving pleasure. The toys and implements were strewn across the table and floor with no care to organization or planning."

"So he's into the kink but not the lifestyle," commented Rique.

"Correct, but have we pinpointed the suspect as male?" asked Rob.

"The M.E. report confirms penetration," responded Baker, eye fucking Rob at every opportunity.

"Was there semen present, or perhaps male DNA?"

"No," smiled Ell understanding where he was going.

"Then I would not make that assumption. Penetration can easily be accomplished by the numerous toys at the scene or even fingers and fists. While it is true there are far more female than male submissives, dominants, be they active in the beliefs of the lifestyle or not, are fairly equal across gender lines. Often, women who are inexperienced in submission seek out female dommes as a sense of security."

"You're talking about bi-sexual women," commented Jones.

"Not necessarily, sexuality lines are often crossed in this type of relationship, especially by those not completely secure in the decision. Deedrie Bouton was very new to it."

"Pardon?" asked Ell a little surprise by this insight.

"I suppose that leads me to the other reason I'm here." He pulled a 64GB USB drive from his pocket and tossed it to Rique. "Bouton had a separate, encrypted partition on her hard drive. I nearly missed it because she had shielded the partition from detection by the primary operating system. I noticed an odd bootlog entry indicating that a second OS was present. It was a Unix backbone but the partition was extremely customized and highly secure. Whoever set it up knew what they were doing and took their time getting it right. I ended up doing a bit by bit backdoor file system scrub and was able to capture about ninety percent of the data."

"What the hell was this girl hiding?" asked Jones.

"Well, that's the thing," continued Rob. "It's a fucking diary."

"Does she have the world's snoopiest siblings?" asked Rique. "Who the hell goes to that much trouble to hide their daily ramblings?"

"No, it's literally a 'Fucking Diary', explained Rob. "It lists every sexual act she's performed in the last eight months. Who it was with, what positions were best, what drugs enhanced or depleted orgasm. This girl was on a mission to seriously get off. It starts out fairly vanilla, standard experimentation. The real kink kicks in about a month and a half ago."

"Lieutenant, I volunteer to read each and every line thoroughly in order to solve this one," said Rique to a round of groans and laughter.

Ell motioned for him to toss her the drive, "I'll take this one. We don't want you having a heart attack. The department can't afford the worker's comp claim. So where does this leave us?"

"Nowhere," responded Baker, "but I'm going back to the security footage of the tattoo parlor. We were looking for a male unsub the first time through. It's time to broaden that search."

"Any word on the operator?" Ell asked Rique.

"Yes, Jane Smith of 225 W Alder St. She's working tonight and I'm heading to M.A.E.'s uptown call centre at ten o'clock for an interview."

"Ok, run it alone, I want to review these new files and see if there's anything there. Baker, Jones, as soon as you're done with the security footage, send me an update and call it a night. It's going to be another long one tomorrow so get the rest while you can."

"Lieutenant, I've got nothing else going on this evening, if it's ok with you I'd like to ride with Detective Shaw and see this through," said Rob.

"That's his call. Wanna babysit the consultant, Shaw?"

"Oh boy! Can I mom?"

Ell laughed, "I guess you're with him. Enjoy!"

Chapter Nine

December 12th

First Anal Experience – It was not at all what I expected. Julie and I hadn't planned on it today. We were set to take the day off and compile our research, but after a couple drinks and a hit of GHB we couldn't help ourselves. The increased frequency of orgasm is definitely leading to a higher sex drive, and Tommy was on the mark with the GHB. Coupled with a few drinks the intensity is amazing.

Jules and I were just playing around really. We were taking turns going down on each other, not planning on pulling out the toys tonight. She was fingering me deep and nibbling my clit, an amazing feeling. The more I got into it, the harder she would suck. My clit was extremely swollen and the intensity of the pressure was amazing. I wasn't really paying attention. I was lost in the ecstasy of it and barely even noticed when she slipped a lubed finger up my ass. I had no idea what she had done. All I knew was that I immediately began to climb towards a massive orgasm. She continued to attack my clit and slowly slid a second finger in. As my ass stretched to accommodate her, I finally began to realize what was happening, but I was too far gone to think about it. My climax rolled over me harder than anything I've felt before. Jules tells me I squirted as I came, but I have no recollection of it. My mind was blank. I could think of nothing but the pleasure I was experiencing.

I'm a little sore tonight but we are planning to try and replicate the results in a couple days. I think we may use some of the smaller toys and see if there's a difference. Needless to say, Anal Expertise is going on the list of requirements.

Dee, B.E.

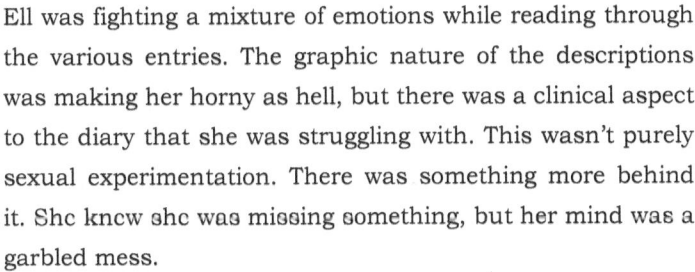

Ell was fighting a mixture of emotions while reading through the various entries. The graphic nature of the descriptions was making her horny as hell, but there was a clinical aspect to the diary that she was struggling with. This wasn't purely sexual experimentation. There was something more behind it. She knew she was missing something, but her mind was a garbled mess.

She pulled out her iPhone and checked the time, 12:45 a.m., no wonder she was dragging. She had expected Rique and Rob to be back from interviewing the operator by now and was contemplating calling when she noticed she had two missed texts, both from Rique. She had been so involved in the diary she hadn't even heard the chime.

Received 11:32 p.m. – "Operator is sending in a voice recording of the booking call. On our way back now. – R"

Received 12:11 a.m. – "Following a lead that just hit, will fill you in when we get back, don't wait up. – R"

It piqued her curiosity but the long day was catching up to her. She considered heading home for a couple hours rest before morning. She was going to need it, especially if Commander Nuez managed to line up interviews with the family. 'Fuck it', she decided, 'no use wasting forty five minutes of drive time.' She headed across the hall to the now abandoned bullpen and stretched out on the sofa against the far wall deciding to catch a few hours and get back at it fresh.

She tried to move but her arms were restrained. Darkness surrounded her, the soft touch of silk caressing her face. A blindfold she surmised. A slight breeze brushed across her naked body causing her to shiver. She could smell him as he moved closer, a wonderful scent, subtle but musky and sweet. Her mouth watered and her senses began to adjust to the lack of sight. She heard his breathing, steady and deep but with a hint of excitement. The touch of soft suede ran slowly across her chest. Too small for a flogger, a crop perhaps? Her senses heightened the experience, sending waves of pleasure coursing through her. The item traced the round of her breasts avoiding her nipples and rising up her neck, over her chin and across her lips. She licked it briefly. Italian leather, definitely a crop. The realization sent shockwaves of anticipation through her skin. Again she pulled to move her arms but could not. The sting in her wrists indicated they were bound above her head by hard metal. Her ankles were free but her thighs restrained and unable to close. Not a spreader, she realized, but ropes tied off to something unknown. The struggle increased her anticipation as the crop slid downwards across her taught midriff, stopping briefly at her pubic bone. Teasing, it continued across the edge of her pussy to her right thigh.

"Please," she begged, and the soft leather snapped roughly, stinging as it connected. She moaned in ecstasy, yearning for more. As if reading her mind, he snapped the crop once more, higher this time, getting slowly closer to the prize.

She began to pant, the want and lust rolling through her. His lips replaced the crop, kissing her welted thigh, his tongue gliding across her skin. She could feel herself dripping, praying for release. Needing all of him. His tongue brushed lightly across her pussy before pulling away, extending the tease. She felt his strong hand cupping the back of her head, loosening the blindfold. It slowly slid free and she gazed into his eyes. Soft blue eyes that pierced her soul.

"Oh Rob," she whispered, as the face slowly morphed until Sebastian was looking down on her.

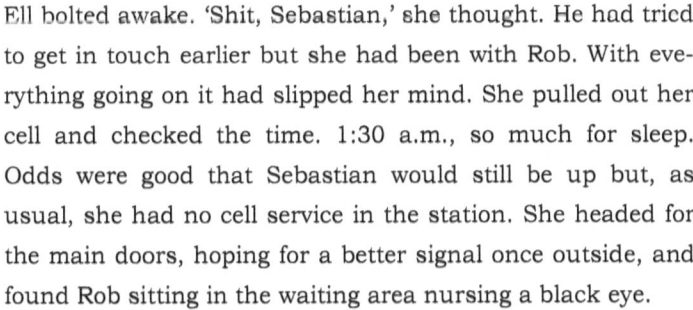

Ell bolted awake. 'Shit, Sebastian,' she thought. He had tried to get in touch earlier but she had been with Rob. With everything going on it had slipped her mind. She pulled out her cell and checked the time. 1:30 a.m., so much for sleep. Odds were good that Sebastian would still be up but, as usual, she had no cell service in the station. She headed for the main doors, hoping for a better signal once outside, and found Rob sitting in the waiting area nursing a black eye.

"Jesus Rob, what the hell happened?"

"Rique and I were following a hunch. Turns out Deedrie had an affinity for a specific dom at Madam Angel's. She'd had two sessions with him this month and had specifically requested him the night she died. The operator told her he was unavailable and she was pretty upset about it. Said she would contact him directly and hung up. We figured we'd pay the guy a visit and see where he was last night. We got lucky, the guy was home but he clammed up tight when Rique identified himself. Refused to answer anything due to client confidentiality. Rique gave him the run down about hindering the investigation but this guy wasn't budging. He reached into his coat for what we later learned was his cell. Rique thought he had a weapon and took him down. The guy reacted as you would expect and fought back. I jumped in to help restrain him and caught an elbow for the effort. Shaw finally got the cuffs on him and drug his ass in for formal questioning. You were dead to the world when we got here so he said he was going to toss him in interrogation and let him stew for a bit before grabbing you."

Ell's blood was pumping now and sleep was the furthest thing from her mind. "You need to get some ice on that before it swells up. Technically you're a civilian so, if you want, you can press charges."

"I don't think that's advisable."

Ell gave him a confused look.

"I'm pretty sure it was Detective Shaw's elbow."

Ell laughed and shook her head. "There's ice in the bull-pen, let's go."

She grabbed his hand and felt the familiar shock of excitement flow through her. They snagged Rob an ice pack and headed down to interrogation. Ell's excitement was growing as they approached Rique in the hallway outside of the room.

"L.T., guy's been less than forthcoming with information.

Refuses to talk about Deedrie due to client confidentiality. Says he was on another booking last night but the alibi's weak. He won't give us the name of the client to verify. He's definitely hiding something."

She gestured to a room just off of interrogation one.

"You can observe from there if you'd like," she said to Rob. "Shaw, you're with me."

Ell started the recording app on her phone as she walked in and began the standard spiel without looking up.

"Lieutenant Frost and Detective Shaw, interviewing person of interest in the Deedrie Bouton homicide. Can you please state your name for the r..."

Ell finally glanced up and her heart nearly stopped as she looked into the deadpan eyes of Sebastian Leriux.

"Hello, Ellison."

"Son of a bitch," she whispered. "Shaw, outside, now!"

Sebastian smiled slightly, and Rique stared at her confused. Ell stopped the recorder, grabbed his arm and pulled him into the hallway."

She paced the hall back and forth as Rob came out of ob servation, a concerned look on his face.

"L.T.? What the hell?" asked Rique.

"Fuck!" she screamed. Her lives were crashing together with no logical way out.

Rob looked over at Rique, "Can you give us a moment, please?" Rique stared at him, exasperated.

"Please?" repeated Rob and Detective Shaw headed down the hall to give them some privacy.

"Ellison, you have to tell him"

She stared at him in disbelief. How could he know?

"I heard what he called you, I know what that means."

She could feel the tears welling in her eyes, the fear overwhelming her, no longer about her job, her career, but rather, Rob. What would he think?

"Ellison," he said grasping her hand gently, "this isn't about us. We'll figure us out later. Right now this is about you, your job, your case and your partner. He needs to know he can trust you just as you do him. You need to tell him."

She felt things begin to focus, her body calming with his touch.

"How do you do that?" she asked meekly.

"Witchcraft." he responded with a smile.

Ell steadied her nerves and flagged Rique to come back. He looked annoyed and was about to launch into something when she held up her hand.

"He didn't do it."

"How could..." she stopped him again.

"His alibi is about as airtight as they come. At the time of the murder he was entertaining a client at the Grand Larriott."

"A client?" asked Shaw suspiciously.

Ell steadied herself again, "He was with me. We were together from shortly after ten until I called you this morning."

"Jesus Christ, L.T."

"Here's the problem. If we go in there and question him on the record about his whereabouts, he's going to clam up and claim client confidentiality because he knows what this could do to my career."

"L.T., it's just sex, everyone does it."

"You know that's not true, Rique. It's not just sex. It's kink, and that alone is enough to have me under a microscope. It's also prostitution, sure they hide behind the legal loophole of paying for an escorted date and everything else is between two consenting adults. It keeps them out of court and we turn a blind eye and collect the tax revenue, but everyone knows what it is. If it goes on the record it could mean my badge. He knows that and he won't let it happen."

"Fuck, I've already got him logged in, if we don't interview him it'll send flags up and brass is watching this case tight."

"So we question him and we try our best to give him another way out."

"And if he decides to bring up your name on the record?" asked Rob.

"He won't," she replied.

"That's a pretty big risk to take, Ellison."

She could see his protective urges coming through and part of her wanted to squeal with joy.

"Would you?" she asked, then, remembering Rique was there, added, "If it were one of your subs in my position."

"No, I can't imagine I would," Rob nodded, giving her a steadying gaze before returning to the observation room.

Ell took a deep breath and looked over at Rique, "Let's try this again."

They entered the room and she started the recording app.

"Resuming interview, please state your name for the record," she said, trying not to look into his piercing eyes as she sat across from him.

"Sebastian Francis Leriux"

'Francis?' she thought.

"Mr. Leriux, I understand you were acquainted with Deedrie Bouton."

"Yes, I was."

"And what was the nature of that relationship?"

"She was a client."

"A client? And what is your line of work?"

"I am employed as a male escort with Madame Angel's Escorts."

"And what, exactly, does that work entail?" Ell was letting him get the legal loophole on the record.

"We provide fantasy dates, such as roleplay."

"Roleplay?"

"Yes, depending on what the client wants. For example," he grinned, "I recently had a client that wished to act out a scene as a high class hooker. She waited in a bar and pretended to solicit an unknown male for a very hefty price. I approached as an undercover police officer, and we played out a scene of arrest and flirtation."

Ell tried not to react.

"And do these fantasy sessions include sex."

"They are usually sexual or flirtatious in nature but the paid services do not include any sexual acts."

Ell's next line of questioning would have normally dug into the 'unpaid' services but she let it go and moved on.

"Did Deedrie Bouton hire you for these fantasy roleplay services?"

"She did not hire me directly, she booked the services through Madam Angel's and I happened to be the escort selected to provide them."

"And what fantasy was Ms. Bouton interested in?"

"I'm afraid I can not divulge confidential client information."

"Mr. Leriux, Angel Demarco has already agreed to provide us all information that her company has on Ms. Bouton. The nature of these services is not in the file, but you are breaking no required confidentiality by speaking of them."

Sebastian paused for a moment, searching for the correct answer. His agreement with Madame Angel's was very specific on what he could disclose. However, Ell knew that he trusted her implicitly. She could see him trying to justify a reason to break confidentiality. She just needed to give him a way.

"I'll tell you what, let's table that question until Ms Demarco can assure you that you are not breaching your contract by answering."

Ell was not looking forward to the next question but knew she needed the answers on the record.

"Were you and Ms. Bouton sexual partners?"

"Not within the bounds of services rendered."

"And outside of those bounds?"

"We had two sexual encounters as consenting adults."

"I assume those encounters, not being part of the paid services, do not fall under the guise of client confidentiality."

Sebastian smiled, recognizing what she had done, "I suppose they do not."

"Please explain to us the nature of those encounters."

"Ms. Bouton was interested in exploring submission. I would not classify her as a natural submissive, but she was curious about the mindset and wanted to know how and why some derive pleasure from it."

"So these encounters were more research than sexual satisfaction."

"I choose to believe that I left her quite satisfied," he smiled slyly, "but your classification would be correct."

"Did she indicate why she was interested in this type of research?"

"No, nor did I pursue it."

Ell steadied herself and prepared for the line of questioning she feared most, hoping Sebastian would understand where she was leading him.

"Madame Angels's records indicate that Ms Bouton attempted to book your services last night. When she was informed that you were unavailable she mentioned that she would contact you directly. Did she do so?"

"Yes, she did," Ell felt like she'd just been hit by a freight train. She had not expected that response. "However, I did not receive the message until this morning. As I told the detective, I spent the evening with another client. Out of respect for my clients, I do not turn on my cell phone when in their company. Ms. Bouton left me a voicemail at 9:43 p.m."

"Do you have a copy of this message?"

"Yes, I saved it and can provide it to you once my personal items are returned."

Ell took a deep breath and looked into his eyes, hoping he understood where she was about to take him.

"Can anyone verify your meeting with this client?" She could tell he was about to say that he could not speak about it due to confidentiality. Her eyes begged him to follow her, to understand what she was looking for. He paused.

"I can't say for sure. We met in the lobby of the Grand Larriott at ten after ten. I booked a room as I planned to stay for the evening. The hotel would have record of the booking and I am sure the concierge would remember me as we spoke at length about the upcoming Collins International charity auction. She is an up and coming artist and had recently donated her first major piece."

Ell breathed a sigh of relief. Ok step one down, now to establish his whereabouts for the time of death. "And where did you go from there?"

"My client proceeded to the hotel bar while I headed up to my room, 1422 I believe. I took approximately thirty minutes to settle in, set up the room and unpack before heading back down to the bar."

"And what time was this?"

"Just after eleven."

"Did you speak with anyone that can verify that timeline?"

He thought for a moment, "The bartender. I ordered a gin and tonic shortly after arriving. In fact, I have the receipt in my wallet. We are required to submit any out of pocket expenses incurred while with a client."

Ell knew the receipt would show that he ordered the drink at about quarter after eleven. She also knew that it would be itemized on her own bill from Madame Angel's. With a twenty minute drive from the Larriott to Deedrie's penthouse he had covered most of the time frame.

"What time did you leave the bar?"

"We stayed long enough for a drink and to play out the scene she requested. I believe we left the bar shortly before midnight."

"And the bartender can verify this?"

"I would imagine he can, we made a bit of a scene when leaving."

Ell glanced over at Rique.

"I'll check it out," he responded.

"Thank you for your cooperation, Mr. Leriux, we would like to make a recording of the voicemail before you leave. If you think of anything else that may help in our investigation, please do not hesitate to call."

Turning to Rique she added, "Cut him loose."

Sebastian smiled at her. It was a grin that would normally

melt her to the core, but in that moment she didn't feel it. She was merely numb.

As she walked into the hall, her emotions in turmoil, she found herself wrapped in Rob's arms.

"You did well," he said, stroking her hair as she fought to regain her balance.

"I..." she stumbled for the words.

"Shhh. It's fine. You're exhausted and stressed, he sees that as well. You need to rest."

"I need to prep for interviews," she responded half heartedly.

"Ellison," he said firmly, "If I need to lock you in a cell and force you to sleep, I will."

She sighed, looking up into his eyes. "The bunk rooms are just around the corner. I'll go grab a couple hours and prep in the morning. Tell Rique to finish up with Leriux and call it a night."

He released her and she turned down the hall, wanting to pull him with her but knowing that would defeat the purpose. Her mind was spinning as she headed for a soft bunk and some much needed sleep.

Chapter Ten

She was restless, asleep but unable to find peace. Then, as if a blanket of security had been placed around her, she calmed. She found solace and with it, rest. She woke three hours later to the sound of her cell phone alarm. 6:00 a.m. like every other day, but today was different. At first she could not make out why. The room was not her own. 'No, the bunks,' she remembered. But why did she feel restrained? Gaining her bearings she could tell what was wrong. An arm lay draped across her, cradling her tight, refusing to let go. She did not need to turn and look to know that it was Rob's, she could feel it. The familiar sense of spark and comfort she had experienced with each touch the day before.

"When did you sneak in here?" she asked, barely awake enough to get the question out.

"Sometime after Rique headed home, about three thirty. I came to check on you, and you were so restless you barely stayed on the bunk."

"And you thought taking up half of it would help?" she teased him.

"Seemed to do the trick," he laughed.

"Thanks, but I really do need to get up. Mind moving this chunk of muscle that seems to be holding me down?"

"I definitely mind, but as you wish, Lieutenant." He raised his arm and allowed her to slide out from beneath it.

"I'm going to grab a shower and a coffee. Do you want anything?"

"So many things, Ellison, but right now I'm opting for a couple hours sleep. We overpaid consultants don't have to be in until nine."

"Pussy!"

"Is that an offer?"

Ell laughed and headed out the door. "Enjoy your sleep, pervert."

After a warm shower and two cups of coffee she was starting to feel ready for the day. She composed a quick email update to Commander Nuez and inquired about interview times for the Bouton family. She was surprised when a response came nearly immediately.

"Interviews are set for 10:30 a.m. at the Bouton Holdings' office. Thanks for the update."

Ell set to work compiling notes on the new information that came to light the previous evening. She had three names that were predominant in Deedrie's diary. Julie, Tommy and Steph. No last names were listed so she cross-referenced them against the contact list pulled from the cell phone found on scene. There were only five possibilities. Julie Downs, Tommy Burton, Tom Drake, Stephanie Winter and Stephane Deluise. The references for Steph were definitely female so she removed Deluise from the list and fired the other four names to Baker and Jones for follow up interviews. She was reviewing Baker's report on the surveillance video, noting that an unknown woman was identified in the waiting room for the duration of Deedrie's visit, when Rique popped his head through her doorway.

"How're you feeling, L.T.?"

"Better," she replied, "How'd things go with Sebastian."

"Not bad, we got him released and I fired the voicemail to Lund for an analysis. Nothing substantial there, just a quick, "Looking to get together, call me.""

"Thanks for letting me handle it last night, and for having my back."

"Frost, I've always got your back. I was a little shocked, and won't even pretend to understand, but hey we've all got our shit. This whole case has thrown me for a loop. I honestly didn't realize how prevalent that lifestyle is. I feel like I've had my head buried in the sand."

"It's not as prevalent as it seems, this case just crosses into it at a lot of angles, but if you really want to learn more about it you should talk to Angel."

Shaw gave her a frightened look.

"Seriously, Rique, the woman is an encyclopedia of sexual deviances. She has a better grasp on the personalities and drives behind every aspect of it than anyone I've met. Besides, I saw your face when she gave you that hug."

Rique rolled his eyes, "Thanks for the attempted setup, but I don't think I could handle her. If the woman's really the kink expert, I'd probably end up bound, gagged and begging before lunch."

"You might enjoy that," laughed Ell, "but you can stow the fears, she doesn't practice most of it. She just learns."

"Seriously?"

"Call her," said Ell dismissively.

"I'll consider it, in the meantime I'm going to run down the concierge and bartender from the Grand Larriott and tighten up Sebastian's alibi for the record."

"Try to nail it down by ten; we have an interview at Bouton Holdings at ten thirty."

"Family?"

"Yup, and likely a half dozen attorney's"

"Fun. Do you think they're involved?"

"Based on what we have thus far, it's doubtful, but we may be able to get some insight into her last couple months."

"I'll be ready. Oh, and L.T., you may want to keep Rob out of the bullpen for a while. I think Baker's still googly-eyed and panting this morning."

Ell laughed and waved at him dismissively, "Get to work."

Having delegated much of the actual investigation, Ell found herself pushing paper and reviewing notes for the better part of the morning, hoping something new would jump out. When nothing did she grabbed the phone and began dialing.

"Christ Ell, it's nine a.m. What the hell do you think I've turned up in two hours?"

"Don't give me that shit. We both know you had lab monkeys working all night on this one, Lund."

"Wish it were true but the monkeys flew the coop at about two a.m."

"Monkeys can fly?"

"Fuck off, Frost, it's too damn early."

"So, what did your monkeys find prior to growing wings?"

"Not much, the prints are a bust on local and state. Feds

are still running them but I expect something from them later this morning. We found lotion residue and skin cells on one of the ropes, both belonging to your vic, so we figure we've ID'd the murder weapon. No usable prints on it, but that's to be expected with nylon. Inventory did turn up a pair a size five black fuck-me pumps."

"She had them in every style going, not much of a find."

"It is when you note that the victim was a seven," he replied smugly.

"Good catch, give the monkeys a banana and call if they find anything else."

She hung up and dialed Browne. After four rings she was transferred to his voicemail and immediately placed the phone back on the cradle. He had a few hours left in the twenty-four hour time frame she had given him.

She headed across the hall to check on the troops. Unlike the morning before, the bullpen was full of detectives. It brought a smile to Ell's face. This was her team doing what they did best. She walked through the desks, briefly speaking with them about their active files, before flagging down Jones.

"Where's Baker?" she asked, not seeing the beautiful redhead in the room.

"Headed down to requisitions. That piece of shit they gave us yesterday broke down on the freeway this morning. I figured she might have better luck flashing those shiny green eyes."

Ell's anger flared, followed by a flash of excitement. Donna Brennan's reprieve had just been revoked.

"When she gets back tell her I'll deal with it. I assume they'll give her a squad car for the time being so don't plan on any anonymity."

"We've got interviews booked from ten till two with the four friends you sent us this morning so it shouldn't be an issue."

"Sounds good, run a photo of the unsub from the tattoo parlor and see if any of them recognize her. Oh, and keep an eye out for a female with size five feet."

Jones laughed, "Cuz that's a short list."

Ell shrugged, "Lund found a pair of size five fuck-me's in the vic's personal effects. It's not her size so it's an anomaly. See if you can match them to one of the friends or the unsub. Rique and I are interviewing the family this morning so if anything hits send me a text, and if they give you any flack drag them in for a formal. We don't have time to play nice on this one."

"No worries there, L.T., nice is Baker's forte, I thrive on bad cop."

"Me too," she smiled heading out of the bullpen and back to her office to call requisitions.

She wandered back in and found Rob sitting on the edge of her desk, his hair still wet from a recent shower. His jeans and tight fitting dress shirt were fresh and new. He looked absolutely edible.

"How the hell did you get a change of clothes?"

He held up three fingers in the Boy Scout salute, "Be prepared."

She rolled her eyes and dropped into her desk chair, "Well, be prepared to wait a moment. I have something I need to take care of." Picking up her phone, she dialed the number for requisitions."

"Requisitions, please hold."

"I believe we've had this discussion, Donna. I have no intention of holding."

"Lieutenant Frost, to what do I owe the pleasure today?"

"I am sure you know why I am calling, let's not play games."

"Detective Baker left moments ago, she was issued a squad car while her unmarked is in for service."

"Lovely. Would you care to explain to me how a vehicle issued at end of shift yesterday requires servicing this morning?"

"Lieutenant, we cannot control when a vehicle is going to have issues. Per your request we rushed the detective's exchange of transpo and ensured they had possession before end of shift yesterday."

"And what good is replacing one piece of crap with another that won't even last twenty minutes on the freeway?"

"They were issued the first available vehicle and it was running fine when delivered. As I said we cannot control when a vehicle will fail."

"Bullshit! If you were doing your job that vehicle would have had a full inspection prior to being issued, and you would not have been putting my detective's in unneeded danger."

"Lieutenant, it was you that insisted the vehicle be delivered in such a short time frame. I informed you that there were procedures that needed to be followed, however, you did not allow us the time required to do so."

"Don't give me that shit, Donna. Requisitions had my request for three weeks. If you'd have dealt with it in that time I wouldn't have had to call at all. As it is, you now have my detectives riding around in a squad car. These are homicide detectives, Donna. They need to be inconspicuous to do their job."

"The squad car is a temporary measure. Their transpo will be repaired and returned within the week."

"Within the week? Not a chance in hell. You are not giving my detectives back that piece of shit. I expect it replaced. Today! And with something new, certified and guaranteed to fucking run!"

"Lieutenant, that's just not possible."

"Make it possible, Donna, or my next call is not going to be friendly."

Ell hung up without giving her a chance to respond.

"Remind me not to piss you off," quipped Rob.

Ell smirked, "What's the matter, afraid a little girl might make you kneel and beg."

"An interesting thought but I don't see you playing switch," his eyes flared with lust and Ell could feel her body tighten.

"You'd be surprised what I can do with the right motivation." The air crackled with sexual energy. Ell was taken aback by the power of it and found it difficult to resist the urge to give in to her primal feelings. His hand brushed across hers and all playfulness was lost. She yearned to be taken. To give him exactly what he desired.

"I think you are plenty motivated, Ellison. Perhaps I should close the door and remind you of your place."

Her mind raced, dual personalities fighting to maintain control. She glanced away unable to hold her composure while seeing the look in his eyes. "Please, not here," she begged quietly.

Rob grasped her chin lightly and turned her eyes back to his. "Then you need to stop teasing. You have no idea how difficult it is to resist you right now."

"Trust me, I do," she whispered.

They stared at each other, lost, for a moment before Rob

took a step back to clear his head. Ell breathed deep, pushing the feelings aside.

"So what brings you to my luxurious office this morning? Shouldn't you be off decrypting data and creating the inevitable A.I. takeover?"

"I most assuredly should," he grinned, "but I wanted to check on you first, and let you know I have a line on the encryption code used on Bouton's hard drive. There's a unique signature that I may be able to pin point. It's definitely a custom job."

"Find me the e-geek that wrote it before you start on your plans for a computer revolution and I'll make it worth your while."

"Already on it but thanks for the incentive. I'll put the T-1000 back in the closet till I've nailed this down."

"Sweet, one more day without being a servant to a robot overlord. Now get the hell out of here before the squad starts gossiping," she flashed him a beautiful smile and nearly melted when his eyes filled with want.

He closed his eyes, took a deep breath and silently headed out and down the hall.

Ell checked the time, and headed across to the bullpen.

"Rique, you're with me," she said turning down the hall, the detective scrambling to catch up.

Chapter Eleven

*T*he Bouton Holdings offices were exactly what would be expected of a billion dollar multinational organization. Dark mahogany and redwood shelving littered the entry way, accompanied by lush Italian leather furniture. A young blond, whose name likely ended in an 'i', sat behind the large, granite top reception desk fielding calls and smiling at anyone that happened to pass by. Ell watched Rique eyeing her up and chuckled to herself.

"Go tell the "i" candy we're here," she whispered, "and try not to drool all over the desk."

"I'll do my best, L.T."

Ell waited a couple steps back, trying to ignore Rique's poor attempt at flirtation while taking in the people scuttling about the office. Unlike the calm wealth presented by the decor, the employees flew by with a sense of urgency and stress. It was an odd dichotomy, but on some level it made sense. A company did not get to the status of Bouton Holdings with expensive furnishings alone. It was those behind the desks that ensured the balance sheet continued to grow.

"If you'll follow us, Lieutenant Frost," blond "i's" sugar

sweet voice interrupted her thoughts. "Mr. Bouton is expecting you in conference room seven."

Ell didn't know what was more disconcerting, the fact that they had seven conference rooms or that they would need one for an interview. She tensed up at the thought of the team of attorneys they were bound to find waiting for them.

Blond "i" led them through the art embossed halls, up two flights of rounded stairs, suited more for an old English home than an office, and into a comfortable room with a midsized granite conference table and six soft leather chairs. Three of those chairs were currently occupied by Mr. James Bouton, his wife Anna and their youngest, and now only, daughter, Stacey. Mr. Bouton was not what Ell had expected. He was an older gentleman, in good shape, with wisps of grey streaking through his well styled hair. All things that spoke of high end business, but his wardrobe, tight fitting jeans and a black turtleneck pullover, seemed out of place. To his left, Mrs. Bouton appeared to be a good ten years younger than her husband though Ell's reports indicated that there was only one year separating the two. She had aged very well, likely due to some medical assistance. She was dressed up, though not formally, in a flower-print sundress and had taken the time to apply a subtle touch of makeup. Still, Ell could see the grief in her eyes. Stacey Bouton, however, was purely professional. Unlike her sister, she did not dress to impress so much as to intimidate. The well cut, professional, skirt and blouse combo coupled well with her pure presence and screamed respect. It was a powerful combination that more than made up for her diminutive frame and small stature.

"Please, have a seat detectives," said James Bouton, gesturing to the empty chairs. "That will be all, Candi."

Ell smiled to herself, having heard the receptionist's name. *Called it.* She was surprised, however, by the lack of counsel in the room. She pulled out her phone and started the recording app.

"Mr. Bouton, thank you for taking the time to see us. I'm Lieutenant Frost and my partner is Detective Shaw. This is not a formal interview but I would like to record it for the record, and I must advise you that you have the right to have council present if you wish."

"Thank you Lieutenant, we want to do anything we can to help. This has been a trying time for the family and we could use some closure." He gestured to his daughter, "Stacey is our general counsel for all personal matters, and I see no reason to make this anymore adversarial than required. We will refer to her for any legal issues."

Ell was impressed, she had expected something different from a man entrenched in the upper echelon of society. In her experience, those with so much to lose took great pride in ensuring the best protection money could buy.

"Sounds good. For the record this is Lieutenant Frost and Detective Shaw interviewing the Bouton family in relation to the homicide of Deedrie Bouton. Can you please state your names?"

"James Bouton"

"Anna Kennedy-Bouton"

"Stacey Bouton"

"Perfect, before we start, I am truly sorry for your loss and I know this process won't be easy so if you need to stop, for any reason, please let me know."

"I believe my parents would agree that we want to get this over with, Lieutenant," replied Stacey. Ell could hear the formality of a legal degree in her voice. She was cold and professional, likely a form of coping, falling back to a place of control. A need to dominate that Ell could not truly understand but certainly respected.

"Then let's begin. Can you please tell me the last time each of you had contact with Deedrie and the nature of that contact?"

"I hadn't spoken with here in about three weeks," replied Mr. Bouton, "and honestly, I had no plans to do so anytime soon." There was regret in his eyes so Ell decided to push it a little.

"And why is that?"

"Quite frankly, she pissed me off. Listen, we've all read the stories floating around in the tabloids for the last few months, the reports of Deedrie gone wild, but I know my daughter and I am more than familiar with the "journalism" that gets into those rags. I've been in them myself on occasion. I didn't put a lot of weight to what was reported. Deedrie has always been a little wild, but, to me, it just seemed that they were starting to focus on her and spinning everything she would do. I threw my publicist on it and asked him to do what he could. Three weeks ago he came back and told me Deedrie wouldn't cooperate, that she wanted her name in the press. In fact, she'd been tipping off the reporters. I didn't know what to think so I went to the condo to see her. I tried to talk to her about it, find out why she was doing it, and reason with her about the effects it was going to have on her from a long term business perspective. She blew me off, told me it was none of my business and if I was worried about her tarnishing the "Bouton" name then I needed to get over it. I tried to explain that the only name I was worried about was hers. My business has a solid reputation and, honestly, her antics couldn't affect that in the least."

"So you fought?" asked Rique.

"No, she fought. Started screaming about what a self centered bastard I was. How she knew what she was doing and one day she'd be twice the person I am. She was seriously pissed, and I stood there and took it. She's my daughter, what else could I do? Eventually she calmed down and told me to get out of her condo and not to come back. We're a close family, always have been, so, trust me, this came as a shock."

"And you hadn't spoken since?" asked Ell.

The regret in his eyes deepened, "No. She's called the house a couple times, but I refused to speak with her until she came to her senses and apologized. She never did and now..." he dipped his head, staring down at the table.

"Did anyone speak with her when she called?"

"I did," replied Mrs. Kennedy-Bouton. "In fact, we spoke last Sunday. She wanted to see if James and I would be attending the Collin's International charity art auction next month. She had modeled for a piece that was being exhibited and hoped we would attend."

"Was that something she did often? Modeling?"

"No, but she seemed fairly excited about it and really wanted us to be at the unveiling. She was such a beautiful girl," her eyes welled up before she could compose herself. "Lieutenant, I don't know who would do this to my daughter or why but, please, you have to find them."

"Were the two of you close?"

"Close? We used to be but lately she's been in her own world and she wasn't ready to share it. I tried to talk to her about it and could tell that something had her pretty excited. I thought maybe she'd found someone special, but I don't know. She just had that spark in her eye lately."

"Can you think of anyone that might be able to shed some light on it? A close friend perhaps? Someone she would confide in?"

"A year ago I'd have said Stacey," she motioned to her daughter, "but now?" she left the question hanging, shaking her head.

"Stacey?" asked Ell, prompting the woman to jump in.

"Mom's right, a year ago I could have told you what she had for breakfast, but I've barely talked to her in the last six months."

"Why's that?"

"I really don't know. We drifted apart. I graduated and went to work for the company, Deedrie hated that, wanted me to get on with one of the big firms in town and 'make my own name'. She's always had a problem with the company. When we were younger, she hated that she was always seen as James Bouton's daughter. The name can open a lot of doors, Lieutenant, but there is always a stigma attached. People don't see us for who we are, for what we've done, they assume we've gotten what we have because of our last name. Dee despised it. In fact, she was so adamant on being her own person that she nearly refused the trust fund. Dad talked her into taking it but, after that, she did everything she could to separate herself financially from the Bouton name."

"We've been digging into her finances and should have a report later today," Ell made a mental note to call Squirrelly if the file wasn't waiting for her when she got back to the precinct. "What we have found seems to indicate that her trust was gone nearly as quickly as she received it, and it would not have made a dent in her expenses over the last few years."

"I hope your forensic accountant is good, Lieutenant," cut in Mr. Bouton almost laughing, "because when it came to tax loopholes and money management my daughter was one of the best. You're looking for her income source, I assume, but what you don't realize is that you're actually looking directly at it."

"Go on," prompted Ell, lost but trying not to show it.

"When Dee was fifteen she started her first private company, an online service allowing people in her school to keep in touch with one another by posting quick updates on what they were doing. Who was going to be where and when, whatever they felt the group needed to know. She offered the service free of charge and included a number of revenue generating ads on each page. She wasn't making much at first, but what she did make was hers alone and she seemed to like that. As the site became more popular with the students, it started to spread to other schools and her revenue grew. Within a year she had a solid online presence. Just after her sixteenth birthday she was approached by an online startup with a ridiculous six figure offer to buy her out. Twitter paid her just under a quarter million, quickly pulled a patent on the technology and rolled a number of her features into their own site. This is when my daughter got her first taste of the true cost of business. She'd been doing it for spending cash and hadn't even thought of incorporating, so when April 15th rolled around and she owed over seventy thousand in income tax she nearly came unglued. That started her down the path. She was determined to protect as much of her money as possible so she started looking into tax code, shelters and loopholes. She became very good at what she did, Lieutenant, and she began marketing and selling her talents to those that could afford them. I was one of her first clients. She's saved my company over two hundred million dollars in taxes in the last eight years, and according to the IRS audit we had last year, everything is above board and legal."

Ell admired the pride in his eyes.

"We've hired one of the best forensic accountants in the city to unravel her personal finances for the estate," commented Stacey. "He's had a last minute emergency but is supposed to start on it in the morning." She passed Ell a business card. "Feel free to contact him if you run into anything you need clarified."

Ell slid the card into her pocket. It was unlikely she'd need it with Browne on the financials, but a second opinion may come in handy.

"Thanks, is there anything else you can think of that may be pertinent here? I know you've all heard about the state in which she was found, we have also recovered evidence that Deedrie was experimenting sexually and it would appear to be more than just recreational fun. Did she mention any of this?"

All three shook their heads. "My sister was a bit of a wild child, Lieutenant, and she's had her share of boyfriends. Hell, we even passed a few back and forth, but the bondage, the whips? That wasn't her. At least, it didn't used to be. I don't know what to think anymore."

"Lieutenant," cut in Mr. Bouton, "I know our name and the press coverage it draws won't make this any easier on you but please, find out who did this and make sure they pay for what they've done."

"I intend to," said Ell, pulling herself to her feet and stopping the recorder. "Thank you for your time, I'll keep you informed as much as I can."

"Anything you need, just let me know," replied James Bouton shaking her hand, a somber remorse in his eye.

***

"So, what's your take?" asked Ell, settling in behind the wheel of the S550.

"Mom and Dad seem genuine and they're definitely grieving. Sister Stacey, on the other hand, is a mighty cold fish. There's more to the sisters drifting apart story than she's letting on. Deedrie may have hated the family name and all that came with it, but her sister certainly doesn't. She's bought in to the Bouton legacy, and I'd wager she knew more about Deedrie's last few months than she indicated."

"Agreed, run me a sheet on her. I still don't see the family involved given the nature of the murder, but let's see what's there. And while you're at it, run down this accountant," she handed him the card from her pocket.

Rique glanced at it quickly and burst out in laughter.

Ell stared at him as if he'd gone crazy so he held up the card for her to read, "Andy Browne, C.A."

"Fucker, he's double dipping on the Bouton's and charging us overtime on top."

Rolling into the precinct, Ell's phone chirped to indicate

an incoming text. She took a quick look as Rique pulled open the precinct door.

"Bringing in a live one, you may want in on this. – J"

Ell quickly texted her back, "Just back from Bouton Int. Put them interrogation two and come fill me in. – E"

"Jones and Baker caught something during the interviews. They're bringing someone in for a formal. Get me a sheet on Stacey and lock up the Leriux alibi. I'll be in interrogation if you need me."

Rique nodded his assent as she headed for her office.

Five minutes later, as she was typing up her interview notes, Jones poked her head through the doorway.

"Baker's got the little bitch down in two. Wanna take this?"

"I'll observe but bring me up to speed on the way." Ell strolled out of her office, Jones on her heels.

"We hit up the Toms first, both came off nervous but sincere. Drake's just a random club hookup that got lucky. Guy was pretty upfront about it, all though his details were blurry. Been about a month since he saw the vic and they don't have a history. Burton's a lot closer. Met Deedrie about five months ago and has seen her pretty regularly since. They took a few rolls in the hay early on but he's got a girlfriend now and claims he's faithful. Baker's gonna dig into it and see if it holds up. The guy was sweating bullets when we first showed up, but he tried to play it cool. Seemed pretty forthcoming, but he danced around the GHB issue. Claims he mentioned it to Deedrie but has no idea where she would have gotten it. It's bullshit and we'll push it if we have to, but I didn't see any reason to get narc involved. I peg him for a low level pervert looking to get off."

Ell smiled as they bypassed the elevator for the stairs.

"Stephanie was a bust. She's been out of state for six weeks on a premed internship at Hopkins. Her roommate gave us her new contact info. We'll run it down this afternoon."

"And our illustrious guest?"

"Julie Downs. From what the Toms say, she and Deedrie were joined at the hip."

'And a lot of other parts,' thought Ell, remembering the numerous entries in Deedrie's diary.

"I assume she was less than cooperative?"

"As soon as we identified ourselves, the little bitch slammed the door in Baker's face and went rabbit. Hauled ass out the window and down the fire escape. Baker pursued and I hit the stairs. When I rounded into the alley Baker had her face down on the pavement, cuffed and screaming. Apparently we've 'violated her rights and we'll be jobless by tomorrow' so I figure we better take advantage of the rest of our shift to shut the tramp up."

Jones was pumped and Ell could tell she was still riding the adrenaline high.

"You and Baker take it, I'll be in observation," she said as they headed towards the stunning redhead waiting outside of the interrogation room. Ell caught a quick glimpse of the mouse just under Baker's right eye and winced.

"That from the door or the aftermath?"

"It's from a four inch heel," she responded. "Who throws a fucking shoe?"

Ell chuckled, pulling open the door to observation as the Detectives composed themselves and gave Julie a few more minutes to stew.

As her eyes adjusted to the dim light of the room, she could see she had company.

"You still stalking me?"

"Oh contraire, Lieutenant," Rob's voice was soft yet firm. "I heard we had some action on the case and wanted to see you at work."

"I'm letting the B squad take this one," she winked turning to the two way glass and flipping the switch to enable the sound system. "Just here to observe and report."

Rob slid in behind her, his hands dancing lightly across her hips and pulling her closer. Ell's heart rate rose, her body beginning to warm and flush at his touch. Instinctively, her head dipped back, resting gently against his shoulder as her eyes closed.

"Perhaps we should make proper use of the privacy," he said, his hands caressing her stomach, his lips nibbling the soft flesh of her exposed neck.

Ell took a deep breath, caught in the moment as the passion and want embraced her. Rob's hand slowly moved up, across her chest, cupping her breast as he pulled her tight against him. Her nipples hardened as his palm brushed across them, pushing against the fabric of her blouse and yearning for a more intimate touch.

"Detective Jones and Baker, interviewing Julie Downs as part of the ongoing investigation into the homicide of Deedrie Bouton."

Ell's eyes snapped open at the sound of Jones' voice. She attempted to pull free of Rob's grasp but he held her firm.

"Relax, Ellison. No one can see you, let's just enjoy the show."

Part of her wanted to fight free but she couldn't. She was lost in his grasp, her emotions running wild. Her thoughts drifting to all the things she wanted to do to him. For him.

Her body relaxed, almost melting into his as she accepted his guidance.

Julie Downs was a petite woman in her mid twenties. Long brown hair flopped across her shoulders in messy waves that appeared overly styled for the atmosphere. In a different locale, she would be considered pretty but under the bright florescent lights of the interrogation room, her over-applied makeup, skin tight jeans and tight, silk camisole just looked slutty.

"Please state your name for the record," said Detective Baker in the sweetest tone she could muster.

"Fuck you, bitch."

Baker smiled politely, "Is that a pseudonym, because your driver's license has you listed as Julie Samantha Downs."

"Ain't you the bright one."

"Is that a yes?"

"Yeah, it's my fucking name, what of it?"

"Thank you, Ms. Downs. As I was saying before you decided to slam the door in my face earlier, we would like to ask you a few questions about Deedrie Bouton."

"Fuck you and your questions, I know my rights and I ain't answering shit."

Jones took the opportunity to jump in, "Your rights? Let's see Ms. Downs, you fled an officer of the law after being told to stop, that's felony evasion. You left that sweet little mouse on Detective Baker's cheek, which would be assaulting an officer. Now, we were under the impression that you'd be co-operative, but if you really want to get into your rights I'll gladly read them to you and start processing your ass through the system."

Julie's demeanor lightened slightly. She leaned back in her chair nonchalantly, but Ell could see a nervous energy in her eyes.

"Is running from the police actually a felony?" asked Rob, his fingers lightly pinching and tweaking her nipples through the soft silk of her blouse.

Ell moaned softly, her subconscious taking over. "In this case? We'd be lucky to get misdemeanor charges."

Rob grinned, watching her involuntary reaction as he continued to caress her.

"Fine," said Julie, "what the fuck do you wanna know?"

"We understand you were close to Deedrie, when was the last time you saw her?" asked Baker.

"Three nights ago, we were kickin' back at 'Maroon' down on third. Was pretty lame but Dee just wanted some down-time. I left with some hottie round midnight and she was still chillin. That's all I know."

"Does "hottie" have a name"

"I'm sure he does but it wasn't embroidered on his pillows and I wasn't looking to get to know him."

Rob chuckled softly, his right hand sliding over Ell's tight abs and worked beneath the edge of her jeans.

Ells breath caught, her eyes rolling back into her head as his fingers danced across her waxed lips.

"Mmmmm no panties, were you expecting me?"

"Some of us don't keep a wardrobe at the precinct", she quipped, as his fingers traced her soft mound.

She wanted to stop him, knew she should, but she was helpless, her body yearning for his touch, begging to please him. Recognizing her growing lust he slid his hand upward, extracting it from her jeans and raising his fingers to her mouth. Without thought, she began to run her tongue across them, her body burning with passion and wanting more.

"I... don't... fucking... know!" snapped Julie drawing Ell's attention back to the interrogation.

"Oh, come on, Julie. We know you've been involved in whatever Deedrie was up to. Her diary outlines every one of her recent sexual escapades and your name is a reoccurring feature," said Jones reasserting herself into the conversation.

Julie's embarrassment and anger rose in unison.

"Fuck you, I'm done with this shit."

Julie stood and started heading for the door. Baker grabbed her wrist, spun her quickly and pinned her against the wall. The move was quick and smooth and before she knew what had happened, Julie was cuffed and detained.

"Ooooo, looks like Red's had some practice," commented Rob and Ell smiled.

"Not nearly enough, and leave my detectives alone you pervert."

"Why settle for a fiery young redhead when I can play with her boss?" Robs fingers pinched her nipples slightly harder than necessary and Ell's knees began to weaken.

"Julie Downs, you are under arrest for felony evasion and assaulting an officer. You have the right to remain..." said Jones running through the Miranda Rights.

"I thought you said the charges wouldn't stick?" asked Rob, kissing Ells neck one final time before pulling back and leaving her in a disheveled state of want and lust.

Ell fought her feelings trying to focus on the job and praying she could regain control before exiting observation.

"They won't but a night in lockup might make her a little more cooperative."

Rob leaned in, his lips brushing against her ear, sending chills through her body. "And what about you? Would a night in lockup make you more cooperative, Ellison."

"Yes, sir," she whispered involuntarily and could feel his desire and dominance pushing to the surface.

She stepped towards the door, a sly grin crossing her face, knowing that she was leaving him hanging and would pay for it later. She couldn't wait.

Chapter Twelve

$\mathcal{S}$ettling back into her office, Ell checked her email. She was slightly annoyed yet pleased to find nothing new. A sly smirk crossed her lips as she snagged her office phone and began dialing.

"Hello?" the frustrated voice of Andy "Squirrely" Browne made her happier.

"Where the hell is my file, Browne."

"Lieutenant, such a pleasure as always."

"Yeah, always here to brighten your day. What's the damn hold up?"

"As I'm sure you are aware by now, Ms. Bouton was quite skilled at protecting her finances. Tracing her income has proven a touch more difficult than anticipated."

"You're trying to tell me that the tabloid queen has you outwitted Browne?"

"Outwitted? No, simply delayed. You'll have the data in about twenty minutes along with my invoice."

"Make sure the 'delay's' not on it, I gave you twenty-four."

"Lieutenant, these things take time. You can't expect me to work for free."

"Just send me the fucking file and make sure to CC Bouton Holdings. They were looking to hire a private examiner for the estate so I let them know there was no need and that we would gladly share our findings."

Dead air filled the line and Ell struggled to retain a laugh. What she wouldn't have given to see his face in that moment.

"If that's all, I have work to finish."

"Just get me the damn file," Ell set the phone back on the cradle and leaned back, pleased.

She was just starting to settle and focus again when Rique popped his head through the door.

"Leruix's alibi is confirmed and on the record." Ell felt some of the tension in her shoulders subside.

"Thanks."

"Don't mention it. I've got a message into your I.T. boytoy to do some digging for me. Stacey Bouton seems to keep things pretty private. I'm hoping Rob can dig in a little deeper."

"I'm expecting the financials back in about twenty minutes, between that and updating brass I'm stuck in the cell for the afternoon. If you don't have anything pressing spend a couple hours helping Jones and Baker run Ms. Downs' background then get some downtime. Oh, and contact Bouton Holdings. You can let them know that they can cancel the forensic accountant for the estate. We'll be sharing our findings."

Rique let out a deep laugh, "Squirrley's gonna love that."

"What can I say, I'm a people person."

As promised the financial breakdown hit Ell's inbox shortly

after Rique headed back to the bullpen. She muddled her way through it as best she could, trying to decipher the cryptic accountant speak and stave off the boredom induced headache.

As expected, the bulk of Deedrie's income came from financial consulting, and her client list held a close resemblance to the Forbes 500. Her annual income had peaked in the previous fiscal year at just under nine point seven million, yet her T2 reflected a taxable income of less than six hundred thousand. The numbers were nearly incomprehensible to Ell. She'd climbed the ladder in her profession, had a bit of a nest egg built up and could afford the things she wanted in life, and her annual income had just recently hit six digits.

From what she could tell, aside from Deedrie's ability to protect her income from the IRS, nothing stood out. In an effort to focus she made a list of the most prominent clients and began a thorough background check on each. Four hours and three pots of coffee later she had thirty two pages of background on seven different clients and no idea what value it could possibly add to her case. 'Such is the glorified life of a detective,' she thought. Checking the clock and noting it was shortly after six she fired off an email to the Commander updating him on the case, saved what she was working on and headed across the hall.

She could hear Baker's laugh before turning the corner. It was a flirty giggle that made Ell's mind wander. She stopped short, taking a deep breath and trying to cease the forbidden thoughts that had crept into her mind. 'That girl's trouble,' she thought as she continued through the door.

The bullpen was once again nearly abandoned. Baker

stood beside her desk gazing deep into the eyes of the man leaning nonchalantly against its edge.

"Christ Rob, don't they have any geek work for you to do?"

"If you recall, someone asked me to shelve my quest to create the robot overlord and dig into the identity of Deedrie's mysterious encryptor."

"Don't tell me, it was a pretty little redhead in PD blues?"

Baker's face blushed as he turned away.

"Unfortunately no, and I really wanted to see her in cuffs," winked Rob as Baker flashed him an embarrassed smirk. "Your partner in crime... solving? asked me to do a side run on Stacey Bouton's background. Turns out my quests crossed paths so I thought I'd better report in. Detective Baker informs me he's gone for the day."

"Sent him home for some downtime, I was just coming to tell you to do the same," she turned her gaze to Baker and felt the familiar rush pass over her.

"Just about to, Jones is down in req swapping out the squad for something else. Hopefully this one makes it home."

"Look on the bright side, if it doesn't you can come watch me deal with it in the morning."

"Oooo fun."

"Ok, hot shot, grab your data and leave the detective alone. My office."

Ell turned back towards the office, her mind in conflict. As much as she wanted to be alone with him she knew this was neither the time nor place. But what if he pushed it? Could she resist him? Did she want to?

She shook off the thoughts and settled into the desk chair. Moments later, Rob slid into the room dragging a leather chair from the bullpen.

"No way in hell I'm sitting on that death trap," he remarked flipping a gesture at the guest chair in the corner.

"It keeps visitors to a minimum," she flashed him a knowing smirk.

"Well, we're touched that you enjoy our company."

"Some more than others," she smiled playfully. "So, did your break from world domination yield anything useful?"

"Perhaps. I was able to delve into the encryption code and begin looking for a signature." He slid her a small stack of paper which appeared to be written in either ancient Sanskrit or possibly the language of the next alien invaders. "Those in the business of creating and breaking these algorithms tend to be cocky and love to leave a little something of their own behind. A calling car, to claim the product."

"Does this mean something?" asked Ell gesturing to the unrecognizable code.

"Yes, but really I just wanted to see that confused look on your pretty face."

She glared and he struggled to hold back a laugh.

"See the bold section at the bottom of page three? It's a redundant piece of cross mapping that is wholly unnecessary for the code. It does nothing but it is recognizable. I reached out to some associates that are, let's say less than law abiding, and was able to pin point the signature. It belongs to someone that's been out of the game for a couple years. Goes by the Greek handle 'Ανάσταση'."

Ell's Greek was pretty much non-existent but a quick Google search helped her out. "Resurrection?"

"Made quite a name for themselves online about five years ago. Rumors suggest it was Ανάσταση that cracked the 'Shadow Factory' Cray."

"The Shadow Factory Cray?"

Rob rolled his eyes, "Sorry, it's one of the most secured systems our government has in place. About five years back it was rumored to be breached but no evidence was ever brought forth. The government claimed the rumors to be untrue, but someone released a snippet online that is believed to be part of the Shadow Factory firewall code. There were a couple big names thrown about but no one ever claimed it. One of those names was Ανάσταση.

"Ok, so I've got a hacker extraordinaire's code encrypting the hard drive that my vic's been storing her sex diary on. This keeps getting better. Any idea who "Resurrection" is?"

"Yes Ell, they have managed to elude federal authorities and keep their anonymity amongst the elite computer community for over six years, but I was able to identify and locate them in the last eight hours."

"Smart ass."

"Perhaps, but at least it's tight and cute."

Ell rolled her eyes but could not argue with his assessment.

"So how does this tie in with Staccy Bouton? You mentioned a crossover."

"So impatient," he said rising from the chair and circling behind her. His hands rested gently on her shoulders and began to knead the tight muscles. "You're tight, you need to relax, Ellison."

"I need to solve this damn case and we shouldn't be doing this here. I mean it, Rob, you have fifteen minutes to stop," she deadpanned, drawing a small chuckle.

"So," he continued, his hands working their way across her shoulders. Ell's body reacted to his touch. Relaxing yet building in anticipation at the same time. "Once I nailed down the signature, I switched gears and started looking into Stacey Bouton. Not much out of the ordinary aside from the family itself. She graduated High School at the top of her class, did three years undergraduate and another three at Harvard Law. Got her J.D. and immediately went to work for the family business. No real trouble in her past and she's kept a low profile."

His hands slowly worked down her back. Ell's body melted into him, her breath stammering as she struggled to maintain focus.

"And the crossover?"

"On a whim I started looking into her career thus far. Aside from the standard contract and rights disputes for Bouton Holdings, it has been rather unremarkable. However, about eight months ago, fresh out of law school, she took on a federal indictment case pro bono. A Mr. Shane Dunder was indicted for illegal breach of a secured system. It wasn't advertised but among the listed aliases in the case file was the name Ανάσταση. The indictment was a fishing expedition and the case was over before it even got started, but it got me wondering."

"Why would a law student fresh off the bar take on a federal indictment?" murmured Ell lost in the relaxing waves of passion that had begun to flow over her.

"Precisely. Care to guess as to Ms. Bouton's undergrad major?"

Her eyes opened, turning to gaze into his for only a moment as his hands ceased their glorious assault. For a second she was lost, filled with want and lust. The stress of the case gone. All thought focused solely on the beautiful smirk before her. She wanted him to take her, to push everything else aside and make her his. He leaned down, placing a gentle kiss on her forehead and whispered, "Soon but not now, not here."

She was torn, disappointed and relieved all at once as he returned to the 'borrowed' chair across the desk.

"B.C.S."

"What?" she asked, shaking off the onslaught of emotion.

"Her major, Bachelor of Computer Science. Three years at M.I.T. pre-law."

"So she knew him."

"They had five classes together over the course of three years. I didn't dig into it much further but it is an interesting coincidence."

"Yes, and given that Stacey and Deedrie were nearly inseparable until six months ago it's reasonable to assume that Dunder was also acquainted with our victim. I need to get him in for an interview," she switched back to her computer and began running a search, a renewed spark in her eye.

"That may be difficult."

Ell shot him a worried glance.

"The feds dug in pretty hard but they had nothing substantial. A few rumors, a five year old IP trace and a lot of assumptions. Stacey got it tossed but the federal government doesn't admit defeat easily. They used the cyber terrorism loopholes to put him under twenty-four hour watch. They tapped every communication he had, accessed full financials, utilized both man power and electronic surveillance and four days after his release he was gone. Not a trace. With the exception of the federal case, his birth, education and employment records, Shane Dunder does not exist. Online or off."

Ell closed her eyes, placing her thumbs on her temples. "Can you find him?"

Rob stared at her blankly. "What?"

"Can you find him?"

"Ell, the federal government, with all their resources, has been searching for six months."

"But they can't go where you can. The 'less than law abiding' won't speak to them."

"Those in deep enough are not much more likely to speak to me, but I'll keep digging. While I do, you need to put this away and get some rest."

Ell stared at him blankly and shook her head. "I'll hit the bunk in a couple hours, I need to keep drilling into the financials and follow up on the forensics."

"No, the bunk is not what you need, Ellison. You need to get away from it. Go home, shut down and regroup. Have you even eaten?"

She could tell he was serious. She could feel her will bending, yearning to be taken care of yet she was fighting it.

"I'll grab something quick and get things wrapped up here, a couple hours at most." She turned back to her computer and pulled up her financial client list.

Rob glared but said nothing. Instead, he reached down and pulled out his cell. After a few moments of tapping a large alert flashed across Ell's monitor. The screens went black and the hard drive silenced.

"I'm afraid the network is experiencing technical difficulties. You may want to call I.T."

Ell, set her jaw and glared. "This isn't a joke, Rob. A woman is dead and it's my job to see that the killer is brought to justice before it happens again. I don't get the luxury of downtime on this one. And I'm not the only one that needs this system."

Rob set his gaze, looking into her eyes with both care and dominance. Her mind reacted instinctively, listening carefully, wanting nothing more than to obey and let him care for her.

"Do you seriously think I would take down the entire network, Ellison? You need downtime, just as your officers do. You need a decent meal, a hot shower and some rest. You're no good to this case if you're too exhausted to focus. This is not a request. You can sit in that chair and pout if you please, but your access and case files have been locked for the evening."

"I'm sorry...," she stammered. "It's ... work. Here... I ... I just can't."

"Relax, this isn't about us. This is about you. I care for you, Ellison, and I am hoping we can explore and expand our relationship but that means I'm going to do what I can to see that you are protected. From everything out there," he waved his hand at the door, "and from yourself. You do the same for the officers in that bullpen because you care. Show yourself the same respect. Go home and get away from this for a few hours."

Part of her wanted to fight, wanted to take control but she knew he was right. Nodding lightly she averted her eyes and took a deep breath.

Rob stood, pulled her to him and she melted into his arms. She felt warm, safe and secure. It was all she really wanted.

"Take care, relax, and I will see you in the morning."

His lips brushed softly across her cheek, his hands caressing her back. She yearned to pull him closer, to have him with her, if only for the night. Her heart raced, her blood warmed her skin with every touch, but within moments he was gone, grabbing the 'borrowed' chair on his way out and leaving her frustrated and stunned.

As she stood there, trying to regain composure, her cell phone chirped. Glancing down she could only laugh

"We're even, for now. – R"

Chapter Thirteen

*H*e had a point. She didn't have to like it but she knew he was right. She was running on fumes and a hot shower and some food would help her refocus. The ride home was quick and uneventful. She decided on pizza and placed an order for a large deluxe on her way. That took care of the food. A quick shower, maybe a glass of wine and she could settle back into her home office in about an hour. Not quite what Rob had in mind, but it would have to do. She had too many loose ends to just let this lie.

Her cell chirped just as she was pulling into her driveway. Glancing down on her way to the door she cringed.

"Ellison, hope everything's ok. Call me. – S"

'Shit.' Why hadn't she thought to call? Granted, she and Sebastian weren't involved but she knew he'd be concerned. She hesitated for a moment and hit dial as she pulled open the front door and dropped down on the couch.

"Ellison?" came a concerned yet firm voice.

"Shit, I'm sorry I didn't call. It's been a long day."

"That's fine, I could see how drained you were last night, I'm just sorry I couldn't be more help."

"It's fine, really. And thank you, I know I put you in an awkward position."

"Would not have been the first cell I've visited for protecting a client, but the irony of that client putting me there was not lost."

She couldn't help but laugh. "It wouldn't have come to that, but thank you for your discretion. The alibi checked out fine and, for now, no one is questioning it. I doubt you'll be hassled any further."

"It's no hassle, Ellison, I just hope you're getting through alright. I've been thinking back to my time with Deedrie and, while the encounters were strange, I don't remember anything that would have led to this."

"I'm muddling through. Long hours and a lot of frustration but I'll get there. Thanks for checking in."

"You sound exhausted. Get a hot shower, some food and rest. You'll focus better."

She almost could not contain a laugh, "You're not the first to suggest it, and you'll be happy to know the food is on the way and the shower's waiting."

"Good, take care of yourself, Ellison, and if you need anything you know how to reach me."

"Thanks, you too."

Hanging up she felt a pang of guilt and remorse flow over her. She did care for him, at least, as much as possible given the circumstances. She had always dreamt of a life with a man like Sebastian yet knew it wasn't possible. And what now? Rob was similar but so very different. She could not deny the feelings she had for him but could it ever be the same? And did she even want that? She had kept her two lives separate for a reason and yet, with Rob, would that even be possible? She laid her head in her hands massaging her temples and tried to push the stress away. She couldn't deal with it. Not now.

The pizza was good, the hot shower even better, and by the time she settled into her desk chair, wrapped in a soft silk robe, Ell felt refreshed and ready to jump back into the slog of research. She fired up her computer, marveling at how quick the new machine booted, clicked on the remote link and was greeted with an 'almost' familiar alert.

"Due to new departmental regulations and the nature of one investigator, the files held by Ellison Frost are not accessible. Please contact Information Services at ext 1911 anytime after 7:00 a.m. or click the following link to work on something more enjoyable."

Her frustration and anger were quickly subdued by curiosity as she focused her attention on the "Enjoyable Work" button. Unsure, but intrigued, she moved the mouse over the button, hesitated for a second, and clicked.

The alert disappeared; the screen went blank followed by a single word. "Enjoy".

Moments later, her frustration began to fade as a beautiful, petite redhead dressed in a black and red leather corset, fishnet stockings and six inch heeled boots filled her screen. A beautiful jeweled collar encircled her neck. The soft leather leash clipped to the front was being held by someone off screen. She knelt on the floor facing the camera, her eyes a deep, captivating blue and filled with lust. Her supple red lips curled slightly into a seductive smile.

While not Baker's twin, there was a definite resemblance.

The footage was good but obviously amateur, lending it a voyeuristic quality that immediately had Ell's body flushing with excitement. A gentle voice from off screen instructed the girl to 'turn' and the leash went taught as she circled, still on her knees. Her ass was firm and beautiful. The soft red skin indicated that she had recently been spanked, though Ell could not determine the implement from the markings. A sharp pull on the leash had the model bending forward, her bare pussy now in view. The moist lips sent a flurry of shivers through Ell's body. Her right hand now pinching her nipples through the silk of her robe.

"Spread", came the voice from off screen and the girl leaned forward, resting her shoulders on the carpet, both hands reaching back and spreading her ass cheeks. Ell's hand slipped inside her robe. Her body ached with want as she ran a finger across her wet lips and began to slowly circle her clit.

On screen, the redhead had begun sliding a finger into her ass, her own moans mixing with Ell's as the two of them enjoyed the sensations. The model reached to her right and produced a long, slim, silicone plug. Ell gasped as she watched it slide gently in. Her body bucking slightly as she continued to work her pussy. Begging for release.

The model's body tightened as the plug slid into place. The voice from off screen requested she 'roll'. Ell licked her lips as the redhead rolled to her back, spreading her legs wide for the camera. Reaching to her right once again she produced a large silver dildo and began running it across her slit. Ell was now lost in passion, her fingers sliding deep inside her, her hips bucking in rhythm to her strokes. The model slowly slid the dildo in, panting and moaning, her head tipping back, overcome with ecstasy.

Ell could not hold back, she fucked herself hard and fast, her eyes closing as she listened to the redhead moan and beg. Her body tightened and began to convulse, her pussy clenching around her fingers as she came. Breathing deeply, her body began to relax and come down from the euphoric high. Her mind lost in exhaustion and joy, she pulled herself to her feet and stumbled across the hall, grabbing her cell phone off the desk on her way. She flopped down on the bed, struggling to concentrate, and sent Rob a text before allowing her body to give out.

"You're stalker's showing. Thanks. – E"

Chapter Fourteen

A night's rest had helped Ell focus, though she hated to admit it. She woke early and was able to get in a quick run on the treadmill, a hot shower and still make it down to PD before 6:00 a.m. To her surprise, when she arrived, the boy-toy was waiting outside her office door with a latte in hand. He was wrapped in tight denim jeans and a loose fitting white T. Not exactly professional but so worth the oversight.

"I thought you overpaid consultants didn't start till nine?"

"It's a rarity but I felt my client would be a little upset if her network access was unavailable when she arrived."

Ell had nearly forgotten. "I'm quite certain you're correct, but I'm sure you could have fixed that with a couple magic words and fancy swipes on your phone. What brings the great creator of the next robot overlords to our humble offices?"

Rob handed her the latte and smiled. "Just wanted to see that beautiful face."

Ell shot him a sarcastic glance and he added. "Where is Baker, anyway?"

She wanted to roll her eyes but a stifled laugh betrayed her.

"Leave the innocent little girl alone you sadistic pervert."

"Oooo, territorial. She's all yours. I just hope I can watch."

Ell unlocked the door and headed into her private cell. Flipping a hand at the computer she asked, "Is this thing back up or do I have to beg... Sir?"

Rob shivered at the thought. "I'm truly sorry to say it is."

"Good, tech's running, suck up latte has been delivered, looks like your work here is done."

"Oh no, Ellison. I'm just getting started."

As hard as she tried to resist it, her body flushed as he smiled and headed down the hall.

Turning back to the computer, she took a sip of the latte. Chai, her favorite. 'Of, course,' she thought smiling to herself.

She pulled up her list of Deedrie's clients and found the file to be twice the size of what she had compiled the night before. Fifteen clients were now listed, each with highly detailed background information, financial data and criminal records. Ell stared at the screen unsure how to react. She grabbed her cell.

"Was this you? – E"

"A vague question but I'll extrapolate. Yes, you're welcome. – R"

Ell stewed for a moment. The case files were confidential but of course Rob had clearance. Yet, somehow it felt wrong. Why? If Rique had finished it up she'd have just been thankful and moved on. How was this different? She struggled with it for a moment before replying.

"Thanks. – E"

She'd deal with the boundary issues later.

She was still reviewing the documents when Rique arrived and popped his head into her office.

"Jones and Baker are going to take another run at Downs in about twenty. She's lawyered up so I doubt it will yield anything useful, but you may want to be there."

"Tell them to take it and keep me in the loop." She handed him a printout of the fifteen client names. "See anything there that stands out?"

He took a quick glance. "Collins International? Wasn't the vic modeling for a Collins' art auction?"

"Yeah, the name keeps popping up. See if you can line up an interview with Ms. Collins later this morning. It's not much but I don't like coincidences. I'll dig into her background and we'll see where it takes us. When you're done, take a look over Rob's notes on Stacey Bouton. I'm going to want to take another run at her but I'm giving him time to dig into it deeper."

"I'm on it." He turned with a slight wince, trying to hide a limp as he headed across the hall.

"Hold up, what's with the hobble?"

"It's nothing, knee's just a little tight this morning. I'm sure it will loosen up." His eyes darted away as if embarrassed.

"Shaw, you lie worse than a twelve year old perp. Go put some ice on it and come up with a better story."

She wasn't sure but, given his reaction, the name Angel came to mind. With a smile she thought she'd play a hunch and grabbed her phone.

"Quit injuring my detectives. – E"

The reply was nearly instantaneous. "Asserting my right to remain silent. – A"

Ell grinned. Oh, the fun she would have with this one.

Virginia Collins was an enigma. Having taken over her family's business empire about seven years prior, she made waves by taking the medical tech and pharmaceuticals company in a new direction. Focusing on high risk research and development had proven fruitful, and Collins International's public stock value had doubled since naming her CEO. She was active in business and social circles but very little private information was available. Aside from the standard business issues, she hadn't experienced any legal problems. At thirty seven she was still single with no major romances of record. Everything about her seemed to indicate that she was purely professional. Ell didn't buy it.

She grabbed the phone and dialed Rique's extension.

"Frost's slaves, how may we help you?"

"Hilarious. Do you really think you could handle that, limpy."

Shaw let out a nervous laugh, "What's up, L.T.?"

"Did you get me a time with Collins?"

"Working on it, thus far 'Ms. Collins is far too busy this morning, but we can certainly meet with her personal assistant who should be able to answer any of our questions'. I'm working my way around the 'empire' right now to try and nail her down."

"Fuckin rich people," mumbled Ell in frustration. "Let me see what I can do from this end. Review the data on Bouton and try and put a fire under Rob's ass."

"I think you'd be far more effective at that than I," mocked her partner.

"Oh, I'm sure Angel taught you a thing or two," the line went silent for a moment and Ell hung up before giving him a chance to respond. She dialed 145 and waited.

"Commander Nuez's office. How may I help you?"

"You can let me speak to him, Keith."

"One moment, Lieutenant Frost, I will see if the Commander is available."

"Gee, thanks."

The line cut to some glorified elevator music and a moment later Keith returned.

"I'm putting you through now, Lieutenant."

The phone rang twice before Ell could respond.

"Frost, just going over last night's review. What's up?"

"I see you're getting the robot trained, I didn't even have time for a smart ass remark."

"Honestly, I think you frighten him."

"Who me?"

"So what can I help you with, Lieutenant?"

"I've been trying to nail down an interview with Virgina Collins and we're getting the corporate run around. Just wondering if you have any pull in those circles?"

"Suspect?"

"Just a curiosity. Her name and the upcoming art auction have popped up repeatedly and I'd like to get a face to face."

"Not really my social circle, but I don't suspect you were thinking of me directly."

"If you want me to go straight to the mayor, I'm more than happy to, but I figured you'd want to handle it."

Nuez laughed at the thought. "Yeah, let's keep the buffer in place for now. I'll take care of it and have Keith let you know when."

"Oh, joy."

"Keep on it, Ell. I know this one's a bitch."

"Aren't they all? Thanks."

Spinning back to her computer she stared at the blank screens for a moment. Full of energy, ready to jump into the fray and she was stuck waiting for information. With a calming sigh she pulled up the case file and began slogging through the data one more time. This was the life of a cop.

With Downs' attorney present, the second interview was pretty much useless. Knowing the D.A. wouldn't bring charges, Jones and Baker were forced to release her. Frustrating but unavoidable. The Commander had managed to wrangle thirty minutes with Virginia Collins at ten-thirty sharp so Ell now found herself entering yet another lush corporate office with Rique in tow. Again, the decor was expensive but Collins International had a very distinct feeling. The offices and personnel were significantly segregated from the reception area, the walls were bright white and adorned with fine art on all sides. The lighting pushing focus to the artwork. The feeling was more that of a high end gallery than a pharmaceutical and medi-tech office.

Waiting was not a requirement as a handsome young man in his mid-twenties immediately escorted them to Virginia Collins' private office upon arrival. The office was beautiful and modern but its occupant was truly breathtaking. Her simple black dress hugged tightly to a perfect hourglass figure and ended just below the knee. Her deep red hair hung loosely across her shoulders and her beautiful smile did little to hide the confidence and determination in her eyes.

"Virginia Collins," she said extending a hand and rising to meet them as they entered.

"Lieutenant Frost and Detective Shaw," responded Ell unable to stop staring at the woman's eyes. "Thank you for taking the time to meet with us."

"Certainly, Lieutenant, I hope you can forgive the run around your department received this morning. I have a very tight schedule and my assistants are under direction to handle as much as possible without my involvement. Had I known this was in regards to Ms. Bouton I'd have ensured they scheduled it immediately."

Virginia gestured to the four leather arm chairs in the west corner of her office. "Please, let's have a seat and see what I can do to assist. Would you like something to drink?"

Both Ell and Rique shook their heads and settled into the soft, Italian leather chairs.

Virginia sat, positioning herself on angle in the chair across from them and leaned back gracefully. Ell was stunned by her poise. The lady took great care to present herself exactly as she wished. She had a calm, yet domineering aura.

"Ms. Collins..."

"Virginia, please."

"Virginia," continued Ell, "can you tell us about your relationship with Deedrie Bouton."

"For the most part, it was professional. I've known the Bouton family most of my life. While our corporate enterprises do not cross paths often, my father and James were part of the same social circles. As such, the families mingled on occasion. We weren't close but we were friendly. Shortly after I took over as CEO I began hearing rumors that Deedrie was working financial magic for her father. I approached her about incorporating her talents into Collins International and have had her under contract as a financial analyst for a little over four years. I can't say that I approved of her public lifestyle but our relationship was professional and, on that front, she was extremely successful."

"Yes, our own analysis suggests that she had a talent for safeguarding corporate assets."

"To put it mildly. The woman was a genius and she will be sorely missed. While we can replicate the procedures she put in place, tax code changes annually and many of our current practices have a very limited shelf life. A first world problem, but her clients will miss her."

"Do you know of any unhappy clients?" asked Rique.

"Only those that failed to take her advice. There are some CEOs that believe they know better, and others that viewed her practices as too risky from a legal perspective. I, myself, questioned much of it at first, but after a review from our tax attorneys I moved forward and implemented her suggestions. I am very glad that I did."

"I understand she was also involved with your upcoming art auction in some way."

"Peripherally. One of the artists that has been accepted submitted a piece which Deedrie had modeled for. Given the situation and the nature of the piece, the artist has withdrawn it from the show. We contemplated leaving it in the collection as it would surely do well and the charity could use the funds, however, we feel it would be in poor taste."

"I'm sorry? You mentioned the 'nature of the piece'?"

"It was submitted for our Fantasy Exhibit. A specific selection of pieces based on sexual exploration."

"And the artist, do you have their contact information?"

"One moment," Virginia rose and walked across the room to her desk. Her dress clung tightly to her hips drawing Ell's eyes once again. She could feel a primal attraction and lust hovering just under the surface, yearning to be set free.

Ell quickly averted her eyes as Virginia turned and headed back to the chairs. Before sitting she reached forward and passed a business card to Rique. "She has a small studio uptown, but your best option is probably catching her at work. She's a concierge at the Grand Larriott."

Rique flashed Ell a subtle look, "Thanks."

"When was the last time you spoke with Deedrie?" asked Ell, trying not to stare at the woman's legs as she sat and crossed them.

"About three weeks ago. She approached me about the painting. The artist has no real experience and, quite frankly, the piece doesn't have a lot of depth, but Deedrie was quite persistent and, with her as the model, it was bound to do well at auction so I agreed to present the application to the board."

"And how was her mood?"

Virginia tilted her head in thought. "Excited. She appeared to be very excited to get the painting into the show. It was odd. In my experience, most models for this type of work prefer to remain anonymous. There is a social stigma that comes with posing for a sexually provocative piece. Deedrie, on the other hand, was pushing to ensure it was well publicized. The board loved the idea, of course, but I got the feeling she had an ulterior motive."

"Did she indicate any other motivation? Anything that may shed some light on her last few weeks?"

"No, it was a brief meeting and, as usual, purely business.

She didn't discuss her private life and it was not my place to inquire."

"This painting, has it been returned to the artist?"

"No, I believe it is still in storage. The decision to remove the piece was made yesterday and it's not set to be returned until end of week. If you'd like I can have my assistant, Trevor, meet you at the gallery so you can see it."

"Please do", replied Ell glancing at the time, "It appears our thirty minutes are up. Thank you for making yourself available on such short notice."

Virginia smiled. A surprisingly genuine smile, to Ell's eyes. "You're welcome. I'll have Trevor give you the address on your way out. Please contact me if you need anything further. I'll see that your calls are put straight through."

The three rose and exchanged nods as they headed for the door.

Chapter Fifteen

*T*he S550 purred as Ell accelerated onto the freeway, heading across town to the auction sight.

"Thoughts?" she asked.

"Not exactly the evil corporate queen we were hoping for. She seemed forthright though far from grief stricken. Didn't bother with an attorney so either she has nothing to fear or wants to make us believe that. She's cold, all business as her background suggests, but friendly enough to make you feel at ease."

'A fair assessment,' thought Ell but there was a warmth there Rique hadn't picked up on. Just under the surface wanting to push through. Ms. Collins was searching for something more.

"This concierge? Safe to assume it's the same one Sebastian was talking to?"

"Yep, Nancy Selox. I spoke to her yesterday morning when I was running down his alibi. I didn't mention Deedrie, discretion and all, but I'm wondering if that was a mistake. I'm curious as to what her response would have been."

"We'll find out soon enough." Ell down shifted and accelerated to pass a minivan.

"Jesus Frost, a little warning before you go supersonic next time."

"Hang on, limpy. Wouldn't want to re-injure that knee. Think how disappointed Angel would be."

Rique got very quiet. He looked like he was trying to say something but couldn't as his eyes diverted out the passenger window.

"Oh, relax Rique. I'm the one that suggested it, remember."

"I know, it's just... weird."

"The real question is, did you have fun?"

"Fun? Definitely but... shit, you can't tell her I said anything, L.T."

"But what?"

"We hooked up to talk. I just wanted to expand my horizons. Things got pretty intense and we played a little, obviously, I was curious after all, but it was more than that. We spent half the night talking. Interests, boundaries, hell everything. I don't know. It's just different than I expected."

"Here's a little inside information that you didn't get from me. Angel may be a student of sexual deviance but she's not promiscuous. The fact that she saw you at all means something to her. One of the things you'll learn quickly is that the sex is not what's important to her. She enjoys it but what she really seeks, what she's looking for, is connection."

"I just didn't expect it. I was up for a bit of kinky education but somewhere along the line it changed. It was different."

"My two cents? Ride it out, just be sure you're ready for where it may take you. Talk to her. Tell her what you're telling me because openness and honesty are the keys to making it work. I think she'll surprise you."

"Just what this week needs, more surprises."

Ell smiled and weaved through traffic as her GPS beeped indicating her exit.

The gallery setting was interesting. It was a beautiful roofed open air venue with a separate dining hall that Ell suspected would be used as the auction house. Given the size and prestige of the location, she was pretty sure it was an event she would not be attending, though the Fantasy Exhibit did have an interesting allure.

Ell glanced around the parking lot but did not see Trevor.

"The kid's driving a three year old Chevy. Given the fact that you broke the sound barrier on the way over, he'll probably be a few minutes."

"If I'd broken the sound barrier I wouldn't have had to listen to your whining."

"I don't think that's quite how it works."

"Whatever Mr. Wizard."

They had a few minutes to spare so Ell pulled out her cell.

"Don't hurt him. – E"

A reply came back almost immediately.

"And ruin all my fun? – A"

"Ok, just a little. – E"

Seeing Trevor pulling into the parking lot, she stowed the phone and the two of them headed to meet him.

"I see that thing handles as sweet as she looks," commented the young man climbing out of his car.

"Yeah, but the badge and gun tend to scare people off," said Rique, Ell snapping him a sarcastic grin in return.

The assistant's face flushed and he forced a laugh.

"The submissions are being stored in a secure facility out back while the venue is being finalized. Follow me."

He led them through the main gallery and out a rear entrance. At first glance, the storage unit appeared to be a well fortified bunker. Ell could spot a number of closed circuit cameras focusing on the area, the building itself was a single room of about seven hundred square feet, concrete construction with no windows and only a single entrance.

"Tight security," she commented as Trevor led them to the entrance swiped a magnetic card and entered a series of numbers into the digital lock.

"Some of the pieces donated are quite valuable. Obviously we are insured against losses, but Ms. Collins prefers not to take unnecessary risks"

The system let forth a combination of beeps and the sound of a vault like locking mechanism could be heard releasing. The door swung inwards and a series of lights automatically engaged within the building.

"The Fantasy Exhibit is in the back left."

Ell slid past him and proceeded into the building. The artwork was well wrapped and organized on a series of labeled shelves lining the walls with only the large installation pieces taking up significant floor space. Knowing the odds of seeing the actual exhibit were slim and intrigued by the notion, Ell took a moment to look over the 'fantasy' works. She was particularly taken by a painting of a random naked man, tied to a bed, blindfolded and gagged. The artist had a gritty edge and had managed to capture a sense of freedom and self-awareness in the eyes. Painted in such a way to make the model indistinguishable yet it drew her in. She was contemplating why when she heard Trevor.

"Oh, god. This must be a mistake."

She didn't need to ask what he meant, she could tell by his tone. "Let me guess. The painting's missing."

Chapter Sixteen

*E*ll cleared the building, passed Trevor, who was now making a series of frantic calls, off to Rique for an interview and called in crime scene. On a hunch, she called Rob.

"Long distance emergency, Rob here. What's your pleasure, Lieutenant."

"I need your pretty little ass over at the new Collins Gallery. There's been a theft at a high security building. Locks and surveillance are all techie and I figured it would be right up your alley."

"Ell, you do realize I'm not officially PD crime tech, right? I'm department I.T., on scenes not really our thing."

"Consider this a house call… without the perks. I'll clear it with Lund but I want you on this."

"Ok, on my way, Lieutenant."

She hung up and dialed Lund.

"Christ, Frost, we're on our way. Keep your panties on."

"Panties?" she replied coyly and heard him stifle a laugh. "I've got Rob coming in from I.T. as a civilian consultant. The security system is pretty high tech and I'd like to get his input on how it was bypassed. Can you work him in?"

"Oooh, sharing your tech slave? Do I get to hold the leash?"

"And here I pictured you on the other end of it. Just get him what he needs for clearance, and thanks."

"Anything for you mistress, just please stay the whip."

Ell disconnected and headed over to meet Rique and Trevor.

"Ms. Collins is on her way down. She's rather upset and has called in the techs that installed the surveillance system to consult," said the assistant.

"Thanks. How long has the art been on sight?"

"Just under a month. Submissions have been funneling in since then but we've had everything selected for a little over a week now. Last inventory was six days ago and all exhibition pieces were present at that time."

"Ok, so we have a six day window," said Rique, "My gut says the piece went missing twelve hours either side of the murder but we'll run the surveillance for the entire window and see what's there."

"Run it," replied Ell, "but don't bet on finding anything. Whoever did this knew the system and how to get past that lock. This wasn't your standard bust and grab. They knew what they wanted and how to get it, and they didn't take it for the value. They bypassed half a million in art just to retrieve that one painting."

Somehow Rob managed to pull on-site a good five minutes before crime scene arrived. Climbing out of his truck, his loose white T blowing gently in the breeze, he glanced over at Ell and grinned. A cold shiver ran through her as she stared into his eyes for just a moment too long.

"Let me guess, happened to be in the neighborhood?" called Ell as he approached.

"You're not the only one with horsepower, Ms. Frost. Just because it doesn't look like a shiny trophy doesn't mean it won't haul when it needs to."

"Yeah, yeah. Big man with big motor," she replied in her best caveman impression.

"I'll show you mine if you show me yours," he winked.

"Later," she mouthed and winked back. "I spoke with Lund and you'll be working with his team once they arrive. The owner has the install techs on their way to consult as well, but I want you to take point on the security system. Trevor here will walk you through basic location of the tech but just eyes until Lund's on scene and clears it for more. You have gloves?"

"Ummm, no. Honestly, this is my first crime scene, Ell. I'm a bit of a fish out of water."

"Two basic rules, don't touch anything till it's cleared and record what you find." She handed him a pair of latex gloves.

"I can think of so many more enjoyable uses," he said sliding them on and snapping them against his wrists.

Ell flushed at the thought and had to struggle to focus. Bringing him on scene may have been a mistake. She needed to keep her wits about her.

With a sly grin Rob grabbed Trevor and headed off to get a feel for the system.

Rique, having witnessed the exchange, raised his eyebrows in question.

"Jesus Christ," said Ell, "is this a crime scene or a schoolyard? When Ms. Collins gets here see who has access and start running them down. If this wasn't a fancy bypass job then someone in her organization is involved. And for the love of god, try to get her to keep a lid on this for a few days.

The press is bound to be circling, but if they find out there is a tie to the Bouton case all hell's gonna break loose."

Ell snuck off as Lund arrived with the crime scene crew and began running down the scene. Pulling out her cell she dialed the precinct.

"PD, eleventh precinct, how may I direct your call?"

"Extension 145 please."

"Commander Nuez's office. How may I help you?"

"Keith, it's Frost, I need to speak to the Commander."

"One moment, Lieutenant, he is just on with the Mayor. Would you like to hold?"

'Shit,' she thought. "Might as well, thanks"

Pacing the parking lot while waiting did little to relax her. She had hoped to catch him and make sure he was informed before this got out. If the Mayor knew then she could only assume the press was all over it.

"Frost?"

"Sorry sir, I was hoping to catch you before this broke."

"Before what broke?"

"Huh? I assumed you knew, Keith said the mayor called."

"Just wanted to relay the praise Ms. Collins had for our fine detectives. What the hell's going on, Ell?"

"There's been a break in at the storage facility for the Collins International art auction. The only piece missing is the one Deedrie Bouton modeled for. Given the nature of the upcoming auction, the press is bound to be all over this. I'm trying to keep the tie-in under wraps but it's bound to break eventually."

"Find out who knew about the painting and see if we can determine if this has something to do with the murder or just some crazed fan looking to profit from it."

"Will do but my gut's telling me it's related. Security at this facility is top notch and it was bypassed not broken. Whoever did this had skills, knowledge and the time to plan."

"Thanks for the heads up, I'll do what I can to calm the waters."

Ell returned to the scene, watching the techs take over the process with methodical precision. Virginia Collins was now on-site and, thankfully, Rique had steered her to a quiet corner of the main gallery. She turned slowly as Ell approached, her soft red hair flipping off her shoulder and catching the gentle breeze. Ell was, once again, amazed by her poise.

"I asssume quiet and private are not going to be options," she remarked.

"Probably not," Ell smiled, "but I am hoping discretion may be. Odds are the press is already on their way but I'd like to keep the nature of the theft quiet, if possible. As we stand, only a handful of people know what went missing and fewer yet understand the significance. I would prefer it remained that way."

"Agreed, a full inventory will need to be taken. I will have Trevor take care of it to keep involvement as low as possible. Our insurance provider will need to know what's been taken and the artist will need to be notified."

"We can take care of notification if you'd like. We'll be heading over the to Larriott shortly to interview her."

"I think it's best if I speak with her first. The security of the artwork was my responsibility and I should be the one to inform her of the theft."

"If you can spare an hour you could come with us, it may help put her at ease to have someone she knows present."

"I cleared my afternoon before heading over here. I'm all yours, Lieutenant."

Ell could have sworn there was a flirtatious tone to the statement and could feel her body flush at the thought. 'Christ, Frost, get a hold of yourself,' she thought.

"Give me fifteen to check in with Lund."

After a quick search she located him just outside the storage facility looking distressed and confused.

"What have you got?"

"Jack shit. This doesn't play. We've pulled a couple partials off the lock pad but I'm betting they match the assistant. Tracking shows no entry in the last six days and surveillance appears to be clean. Rob's taking the system in for a full scan, but we have nothing to indicate anyone's entered or been in the area since the last inventory. Tech can be breached but this place is a bloody vault and the system is top of the line. Those capable of pulling the job aren't about to leave half a million in possible profits behind. Worst part is, they did a full video sweep as part of the inventory and every slot was filled. I've got the monkeys running prints and treads but I'm not very hopeful. Based on the evidence, you're looking for someone who can teleport through two feet of concrete because, at this point, it's the only way in."

"Great, I'll put out an APB on Nightcrawler. In the meantime keep on it."

Lund stared at her smiling and confused.

"What?"

"Sorry, I'm just surprised by the reference."

"Yeah, I'm a veritable refuse of useless information. I'm on my way to talk to the artist before the press starts swarming. If anything important pops up, text me."

Ell headed back to meet up with Rique and Virginia. Rounding the corner to the parking lot she could see Rob leaning against the side of his pickup, a cool smile across his face as he chatted with Ms. Collins. She was enthralled and relaxed. A side of her Ell knew was there but had not seen. She flipped her hair casually, reached out and touched his shoulder, the flirtation subtle but unmistakable. Ell's mind began picturing the two of them together. Their beautiful bodies entwined as he introduced the lady to a passion she did not know existed. Ell snapped herself back to the moment and smiled. The man certainly had good taste.

"If you're done trying to whisk away my I.T. slave with promises of fame and fortune, we're ready to go."

Virginia smiled and looked unsure what to say.

"Slave?" asked Rob saving her

"Servant? Underling? Sub?" asked Ell, faking a look of confusion.

"A pleasure as always, Lieutenant. I'll get you the data on the security as soon as I have it. And it has been a great pleasure to meet you, Ginny."

'Ginny?' thought Ell.

"Thank you, and you as well."

"Do you want to meet us down there? If not I'll have Rique take a squad and you can ride with me," said Ell as they headed towards her car.

Rob poked his head out the window of his truck as he was pulling out.

"Save yourself the heart attack. Meet her down there."

Ell shot him a finger and all three laughed in unison.

Virginia drove herself, more for the convenience of having her car than the fear of riding in Ell's, but the fact that the Lieutenant arrived at the Grand Larriott nearly ten minutes before her likely reinforced that she'd made the correct choice.

Ell and Rique let her take the lead knowing that she wanted to handle the theft personally. Virginia, or one of her assistants, had called in advance and a man whose name tag identified him as the 'Day Manager' met them upon arrival and led them to a series of offices behind the concierge desk. Nancy Selox was waiting for them and appeared to be nervous. She was young, perhaps twenty-two at the upper end, had short black hair and wild eyes lined in heavy purple shadow. Ell recognized her immediately and was instantly on edge. She hadn't considered the scene her and Sebastian had made in the lounge and lobby three days prior. Now that she had she was unsure how to deal with any recognition that may arise.

"Nancy, I'm sorry we had to drag you in here without more warning."

"Ms. Collins, is something wrong? Did the board change their mind about showing the painting?"

"I'm afraid not, there has been a theft at the storage facility. I'm sorry to have to tell you that your painting is missing."

"Missing? Oh god, is the exhibition still on track? How many pieces did you lose?"

Virginia was unsure how to respond and glanced at Ell who nodded.

"Yours is the only one missing. Lieutenant Frost and Detective Shaw," she motioned to them, "believe it may have something to do with Ms. Bouton's murder and they'd like to ask you a few questions.

"Of... of course," she stammered.

"Thank you," interjected Ell, taking the lead. "I'm sorry to throw this on you out of the blue but the theft was just recently discovered and we feel it may be related. How did you know Ms. Bouton?"

"I didn't, well... I guess I knew her but I didn't really know her." She was staring at Ell confused as if something about the woman was out of place. "Sorry, did that make any sense? I met her here, at work, about two months ago at a gala. She overheard me talking to Jon, umm he's a bellboy, anyway, she overheard us talking about the art auction and how I wanted to submit one of my paintings. I had heard about the Fantasy Exhibit and most of my stuff is pretty erotic so I was thinking about it."

She stopped for a moment, staring at Ell again as if trying to place the face. "Anyway, Deedrie overheard and asked me about my work. She was looking for an artist to do some work for a new business venture. When I started to talk about the stuff I do she pretty much insisted that I paint her and submit it. She had the scene all worked out and knew exactly what she wanted. I don't usually work from models, I tend to free flow, but this was Deedrie Bouton, the name alone would get my piece in the auction. To top it off she wanted to commission the work so she could use the image in future promotions."

"You said this was about two months ago?"

"Yup, we set up in her condo and finished the painting about two weeks later. I still can't believe she posed for it and actually wanted it out there, but I suppose if she was looking to use it as a corporate logo it was going to be seen."

"Corporate logo?" prompted Ell.

"I'm not sure what the company was but she wanted the painting as the logo, paid me a hefty commission to use it."

"Do you happen to have any photos of the painting?" Ell's instincts were kicking in hard and fast.

"Sure," replied Nancy digging out her cell phone. "It's not my best work but it was definitely going in the portfolio."

She handed the phone to Ell and, as expected, there was Deedrie Bouton in the exact pose she'd been found murdered. Ell handed it back and had Nancy text her a copy.

"Do you have any idea what business she was planning to use this for?"

"Not really, she was pretty secretive, but the contract for rights and commission was in the name D. B. E."

Ell made note and thanked her for her time, leaving a card in case she thought of anything pertinent. Virginia Collins stayed behind to discuss the insurance issues and valuation of the painting. Nancy seemed relieved to know she would be compensated but concerned about being in the middle of a murder investigation.

———————

"Run a corporate search on D.B.E," she instructed as they settled back into the S550. "Nothing showed on the financials so it has to be recently incorporated."

"On it," said Rique pulling out his cell as she accelerated into traffic.

"We need to know what the hell this girl was doing and who else was involved."

"Corporate records show registration of D.B.E Corp. less than four months ago. Incorporator of record is listed as BabyBird Inc. I can't pull the articles and bylaws until we hit the office but I'm pulling up BabyBird now."

"Don't bother, it will lead to another corporation, likely out of country, but they all lead back to Bouton. BabyBird is the central US Corp on Deedrie's T2."

Ell, slammed down the accelerator weaving through traffic.

"Shit, Frost."

"Sorry, hang on, limpy"

"I'm pretty sure we have to survive the ride back to office if you want to solve this thing."

"Three years, Shaw. Have I killed you yet?"

"I'd like to at least make it through the day in one piece. I'm supposed to see Angel again tonight."

Ell sat there stunned as if something just hit her. "Angel. Son of a bitch. How did I miss it?"

"What?" asked Rique, thoroughly confused.

"She wasn't out getting her freak on for the last six months. She was doing research and drumming up free publicity. D. B. E. - Deedrie Bouton Escorts."

Chapter Seventeen

"*P*ull the articles," said Ell as they stepped back into the precinct after wading through the onslaught of press that had, once again, began to circle. "Odds are this was Deedrie's show but let's check for additional officers or directors. Someone else had to know what she was doing and I want that person in the box by end of day. Get Baker and Jones running trademarks, licensing and whatever else she would have needed to start this up."

They separated at the bullpen and Ell headed into her office. She grabbed her cell and fired off a text.

"My office, bring what you have. – E"

Rob's response was quick.

"Oh the options. On my way. – R"

She smiled, wishing the visit was personal, and pulled up Deedrie's diary, scanning it quickly with a new found eye. She could see how the methodical and experimental nature made sense. It was a series of tests digging into sexual psychology, wants, needs, and kink. It was market research. She made note to contact Angel and have her put out feelers in the community.

"You're beautiful when you're focused," said Rob from the doorway. "What's up?"

"Bouton was starting an escort agency. She commissioned the painting as a corporate logo, the sex was basically market research and the wild girl publicity was pre-launch promotion."

"Makes sense, what we know suggests she had a flair for business. Given her public popularity it would have generated plenty of interest."

"Yeah, and it looks like someone wasn't too please about it, which means it wasn't a secret and I need to know who else knew about it."

"Seems reasonable in an unreasonable sort of way. So how can I help?"

"Can you reach out to the community and see if anyone heard rumors of a new agency on the scene?"

"Sounds easy enough. I have some friends that use the services. May be a good idea to reach out to those you know as well."

Ell thought, for a moment, that she could sense a ping of jealousy in the words. Could she be reading something into it?

"I'll be talking to Angel again shortly, if there were rumors of competition she'd have known."

"It's a pretty competitive business, Ell. The solid escorts are difficult to find and constantly being poached. If she was just starting out she'd need to build a team and I doubt she'd be looking for streetwalkers and strippers. She'd want the elite. We can't rule it out as a motive."

"Yeah, it's on my list but for some reason this still feels more personal. Any luck with the footage?"

"Yes and no. I have a deep scan running on the video.

The footage doesn't show any activity around the building for the last six days. The timestamps solid and there's nothing missing but a bit by bit comparison has flagged two very distinct loops. Someone's replaced two sections of footage and looped in previously recorded data. Whoever did it was talented because, to the eye, there's not a single determining factor in the visual. I'll have a record and timeline for the missing footage in about an hour."

"What about entry?"

"No evidence that the card and keypad tracking was tampered with so they either bypassed the system altogether or found another way in."

Ell rubbed her temples and leaned her head back.

"We're back to NightCrawler," she said, eliciting a questioning look from Rob which she simply shook off.

"I'm still missing something."

"You're running at a hundred miles and hour trying to make sense of the landscape whipping past. Slow it down, Ell."

She glanced up, admiring the calm presence in his eyes and wishing she could reflect it.

"How the hell do you do that?"

"One piece at a time, you can't finish the puzzle without taking the time to examine each piece and figure out where it fits."

"And when the box has been torn and there are pieces missing?"

"You extrapolate."

"Sounds easy."

"The puzzle may not be easy, but the process is established. Slow down and go back to it."

"Fuck, I'm beginning to hate it when you're right."

Rob smiled as if he was privy to some inside joke. "Sounds like a solid relationship to me."

Ell smirked and he took the opportunity to retreat and get back to work.

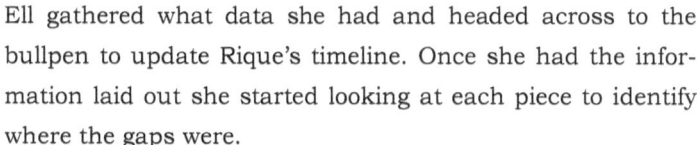

Ell gathered what data she had and headed across to the bullpen to update Rique's timeline. Once she had the information laid out she started looking at each piece to identify where the gaps were.

She took a step back analyzing the board, looking at it as a business start-up process. Capital wasn't an issue. Market research and publicity lead-up were there. Legal and setup were in place. Corporate branding had begun and, with the art auction and the paintings reveal in four weeks, a public launch would likely follow shortly. She was staring at the board when Baker slid in beside her.

"Rique filled me in on the theory. Looks like she was ramping up towards a grand opening, so to speak."

Ell couldn't contain a grin, "Yeah but something's missing. Something doesn't fit."

"Auction's in four weeks right?"

Ell nodded.

"Ok, so assuming she was planning to tie the launch to the reveal she'd need staff. Four weeks isn't a long time to recruit. She had to have approached some of them by now. And what about clients? She's been promoting subtly for months but she'd want a small client list in place prior to launch, right?"

'Missing pieces,' thought Ell.

Rique hobbled up next to her, trying to hide his limp, and held out a small stack of paper.

"Organizational docs. Nothing out of the ordinary but the articles do list a second director."

Ell flipped through the pages until she got to the assignment of directors.

'Vice President – Julie Samantha Downs.'

"Son of a bitch." Take Jones and get her back in a box. Lawyer or not, she has some questions to answer. I'm taking Baker down to Madame Angel's."

Rique raised his eyebrows and gave her a cheeky grin.

"Mind out of the gutter, Shaw. I need to talk to her staff and find out who, if anyone, Deedrie was planning to poach. If you wrap up Downs before we're back let her stew in holding. The bitch is mine."

She headed out, Baker in tow, and fired a text to Lund.

"What's the timeline? – E"

"2 hrs for basics – 24 if there are prints. – L"

"Connect with Rob and get his data in the report. – E"

"Yes, mistress. – L"

They exited the front door to a swarm of reporters, "Fuck. Look casual and don't give them a reason to attack."

Baker laughed, her giggle sending waves through Ell. "Not sure bear defense works, Lieutenant."

A young female reporter pounced in front of her as she turned and headed for the parking lot.

"Lieutenant Frost, can I get a comment on the Collin's Gallery robbery?"

"No comment," replied Ell trying to ignore the microphone being shoved in her face.

"My sources say it was discovered while investigating the

Bouton homicide. Would you care to confirm the relationship and explain how it came to light?"

Ell stopped dead in her tracks, grabbed the microphone and turned it off.

"Listen... Cindy," she said, looking down at the reporters press badge. "Off the record, I'm not sure who your 'source' is and quite frankly I'd run you in right now if I thought you'd give them up, but your information is rumor and speculation. If you decide to go live without proper corroboration I'll be running your ass in for obstruction, inciting public panic and anything else I can get to stick. Is that clear?"

The reporter may have been taken aback but she stood her ground. "I have the right to report the facts and I intend to do so, Lieutenant. You can wave all the threats you wish, but we both know they're empty."

Ell took a deep breath, realizing that she'd taken the wrong tactic. She had assumed she could intimidate the girl and had failed miserably. She glanced at Baker, who looked unsure how to react. The other reporters were starting to mull in their direction so Ell grabbed Cindy by the elbow.

"Walk with us, Cindy."

She was unsure but decided to go with it, and the three headed deeper into the parking lot.

"Still, off the record. We believe there is a correlation but at this point it's speculation and we'd rather that speculation wasn't made public. We are pursuing a killer, likely one that will be following news reports and, if our assumptions are correct, the further they think we are from tying things together the less likely they are to react, hide, or bolt."

Cindy looked at her speculatively.

"I'm not going to ask you to bury what you may or may not know because you have a job to do, but you need to know what that report is going to do. Quite frankly, I'd rather it came out later than sooner. So what's it going to take for you to take your time putting it together?"

The girl caught on quick. "Well, if I were busy prepping for a one on one exclusive with the lead investigator it would be really difficult to get my story in before deadline."

"Give me forty-eight hours and you'll have your interview."

Cindy smiled as if she'd just won a Pulitzer.

"And if your source is inside those walls," Ell gestured at the precinct, "you can let them know their days are numbered. You may not give up a name, but I'll find it and make sure the leak is sealed permanently."

Cindy looked at her intently as if making a decision. "They're not," she said, to Ell's surprise, "but I won't break their confidentiality. A pleasure doing business with you, Lieutenant Frost."

She grabbed the mic out of Ell's hand and headed back towards the main entrance.

As the Mercedes pulled out into traffic, Ell glanced over at Baker. Her red hair was pulled back into a tight pony that lay across her shoulder. She was quiet but observant. Ell was taken by her natural beauty. A young, innocent look that she simply could not resist.

"There are a couple things you should know before we see Madame Angel."

Baker flipped her attention from the road to the driver. Ell tried to focus on traffic as looking into Baker's eyes was too distracting.

"Angel and I have a pre-existing relationship. We were

college roommates and have remained friends over the years. That's going to make this process both easier and much more difficult. There is a good chance some of her employees were involved in Bouton's venture and I need you there as an unbiased set of eyes."

"Which is why I'm here and not Rique." Her response was unexpected.

"Pardon."

"I overheard him calling Angel before leaving last night. He asked if she was interested in dinner. Given the limp he's been hiding today I assume it went... well."

Ell paused for a moment. "You're a good detective, Baker. Observant, understanding and quick. Those traits will take you somewhere. Hold on to them."

The detective's face grew to a shade of red rivaling her hair. Ell could see the formation of tears in the corner of her eye.

"If you say 'Awe, schucks.' I'm tossing you out without slowing down."

The line helped to break the tension and the two of them broke out into laughter.

"Thanks, I've had good teachers."

Ell checked the time. Angel's wouldn't be open for a few hours yet. She engaged her Bluetooth.

"Call speed-dial eight."

The phone began to ring across the Mercedes sound system.

"Hello?" Angel's voice filled the car.

"Angel, we need to chat. I'm en route now, any chance you're at the office?"

"I just left for the day. I was heading home for a quick soak and some downtime. What's up?"

"I'd rather not say over the phone, where can we meet?"

"Shit, Ell I'm almost home do you need me to head back into the office."

"The house will work, you still in the ranch style on 53rd?"

"Yeah but they've gated the community so I'll have to buzz you in."

"I can bypass with my badge number, we'll see you in about fifteen."

Ell disconnected and turned to Baker.

"Hang on," and with that she whipped a u-turn and accelerated north.

She made the trip in just under ten minutes and, unlike Rique, Baker smiled and enjoyed the ride. The joy present in her eyes with every shift, swerve and jolt drew Ell in. This girl reveled in the anticipation and excitement. Ell couldn't help imagine how fun she would be in a more intimate setting. It made her body shiver and her blood warm as she imagined Rob, standing over the two of them, leashes in hand.

Trying to regain her bearings, she pulled into the driveway of a beautiful ranch style bungalow on three acres of well-manicured land.

"Jesus, I'm in the wrong business," said Baker. Ell nearly laughed due to how well the comment coincided with the fantasy she was just shaking off.

Angel met them at the front door, her petite frame silhouetted by a beautiful yellow sundress and burgundy, high-heeled boots.

"Angel Demarco, this is Detective Baker."

Angel extended a hand, "Pleased to meet you, Detective. Please come in."

She led them through the main foyer to a large sunroom

and gestured towards a leather couch, taking a seat in the armchair across from it.

"Ok, what's the emergency, Ell? I'm hoping we can make this fairly quick, I have dinner plans in about two hours and need to get ready."

"I'm willing to bet you're date's working late so I'm sure we'll be fine."

"Gee, thanks for clearing my schedule, Lieutenant."

"Sorry, unavoidable perks of the job."

As if on cue Angel's phone chimed and she shook her head as she read the message from Rique.

"Looks like my evening just cleared up, what can I help you with, Lieutenant?"

"Deedrie Bouton Escorts."

Angel looked confused and worried. "Pardon?"

Ell sensed that she wasn't nearly as surprised by the reveal as she should have been. Her gut told her to push. "How long have you known."

Angel went silent; Ell could see her weighing her options and her own heart sank. This was a reaction of guilt. One she'd seen a number of times.

"I..." Angel stopped. "I believe I'd like my attorney present before we continue."

Ell was floored. What the hell was going on? She glanced at Baker, who was watching the woman with great intensity.

"Ms. Demarco," the detective stepped in, "If you would like an attorney present we can certainly accommodate, but I must advise you as to what that will mean. In order to ensure all parties are protected, we will need to perform this interview at the precinct. You may not know this but the press has descended heavily on the eleventh due to an art theft that was discovered earlier today. We will not be able to protect your identity.

"I understand but I have been advised by council to answer no questions in regards to this matter unless they are present." She shifted her gaze to Ell, there was a slight tear in her left eye and a sincerity in her voice. "I'm sorry, Ell."

Chapter Eighteen

E ll was pissed, she wanted to slap the cuffs on her and accidentally miss the doorway on the way out. Unfortunately, they didn't have anything on Angel and no cause for an arrest so they were forced to rely on a 'promise' that she and her attorney would meet them at the precinct. She took her frustration out on the accelerator and fellow travelers. Despite the confusion and concern for Ell, Baker grinned the entire way.

Ell glanced over, saw the grin and began to relax.

"Sorry, I don't mean to downplay what just happened but this car seriously rocks."

Ell broke out into uncontrollable laughter.

Baker flushed red but her smile never ceased.

"Tell you what, next time you can drive," said Ell as she hung a left into the precinct parking lot. The press was still swarming but Cindy was nowhere to be seen. Ell made a silent prayer for a major emergency in the next fifteen minutes in hopes they'd disperse but knew it was futile. She didn't know what Angel was wrapped up in, and she was still supremely angry, but she didn't want her friend's name drug through the mud. As they made their way into the precinct another thought hit her like a brick. If Angel was seriously involved their background together was bound to come out. Her head began throbbing as the stress hit full force. What the fuck did Angel do?

She was on the brink of screaming when she walked into her office and there he was. His eyes glowing with a calm security she desperately needed. Without a second thought she melted into Rob's arms and broke down. He said nothing and no words were needed. He simply held her close, his arms wrapping her tight and helping to alleviate the pain. After what seemed an eternity, she slowly pulled herself free.

"Thank you," she said wiping the tears from her eyes.

"What happened?"

She didn't know what to say. She slumped down in her chair and sighed deeply.

"We went to interview Angel. I don't know what's going on at this point but the moment I mentioned D.B.E. she went white and lawyered up. She's one of my oldest friends and I don't even know what to think."

"Start by giving her the benefit of the doubt."

"I want to, I refuse to believe she could do this but ... I don't know. She and her lawyer are on their way down for an interview."

"You need to step aside, Ell. You're too close to it and too shook up to be in that room. Let Rique handle the interview."

Ell started laughing, Rob looking at her as if insanity had suddenly kicked in.

"Rique's not an option. The two of them hooked up last night and he just postponed a dinner engagement with her minutes before all this hit."

"Under different circumstances I'd almost find that humorous. Let Jones and Baker take it, you can monitor like you did with Downs."

"I'm not really in the mood for that kind of monitoring," she jabbed.

"You know that's not what I meant."

"Relax, stud. I'm just playing with you. I need to take this interview. I need to face her and find out what the hell is going on."

"Ell, if she is involved your background together jeopardizes the case. I know you want to face this, and yes, we need to give her the benefit of the doubt, but you also need to do what's right. Jones and Baker are solid detectives. They don't have a personal connection here, and they will do what needs to be done. Pass the interview off."

"You know this 'always being right' thing is starting to piss me off."

"I promise to be wrong at least once a month." He held up three fingers in the 'Scouts Honor" signal.

"Ok, I need to see where Jones is. She and Rique were looking for Downs to drag her ass back in here."

She pulled out her cell and fired Jones a text.

"ETA? Need you back at the house. – E"

Her cell chirped a couple seconds later.

"Ten minutes. Downs has gone rabbit but we've got feelers out. Explain soon. – J"

Ell took a deep breath and looked back up at Rob. He had a quiet strength about him. A security she had been missing.

"How'd you know?"

"Would you believe stalker tendencies?"

Ell gave him a skeptical look.

"I'm not sure I should be telling you. Baker texted me on your way back and said I should be here when you arrived."

Ell stared at him, dumbfounded.

"She didn't give me any details but I do what I'm told," he winked and his smile grew.

"Wait, what? How the hell does Baker know? Actually, what does Baker know? I don't even know what this is."

"For that answer you will need to ask her. I'm just following orders, Lieutenant."

Ell made a mental note to have a heart to heart with Baker once this was all over. If she somehow picked up on the connection then it was possible others had as well.

Angel Demarco arrived with her attorney five minutes later. Jones and Rique were still en route so Ell had Baker escort them to Interview One and get them settled. Ell was nervous and still running on adrenaline, but she tried to reign it in and focus. When the detectives arrived she asked Jones to wait in the bullpen and pulled Rique aside.

"I've got Angel Demarco in Interview One. As soon as we mentioned Bouton Escorts she got really nervous and lawered up."

"L.T. you don't think..."

"No, I don't, but she's obviously been hiding something. Given our connection I'm having Jones and Baker take the interview. I need to know I can count on you to stay clear of this for now."

"You know you can. I... hell I don't know what to think."

"Welcome to the club."

The two of them crossed the bullpen to Jones and the recently returned Baker. She gave them a brief run down on the plan and asked if they had any questions prior to jumping in.

"Just one," asked Jones. "How should we play this? Right now we don't have any evidence that suggests involvement. How hard do we go after her?"

"As hard as you need to. She has an attorney in the room so that's bound to make it difficult. Do what you need to do. I want to know what she's hiding and why she's escalated this. Until we have those answers you keep pushing."

"Are you observing," asked Rique.

"Yeah, care to join?"

He considered it for a moment. "No, I don't know what's going on but either way I don't think I want to see it. Let me know how it plays out and I'll go from there."

The three of them made their way down and Ell slipped into the observation room. Rob, of course, was already there. She positioned herself in front of the glass and he gently wrapped his arms around her from behind. It was a tender embrace, precisely what she needed.

"Detectives Jones and Baker interviewing Angel Demarco as part of the Bouton homicide investigation. Ms. Demarco has elected to have council present. Please state your name for the record, sir."

"Dallas McDermont J. D. I have instructed my client to answer only upon my approval, but I will allow her to do so in her own words,"

"That's very kind of you Mr. McDermont," replied Jones with a touch of sarcasm. "It makes our lives so much easier when we can interview the actual party in question."

He was about to reply but Jones ignored him and immediately addressed Angel. She ran through the standard Miranda rights and asked if she understood them.

"Yes."

"Ms. Demarco, as my colleague was inquiring before you insisted on formalizing these proceedings, please tell us what you know of Deedrie Bouton Escorts."

The lawyer nodded.

"Until this evening I had never heard the name."

"Have you heard any rumors in your community about a new, elite service planning to open its doors?"

The lawyer nodded.

"There are always rumors, very few of them come to fruition, and those that do find out quickly that this is not an easy business to jump into. As with anything, you need a niche and you need time and money to build up your name as a respectable service. So, yes, I've heard rumors but nothing that overtly concerned me."

"And if those rumors had revolved around someone with the name recognition and capital of Deedrie Bouton, would that concern you."

"Detective, my client has already stated there were no rumors that concerned her. Let's keep this interview on the facts as I doubt speculation will help your investigation."

"You'd be surprised how often speculation is rooted in unknown fact, counselor. So you were not aware that Deedrie Bouton was attempting to set up a rival escort agency?"

Angel glanced at her lawyer who seemed unsure how to proceed. "I am afraid I am advising my client not to answer that question. We are treading onto grounds which may encroach upon a legally binding confidentiality agreement."

"Pardon?"

"My client is under contractual obligations not to speak on certain matters."

"Counselor, this is a murder investigation. Whatever civil

contract may be in place is trumped by the protection of the citizens. We both know that, if needed, we can have a judge force her cooperation." Baker had now joined the conversation.

"Perhaps, but until that time I am advising my client not to answer."

"And who is party to this confidentiality agreement?"

Ell smiled, she could tell Baker was looking for a legal loophole to back him into a corner. It was unlikely to work but it was a solid tactic.

"Obviously that can't be discussed."

"Actually it can. The names of the parties involved in a confidentiality agreement are not held as confidential unless done so via a separate agreement. While the content of said agreement cannot be discussed, there is nothing stopping us from discussing its existence or the parties bound by it."

The lawyer looked thoroughly confused. After some thought he responded, "The agreement was signed by both my client and Deedrie Bouton. If you would like any further information you will require a court order."

"Deedrie Bouton. Not Deedrie Bouton Escorts?"

"As stated my client was unaware of the existence of Deedrie Bouton Escorts," responded the lawyer assuming she was attempting to indicate otherwise.

"So the only party that could bring action against your client for breach of contract is deceased. Please explain the justification for stonewalling this investigation."

Angel quickly snapped her head towards the attorney. "Is that true?"

"The terms of your agreement do not expire upon death of one of the parties."

"Perhaps," said Baker. "But, who listed in said agreement

would have the right to bring forth a lawsuit in regards to a breach?"

"Only those parties bound by the agreement," resigned the attorney.

"One of which is dead. So unless you plan on bringing a breach of contract suit against yourself, Ms. Demarco, there is no reason said contract needs to be upheld."

Angel again snapped her eyes to the lawyer. Ell had seen the look before and she could tell the woman was pissed.

"Regardless, I still advise not speaking on these matters without being compelled to do so by a court of law."

"And the reason for that advice?" asked Angel.

"There are additional concerns. It is not in your best interest to get involved in this investigation."

Angel's fury was growing and Ell was relieved to see it. "My best interest? Do I, or do I not, have a legal obligation to remain quiet?"

"It's a grey area at this point but you have no obligation to speak to the detectives whether the contract is still binding or not."

Angel was on the edge, and Dallas McDermont was beginning to sweat.

"What is my exposure should I choose to ignore the agreement?"

"Ms. Demarco, this isn't really the place for this type of discussion."

"No, the right time would have been when you were advising me not to speak but as you did not feel it pertinent to explain the actual legal position at that time you can damn well do so now. What is my potential exposure?"

"I assume you mean other than possibly becoming a person of interest in an ongoing homicide investigation along with the negative press and issues that will certainly arise from doing so?"

"What is my financial exposure in regards to the contract?" Angel was doing everything she could to hold her anger in check.

"Should the estate decide to sue, you will incur significant legal costs along with damage to your reputation."

"Since I didn't hear anything in regards to a settlement, am I to assume I have no legal obligation to remain silent."

"It's unlikely a suit would hold up but I still advise you to remain silent. There is nothing gained by speaking."

Angel lost it. "Nothing gained? Nothing gained? Do you have a shred of human decency? What I know could help an active homicide investigation. You know damn well that contract was the only reason I withheld the information. Get out."

"Pardon?"

"Get the fuck out of this room and advise your firm that they are to expect a termination letter as soon as I am finished speaking with the detectives."

She was livid, emotions were high and rising but to Dallas McDermont's credit he said nothing. He methodically packed his belongings and left the interview room.

Ell leaned back into Rob's arms a sense of relief filling her yet still battling concern, and desperately wanting to rush into the interview room and take over.

"Relax, they've got this," he whispered, feeling her body fighting with itself.

"It was a good play."

"Baker has good instincts and she reads people well. She saw something there, knew Angel wanted to talk."

"She saw it back at the house, too. I missed it but she made a play to scare Angel into talking. Not the right tactic at the time, Angel's a fighter and if you give her a chance she will fight back like a stubborn mule, but Baker doesn't know her."

"Sounds like someone else I know," he teased, his arms still wrapped around her from behind but now loosening.

Ell slipped her heel onto the tow of his shoe and shifted her weight.

"Owww. I take it back, you're not stubborn at all," he mocked as she grinned knowing that too would cost her.

In the other room, Baker set a glass of water in front of Angel and Jones took over.

"Ms. Demarco, for the record, are you now waiving your right to have counsel present for this interview?"

"Yes, and I'm sorry I put you all through this."

"Ok, where were we? Right, were you aware that Deedrie Bouton was attempting to launch a rival escort agency?"

"Quite frankly, no, but I did know she was interested in getting into the business. Five months ago she approached me with a business opportunity, as part of that discussion we each signed mutual non-disclosure confidentiality agreements."

"What was the business opportunity?"

"Deedrie had aspirations of a nationally branded, full service escort agency but felt starting from the ground up would be too difficult given the need for elite staff and reputation. She approached me with an offer of becoming a full partner in M.A.E. She had the capital to make a massive expansion a realistic possibility. There are some serious legal concerns in my business and addressing those on a large scale is a very costly scenario. It is one of the major issues I have come across as my business has grown. The offer intrigued me, and we spent about three weeks in discussions."

"As she moved on, can we assume the negotiations fell through?"

"She was very naïve when it came to the industry. It became apparent rather quickly that she did not have a realistic understanding of the business and how we are forced to operate. Had she been looking to be a silent partner, that ignorance may have been alright but she wanted to take on an active role. It simply wasn't feasible. My primary concern, however, was that she planned on going very public with the expansion. Large scale marketing, online campaigns, launch parties. This is not an industry that works well with publicity. Our clients demand and require a level of discretion. In the end we simply could not come to terms and went our separate ways."

"And you weren't worried? Knowing she was looking to build a highly promoted, competitive service?"

"Not in the least. Her business model was out to lunch and she had no clue as to the industry or the psychology of the clientele. She didn't even have practical experience in most of the services she wanted to offer. Then, after seeing her tabloid implosion over the last few months, I assumed she'd given up on the idea and gotten herself wrapped up in the same never-ending spiral we have seen so often before."

"So given the knowledge that she was, in fact, moving forward does anything stand out?"

Angel thought for a moment. "I did have three escorts leave in the last two months. It was unexpected but not uncommon.

Eventually many of them want out of the life. They fall in love or save up the cash to move on. Aside from that I don't think much has changed. Our client list has been steady and there hasn't been much turnover there."

Ell tensed at the mention of the client list. Jones' questioning was leading back to a request for it to be provided. She knew what Angel's response was going to be but once the request was on record she'd be forced to follow up on procuring it through legal channels.

"Do you know if any of your employees have been approached directly in regards to moving?" asked Baker.

"No, but poaching is pretty common, and the employees rarely mention attempts. They like to keep their options open."

"We would like to speak with them."

"I'll have the list sent over so you can begin arranging interviews."

"Thank you, I think that's all we need for now but please let us know if anything new comes to you. We appreciate your help, Ms. Demarco."

"Call me Angel," she replied extending a hand to the two of them.

Jones flashed her partner a questioning glance as if confused as to why she had cut the interview short. Baker smiled but said nothing.

Rob released his grip on Ell, assuming she would want to leave and speak to her friend in private but she didn't move.

"Go, Ellison."

"And say what?"

"Whatever needs to be said." He pushed her forward and watched her slowly walk out the door.

Chapter Nineteen

*T*he conversation with Angel was awkward and quick. Ell needed time to process and Angel was unsure what she could possibly say. Having promised to talk again once things settled, Ell crashed into her desk chair and rubbed her temples. Seven twenty-three and she felt like the day was spinning out of control. She spent a few moments silently cursing the case before pulling herself together and heading across the hall.

"Jones, Baker, good work in there," she said entering the bullpen. "Rique and I will start running employees, what the hell is up with Downs?"

'Up with Downs?' she thought, fuck her mind was mush.

"Little bitch went rabbit as soon as she was sprung," said Jones. "Hasn't gone home and no one has a clue where she is. We've been monitoring financials and so far she hasn't touched any of her accounts. The bank was friendly and set up a flag, so if she uses it we'll know."

"Ok, end of shift has come and gone so if nothing is pressing grab some rest and we'll start running again first thing tomorrow."

"Jones and I were talking about grabbing a drink and a bite to eat at Sully's before heading home. Rique shot us down but you're welcome to join."

Ell really didn't want to take the time away from the case but she did need to eat and, honestly, how could she say no to those gorgeous eyes Baker was batting at her.

"Sounds perfect, give me fifteen to wind down here and I'll meet you there."

She headed back to her office, saved her files and sent the commander an update before logging out. She contemplated sending Rob a text but held off. It was bad enough Baker had made the connection she didn't need to be seen walking into Sully's on his arm right now.

Sully's was a neighborhood style pub about two blocks from the eleventh. It was a classic dark, wood finished pub. The patrons were a mixture of blue collar working stiffs and off duty cops. The atmosphere was welcoming and relaxed. As much as she wanted to like it, Ell always felt out of place. With a slight sigh she pulled open the door and headed in.

Baker and Jones had chosen a quiet table in the back, just across from the rarely used pool table. Ell slung her leather jacket over the back of a chair and settled in across from them.

"Thanks for coming, L.T. I know it's piss poor timing but at some point you need to shut it down and grab a beer," said Jones as the waitress arrived on cue. She set down a bottle of Coors in front of Jones, a Bellini for Baker and asked Ell what she'd like. Technically she was off duty but she wanted to head back and get some research in afterwards. 'Ah, what the hell," she thought and ordered a scotch neat. Baker and Jones exchanged a surprised look but Ell missed it.

"So where the hell did you get an education in contract law?" asked Jones.

Baker looked at her confused, "Huh?"

"All that shit about the confidentiality agreement not protecting the names of those signing it. How'd you know that?"

Baker smiled shyly. "Know what? I don't have a clue what it covers, but the guy was young and eager so I figured if I grabbed something obscure and spoke with authority he'd be too scared to admit he didn't know it with his client staring him down."

Jones let out a cackle like laugh, taking a deep slug of her beer. "Fucking beautiful. I tell you, L.T., this one's got the shit."

Ell looked at the beautiful redhead, she had a whole lot more than 'the shit'. "Yeah, I'm already watching over my shoulder. I may have to bust her back down to patrol just to make sure my job's safe."

Baker blushed slightly and took a sip of her drink to try and hide the embarrassment.

The waitress returned with Ell's scotch, it wasn't single malt but it had a rich smoke and was smooth for a blend.

"Ok, boss, gossip time."

Ell's heart rate soared in dread.

"Inquiring minds want to know, what's going on with Rique and that little fireplug femme fatale?"

'Thank god,' she thought. "I'm not sure but the boy better be careful and hide his cuffs."

The girls broke out into laughter, finished their drinks while each took turns with a pot shot at Rique's expense and ordered another round. They were just starting back in when Baker stood up and waved someone over. Ell, her back to the door, had to twist around to see. Her body reacted instantly at the sight of Rob approaching. He was breathtaking. Loose fitting jeans and a tight black dress shirt hugging his frame. He had the top button undone and, with two scotches under her belt, Ell could barely fight the urge to undo a few more with her teeth. He smiled as he took a seat next to her causing every nerve ending in her body to begin to jump.

"Thanks for the invite, Jamie."

It took Ell a moment to recognize Baker's first name and she nearly laughed at the absurdity.

Baker smiled back at him, a shy flirty look. "You're part of the team, it only seemed right. Besides we needed someone to offset the overload of estrogen at the table."

The waitress returned with their third round and a diet Pepsi for Rob.

"Who invited the sober buzz kill?" asked Jones, coaxing laughs from everyone. Rob seemed unaffected and raised his glass in a toast.

"To the best crime fighters this side of Gotham."

They all chimed in and Ell tossed back her third scotch in one quick gulp. She had to admit, it was nice to get away from the death and mayhem for a bit. She didn't do it often enough.

Rob eyed up the pool table and turned to the girls. "Who's up for a game?"

Baker begged off quickly and he turned to Ell. "How about it, Lieutenant, care to learn a thing or two?"

Ell admired the smug look in his eye. "I'd hate to embarrass you on your first night out with the team."

Rob smirked, "Is that so? Those are mighty strong words, how about a wager."

Ell's interest was piqued, "What do you have in mind?"

"Let's say two hours of services rendered. If you win I'll be your dancing tech monkey free of charge and if I do... we'll find some way for you to work it off."

Baker and Jones let out cat call whistles egging her on.

"You really don't want to do this."

"Oh, but I do, Ms. Frost."

"Rack em!"

Rob racked the balls and Ell selected a cue, trying to find anything remotely straight with a half decent tip.

"Standard 8-Ball?"

"Sounds good, soon to be slave boy, feel free to break."

Rob took a step back and held out the cue ball. "Ladies first, I don't want you complaining about an unfair advantage."

Ell wanted to warn him but the smug look and cocky attitude made her smile and take the ball. She settled in, rolling the cue ball with the tip of her cue until she found the sweet spot. She took a moment to steady herself and then let loose with a shattering break sinking the one, four and thirteen. She looked up and Rob was smiling.

"Nice break."

She shrugged, circled the table twice planning out her course of action and settled back down. Three to the side, six to the corner, two cross bank to the corner, seven long cut cross table to the side, five quick jab to the corner with a little left hand English bringing the cue ball back behind the eight.

She looked up and the smile on Rob's face had been replaced with utter shock and just a touch of fear. Ell lined up the eight ball, shifted her gaze to the side so she was looking directly into his eyes and drained the shot without so much as a glance. She handed him the cue, said, "Thanks for the game," and casually took a seat back at the table. Baker and Jones were in near hysterics.

Rob sat back down shaking his head but the smile slowly returning.

"I tried to warn you."

The waitress brought another round and the four of them nursed their drinks, harassed one another and focused on anything and everything but work. It was relaxing and enjoyable, but Ell could not shake the feeling that she should be back at the precinct pouring through case files. As they finished off their fifth, or was it sixth, round? Jones gestured back at the pool table.

"Want to keep that losing streak alive?"

Rob agreed and the two of them went about racking up the balls. Baker, now extremely intoxicated and looking more and more appealing with each moment, set down her glass and looked into Ell's eyes. It was an alluring glance which made Ell want to leap the table and devour the young woman.

"So, I've been meaning to ask, are you two exclusive?"

Ell nearly spit out her scotch.

"First, what makes you think we're anything?"

"Someone once told me I'm a good detective."

"Indeed, and thanks for texting him earlier."

"I thought you could use a friend and he seemed the logical choice, but you're avoiding the question."

If she had her wits about her she'd have kept avoiding it but the scotch had long since destroyed her good sense. "I don't know what we are. At this point neither of us does, and we're not pushing it. That said, I've seen the look in your eyes when he's around and you should know I'm not a jealous person. Exclusivity isn't really my thing. I can't speak for Handsome McFlirty over there, but I don't own him and if he's interested don't let anything about him and I hold you back."

Baker smiled as if there was an inside joke Ell was unaware of. Her phone chimed and she gathered her coat. "Looks like my cab's here. Say goodbye to Jones and Handsome McFlirty for me."

Ell nodded. As Baker walked passed she leaned down close to Ell's ear and whispered. "It wasn't just him I was interested in."

Ell was stunned, her body flushed at the thought, her mind's eye racing through all the possibilities as the alcohol killed her internal filter. The passion and want pushing through her cognitive thought, her mind and body racing out of control.

Baker slid her coat over her shoulders, flipped her hair to the side with a deeply seductive look and stepped away.

"Have a good night, Lieutenant."

Chapter Twenty

*T*he rest of the evening was a blur. Rob and Jones returned to the table but Ell's mind was lost. At some point Jones called a cab and Ell remembered walking out of Sully's, and back towards the precinct, barely able to stand. Everything else was like a dark chasm lost to time. She awoke to the sound of her cell chirping. She was home, in bed and not alone. She took a quick glance at Rob lying next to her, still fully dressed with his hand resting gently on her thigh, and then turned her attention to the clock on her night table. *Four oh three, who the fuck was texting her?* She reached out, still half asleep and grabbed the phone.

There were two text messages. The first was an alert from P.D. tracking.

"Subject card use in progress – Julie Downs – Masion Villages on 17th"

The second was from Rique.

"I'm on it, will contact if required. – R"

'Thank god for partners," she thought, her head beginning to throb. She grabbed the bottles of water and Tylenol conveniently located beside her clock and took two.

"Everything ok?" mumbled Rob, barely conscious.

"Rique's got it," she said as she rolled back over, her mind struggling to make sense of the evening and coming up blank. 'Not the time,' she thought and let herself drift off.

Her alarm went off at six and she was tempted to toss the damn thing out a window. The drummer that had been playing her temples like snares had subsided thanks to the Tylenol, but the rest of her body was very sore.

"Is sleep even an option in this house?" asked Rob, stretching and rubbing his face.

"Uhhhnnn," groaned Ell as she pulled herself from the bed and headed for a warm shower.

She let the warm water rush over her and begin to wash away the fog, stretching her muscles while it did. The night was a blur. She had no idea how she had gotten home though she assumed Handsome McFlirty had something to do with it, and god knows what happened after that. Fifteen minutes later, warm and far more alert, she walked back into the bedroom in a short silk robe. The bed was made and there were clothes laid out for her, three separate outfits. There was no sign of Rob. She perused the options and decided he had at least semi decent taste. Letting the robe fall to the floor, she decided on a pair of tight jeans, a black tank top and a long, form fitted, olive green sweater. He had neglected to layout underwear so, with a sly smile, she neglected to wear any.

She snapped her badge onto her belt, grabbed her shoulder holster and beat up brown leather jacket and headed down the stairs. The aroma of coffee floated through the air as if calling her. He handed her a cup without looking up as she entered the kitchen.

"How do you like your eggs? Scrambled or more scrambled?" he asked while flipping some bacon.

"Let's go with scrambled." Ell took as seat at the island watching him in silence. She could get used to this.

He slid a plate in front of her and finally looked up. He looked at her with passion and approval causing her heart to quicken. "That looks good on you."

"Thank you, but you know I've been dressing myself for mumble mumble years now, right?"

"Mumble mumble years?"

"Yup, it's a while."

"But think how much time it saved you and from the looks of it," he said, slowly circling around her and taking a seat to her left, "I did well."

"You know most guys would be trying to get me *out* of these clothes. You may lose your membership."

"I've built up some man-cred over the years, I'll be fine."

Ell dug into the eggs like it was her last meal.

"Damn, these are decent," she said, almost surprised.

"Decent? Such high praise. You're welcome."

Rob sipped his coffee and she realized he wasn't eating.

"Afraid of your own cooking?"

He laughed, "No, just can't eat at this ungodly hour. Us overpaid consultants are usually still in bed about now."

Ell was quiet for a bit, finishing her breakfast and sipping her coffee. Finally, after stewing about it for too long, she asked, "Speaking of bed, did we…?"

She could see an annoyance in his eyes. "Yes Ellison, I wanted our first time to occur while you were semi-conscious and ready to hurl on my shoes."

'Shit,' she thought. 'Had to ask.'

"I'm sorry, bad question. The nights a giant blur and I kinda lose all discretion when I've had a few."

"Hmmm, good to know," he grinned like a devious child, "and apology accepted. You can rest assured, Ellison, when the time comes, you'll remember it."

The thought sent a chill down her spine and had her heart pumping. "You may not get to make that choice. Unless I'm mistaken, you owe me two hours of services."

"Ah, so I see the *entire* night's not a blur. I believe that's two hours of 'dancing tech monkey' services."

"Yup, but just wait until you see what I do for my dancing tech monkeys, Sir," she ran a hand slowly up the inseam of his jeans stopping just short of the prize. Then hopped up, flipped her coat over her shoulder and headed out.

"Lock up on your way out, monkey boy."

He motioned as if to call out after her but instead just rolled his eyes and laughed as she walked out the door.

Ell was grinning smugly as the door closed behind her and she noticed that her shiny S550 was nowhere to be seen.

'Well shit, way to ruin an exit, Frost.'

She ate crow in the most dignified manner she could find, and he let her do so with minimal ribbing.

The ride to the precinct was uneventful but she took the time to message Rique and get an update on the early morning alert. Julie Downs had finally surfaced. In a drunken stupor she had wandered into Masion Villages, an upscale hotel downtown, and attempted to book a room. She was paying cash but her credit card had been swiped as a security measure and was, subsequently, flagged by P.D. tracking. When Rique arrived on scene with two patrolmen, she was passed out and barely cognitive. He'd tossed her in a cell to sober up and notified her attorney. Ell could not wait to get the little bitch in the box.

Rob dropped her at the precinct front doors and headed home for a change of clothes before starting his shift. Luckily, at this hour, the press was not yet swarming and no one saw her as she hopped from the pickup and headed inside. She could just imagine the rumor mill beginning to grind.

She popped her head into the bullpen on the way to her office. Rique was alone, staring at the timeline trying to get prepped for the day.

"Quiet morning."

"For some," he replied. "I just came back up from 'the Tank' and Downs is screaming bloody murder."

"You know just what a woman wants to hear. Speaking of which, how was the night."

"It was good. We went for dinner and cleared things up. She feels like shit, Ell. You should talk to her and get it sorted."

"I will. Emotions were running pretty high last night."

"Yeah, from what I hear the four of you worked that out the hard way."

"Every joint in my body is reminding me of that right now. Thanks for taking the call this morning. I owe you."

"Sweet Jesus, let me get a recorder so you can say that again."

"Bite me, limpy."

She was just turning to leave as Baker walked in. As beautiful as she was, walking death would be a good description of her that morning. Her entire body appeared to scream in pain with every movement. Her naturally pale skin was almost ghostlike and she had dark sunglasses covering her eyes to block out the glare of the lights.

Ell immediately broke out in laughter.

"Respectfully, fuck you, Lieutenant."

Leaning in close, Ell whispered. "Is that what you were hinting at last night?" and Bakers pale face flushed a deep, dark red.

"Looks like your color's coming back."

With a wink she headed to her office, pulled up her notes and began prepping for the Downs' interview.

Julie Downs' attorney arrived at nine and demanded to see her client. Ell had Rique escort her to holding for a short conference before the two of them were brought up to Interview Two.

Since Baker was in no shape for an interview, and Ell was itching for a piece of Downs, she had the detectives follow up on the list of M.A.E. employees and headed down to meet up with Rique.

"What's the mood?" she asked, seeing him waiting for her in the hall.

"Downs is bitchy as hell. So... normal. The lawyer's not helping. She read me the riot act for holding her client blah blah blah. I'd say this is gonna be fun."

Ell entered the room and engaged the voice recorder on her phone.

"Lieutenant Frost and Detective Shaw interviewing Julie Downs in relation to the Bouton homicide. Ms. Downs, I see you have executed your right to counsel for these proceedings. Please state your name for the record, ma'am."

Shirley Greene, and you had no right to detain my client, Lieutenant. I demand she be released this instant and you can expect a formal complaint to be filed with your superiors."

Ms. Greene would have been a pretty lady if not for the bitch like sneer that appeared to be permanently etched on her face. Ell disliked her immediately.

"Sounds fun, feel free. Your client was reported drunk in public. She is a material witness in a homicide investigation and Detective Shaw was bringing her in for questioning. As she was highly intoxicated and had previously demanded an attorney he had no option but to detain her until such time as said attorney arrived. If you were concerned, perhaps you should have shown up when you were notified at five a.m. and not four hours later."

The attorney went on the defensive, "We will not be answering any questions. You can release my client and quit harassing her."

"Your client is a material witness and person of interest in a homicide. Her release is being processed but until that is complete she's not leaving. You can feel free to ignore my questions if you wish, but I will be asking them for the record."

The attorney turned to Julie, "As we discussed, you say nothing."

"Ms Downs, as Deedrie Bouton's business partner you have intimate knowledge into the symbolism of this image, correct?"

Ell slid her a crime scene photo of Deedrie Bouton strapped and tethered.

Downs stared at it but didn't move. The lawyer took a

quick look and instantly pushed the image back at Ell. "My client knows nothing of these events and attempting to frighten her with this image is highly unprofessional."

"Oh, but that's not true. Your client is very familiar with the image in question. It's a replication of the corporate logo for a company of which she is now the sole director. I have a difficult time believing that the symbolism of the pose is co-incidental. Who else had seen this image, Ms. Downs?"

Julie was about to answer but Shirley Greene immediately jumped in. "Not a word."

Ell could tell this was an effort in futility.

"Well, this has been fun, Detective if you could see that Ms. Downs is released and escorted home." Ell stood and headed towards the door. "Oh, just one more question. What's your shoe size?"

Julie stared at her confused but her attorney stopped her, once again, before she could answer. "It's been a pleasure, Lieutenant."

Rique followed her out, "What was with the shoe size?"

"Just wanted to see her reaction. She's scared shitless and she wants to talk, we need some leverage. Process her out and put a black and white on her. I don't want her disappearing again."

"Might be better off putting a couple plain clothes on her. If she knows she's being tailed she's more likely to try and give them the slip."

"Good point, see what you can do, the budget's open on this one."

Chapter Twenty-One

The morning was dragging and Ell was pretty sure the scotch was to blame. Her headache was slowly returning and the pills were doing little to null the pain. She felt like she was spinning her wheels. She reached for her phone but decided a reprieve from the office would do better. Pulling herself out of the chair, she headed through the door and down the hall to the elevators. Might as well brave the second floor and go pay Lund a personal visit. She waited for a moment while the elevators slowly crept towards her floor before impatience took over and she headed for the stairs. Her energy level was still dragging but she took them two at a time in an effort to force a little exertion and some much needed adrenaline flow.

The second floor was a litany of chaos and confusion. It housed Crime Scene, I.T. and a number of administrative divisions. To her, it was like walking behind the wizard's veil and seeing a skinny white guy pulling the levers. Disappointing but still rather impressive.

She found Lund in one of the various labs speaking to a young tech about god knows what. It sounded vaguely like

English with a whole lot of 'itis', 'oric' and 'lum's tossed in. Geek speak at its best.

"Lund, where's my data on the Collins' job?"

"Jesus Christ, who invited the muggle into the batcave?"

Ell gave him a smirk but, despite the easy setup, she couldn't come up with a quick reply. Fucking hangover was killing her repartee.

Lund just laughed, "Remind me to catch you after a night out with the girls more often. It's good for my ego."

"Shit, is my entire life on record now? Can't a girl even have a night out without the rumor mill going into overdrive?"

"Not if you do it at Sully's," chuckled Lund as he led her down an equipment-covered hall towards his office. It wasn't much different from her private cell, tiny and tight, but at least Lund had managed a window. He headed over to the desk. Ell eyed up the guest chair but thought better and leaned against the door jam instead.

"What have you found?"

"Results are just funneling in," he said, giving his mouse a wave then looking back up at her.

"And?"

"And, I'm pulling it up, give it a moment, we don't all have the ass... ets required to get high speed upgrades out of I.T."

"I think you'd be surprised, bat your pretty little eyes next time they're here and see what happens."

Lund snorted and returned to the computer, which was now following orders as it should.

"Ok, we should have pulled over two hundred prints from the artwork given the amount of people handling it from creation to move, but there were only seven, three of which are partials, five were a ninety-eight percent match to your boy Trevor. One, pulled off a rather intriguing painting, belonged to Lieutenant Ellison Frost," he raised his eyebrows with a smirk, "and one, is yet unidentified. The unidentified print was pulled from the release catch on the surveillance cage. It's an electrostatic release that works similar to your smartphone's touch screen and requires a conductor to operate. Odds are pretty good it's our thief's. There was a solid attempt to wipe down the unit as well as the artwork and storage bunker, which is why it's only a partial. Local and state runs have come up empty and the fed's not in yet, but I don't expect much. If you get me someone to match it to we can use it in the end but it won't help you solve this thing."

"What about the surveillance?"

"I have Rob's preliminary report. Looped footage two days before the murder and again the morning after. It's a total of twenty-two minutes the first time and just over an hour the second. He's running a shadow reconstruction to see if there is anything on the edges of the loop that can be recovered. He's not hopeful. He's also running something I can't even start to understand on the locking mech and software. Said it was a hunch but doesn't expect anything for at least another twenty-four."

"Anything else fruitful?"

"Perhaps. What shoes were you wearing at the scene?"

Ell had to think back. "My Cydwoq Drills, why?"

Lund looked at her as if she was speaking a foreign language. "What the fuck is a sidewalk drill?"

Ell almost laughed but managed to retain her composure. "C. y. d. w. o. q. is a brand of shoe. Something you don't pick up at the nearest Target," she said, pointing to his sneakers.

"Drills are a calf high leather boot with a flat, soft sole."

"Women," muttered Lund. "Size?"

"Thirty-seven." Again Lund's look glazed over into confusion. "They're European, it's about a six and a half to a seven."

"Thanks for the 'edumacation'. In that case, I also have a couple footprints lifted from the loose dirt behind the building. Woman's size five, slight heal and no distinguishing tread. Since surveillance shows no activity in that location in the six days prior to discovery, odds are they were left by the thief or an accomplice."

"Accomplice?"

"Can't rule it out. Nothing suggests it had to be a two person job, but there's nothing pointing to a solo either."

"Same size as the heels left on scene."

"Yup, narrows the suspect pool to what, two billion?"

"Ok, let me know if the fed's flag anything on the print, and fire me and Rique the report as soon as you've finalized."

"Yes, mistress." Lund deadpanned and Ell turned on her heels and headed down the hall.

She stopped briefly at the elevators then had a second thought and headed back down the east corridor. She had no idea where his office was, or if he even had one for that matter, but the east wing was I.T. so Rob had to be there somewhere. After five minutes of wandering aimlessly she finally gave up and grabbed the nearest geek.

"Where can I find Rob in this maze?"

He was engrossed in what appeared to be the base components of a robot overlord and answered without looking up.

"Dixon or Faeye?"

Ell stood there stunned and speechless. She didn't know his last name.

"Five foot tenish, wavy brown hair, ice blue eyes."

"Faeye. Next left, second door to the right. Not sure if he's there though, he's been running a pile of tech data for some hot Lieutenant down in homicide."

Ell smiled at the description, thanked him and headed back down the hall. The door to his office was open but Rob was missing. She was going to call it bad timing and head out but the office itself caught her attention. It was easily five hundred square feet with two windows and modern, elegant furnishings. The desk held three workstations of varying configuration and the walls were lined with shelves of computer components meticulously organized. The north wall was a solid redwood bookshelf lined with more tech manuals and journals than she knew existed. She was in awe and for the first time in a long while she felt the ping of jealousy. She was standing there slack jawed when he strolled through the door, latte in hand.

"Lieutenant, had I known you were here I'd have brought a chai. What brings you to the slums of the second floor?"

"What the serious fuck, Rob."

He stared at her confused and slightly worried.

"Pardon?"

"I spend my days in a ten by ten cell working my ass off to put murderers behind bars and you have your own private penthouse?"

"Better negotiating skills?"

"Fucking consultants."

A sly grin crossed his face.

"An interesting idea. If you'd like to lock the door I can certainly take care of that request."

Ell flushed at the thought. Was he serious? What she

wouldn't give to be forced over his desk, her hair pulled back as he took her. She glanced over at the door briefly then took a step towards it. His hand grabbed her arm holding her in place. The grip both restraining and freeing at the same time. He pulled her close, his lips brushing her cheek as he whispered, "I was kidding, Ell, not here but soon, I promise. I want to do this right."

"Fuck right," she whispered back, the passion building hard and fast.

"Soon, I promise."

She stared at the floor, pulled back, took a couple deep breaths to steady herself then grabbed his latte and took a deep swig.

"Not bad," she said taking a seat in a plush leather guest chair. "I could get used to this."

Rob could not help but laugh at the transformation. The woman could pretend well, a roleplayer at heart, but he knew the switch could not be flipped so easily.

"So, back to my original question, what brings you to the slums?"

"Escape. I needed out of the cell so I came up to check in with Lund. He tells me you're running something on the footage and locking mech."

"The footage was seamless to the naked eye but I figure whoever did it was under time restraints so there may be a shadow."

"A shadow?"

"Overlapping footage at the seams of the insertion. I'm running it through a video analysis now and should have the results in the next hour. The locking software will be about twenty-four at best. The bypass was brilliant and I still haven't been able to trace the work around. If I can, there may be something to work with."

"Busy boy."

"Nah, those two pretty much run on their own, it's the search for your suspected hacker, Shane Dunder, that's been fairly hands on."

"And"

"And, it progresses. Slowly."

"Anything I should know?"

"Not yet, but I have some threads I'm pulling on. Gently. If he is Ανάσταση I don't want to tip my hand."

"Ok, let me know when you've got something or if there is anything you need from our end."

"There is so much I need from your end, Lieutenant."

"Sorry, Sir. You missed your chance. I need to get back to the cell. Too much time in luxury and I'll lose my edge." She handed him the latte and, without thinking, rose up on her toes and gently kissed his cheek.

It was a simple gesture but one that made him smile as he watched her leave.

***

Rique flagged her down before she could get back to the office. "Baker and Jones just tagged me. They've talked to four escorts with six more to go including Sebastian Lerieux. They wanted to know if they should bother with him since he's already been interviewed."

"Shit, tell them to get a statement on possible poaching. We need to be thorough. In the meantime, I'll touch base and let him know they're coming."

"Will do, when you're done swing by the pen, I just got the full access list from Ms. Collins and there's an oddity."

"Oddity?"

"Let me keep running with it and come see me when you're done."

Ell pulled out her cell and, as usual, had no bars. Thank goodness for wifi and messaging or the fucking precinct would be a telecommunication free zone. She considered her options. It wasn't a call she wanted to make from the PD landline and messaging seemed a little cold given the circumstance. She hadn't seen the front of the precinct since start of shift, but there was bound to be a couple camera crews still circling. With no other option she would be forced to face them. She cleared the front doors and was relieved to see only two press vans still on-site. God, she'd be glad when this was over. She pulled out her cell and dialed Sebastian, hoping he was available.

"Ellison?"

"Sebastian, thanks for picking up."

"What's up?"

"I'll give you the short version without details so you can be genuinely surprised. I have two detectives coming to interview you."

"Again?"

"There have been some developments. Try not to get into a wrestling match this time. I'm pretty sure either of them could take you."

He laughed and she continued. "We're interviewing all of Angel's staff, and it would look odd if I chose to leave you out of the mix. Your alibi's on record so there shouldn't be any issue there. This is just more background on Bouton."

"I'm pretty sure I've told you all I can, but I'll talk to Angel about it since some of the questions may fall under client confidentiality."

"It's possible, but the detectives know you've given a formal statement so this should just be routine follow-up."

"I'll play nice. Thanks for the heads up."

"Do me a favor when you're done."

"What's that?"

"Let me know what you think of the redhead."

"Ahhh, do I sense an interest?"

"Just want to know if my instincts are still up to par."

"Will do, enjoy your day, Ellison."

She disconnected and headed back in to check on Rique.

"All squared, what's the oddity?"

We have four employees, two board members and Ms. Collins who have access to the storage unit. The board members check out, I did a quick run on Trevor which came up clean and figured no use digging further on Virginia. Of the other three staff, one is another assistant, Jon Gilam, and has been with Collins for twelve years. The other two are part of the restoration and setup crew. Brianna Handen and Rosee Currtin."

"Ok, so what popped as odd?"

"Currtin doesn't exist. The company hired for restoration and setup, GPrep Inc., has never heard of her. In fact, they were only issued one access card which is in the possession of Handen. She's coordinating the setup."

"Who issued the cards and codes?"

"Collins, and she forwarded me the email request from GPrep Inc. for the second card. She ran the activation and left it with the receptionist for pickup a week ago."

"So someone spoofed an email and got their hands on a card and code. So much for hi-tech security."

"Yeah, but why not just use it? Logs don't show the card ever being used, why bypass the system when you don't need to?"

"Maybe they didn't, Rob's been having no luck pin pointing how they bypassed the system, what if all they did was tamper with the logs and surveillance?"

She pulled out her cell and sent him a text to that regard.

"Do a run on Rosee Currtin and see if there is anyone in the system that jumps. It's likely and alias but we better rule out the obvious first. I'm going to take Rob and see if we can locate any footage at Collins International. Given the cost of artwork in the foyer, they're bound to have surveillance. If we're lucky, 'Rosee' didn't take that into account."

Rique gave her a nod and she headed back to her office to make the call. Virginia was out of the office but Trevor put the call through to her cell as instructed.

"Hello?"

"Ms. Collins, it's Lieutenant Frost."

"Lieutenant, feel free to call me Virginia. What can I help you with?"

"Sorry, professional habit. We're running down the secondary access for GPrep. You mentioned the card and code were picked up at the reception desk, do you have security footage of that area."

"With the exception of my office and the restrooms, I have footage of every area. I assume you would like to see it."

"Yes, I'd like to bring my I.T. tech down right away and see what we can locate."

"I'm about forty minutes from the office, but I can free my

schedule for the afternoon and meet you there right away."

"You really don't need to go to the trouble, if you can just advise your people we are on our way I'm certain we can handle it."

"Lieutenant, if you're bringing that sexy tech from the gallery it's no trouble, it's a pleasure. I'll see you there."

Virginia hung up and Ell let out an audible laugh. If Rob capitalized on all the women swooning over him he'd be a very busy man.

She pulled out her cell and fired him a message

"Grab your gear and meet me in the parking lot, you're going back out in the field. – E"

"And here I had my hopes up for so much more after the first half of that message. – R"

"You had your chance in that swanky office. I've got work to do now. – E"

"You'll have plenty of work to do then as well. Best start saving your energy. – R"

Ell's body tingled at the thought.

"Yes, Sir. – E"

She was waiting beside the Mercedes when Rob came around the corner lugging two giant bags of god knows what.

"Christ, did you pack up half your office?"

"Well, I wasn't privy to where we are going or what we are doing so I grabbed my gear as instructed."

She popped the trunk. "Toss it in. I'll explain on the way."

"Good call on the bypass, by the way." He slipped into the passenger seat beside her. "A simple log wipe explains a lot and I was as able to modify my search significantly with that assumption. If there's evidence of tampering I'll know when we get back."

"Sounds good, in the meantime we are making a run over to Collins International to check on a secondary bit of surveillance." She gave him the run down on the extra GPrep access card and how it was obtained.

"Social engineering, still the number one source of breaches worldwide. Given the level of savvy used on the gallery footage I'll be surprised if we find anything, but if it has been tampered with, each new piece will help us nail down a signature."

"That was my thought. Your not so secret admirer 'Ginny' should be there in about another fifteen minutes so we should get all the access we need."

"Why Lieutenant, was that a hint of jealousy I detected?"

Ell laughed. "Not likely, but if she does manage to sneak you of for a quickie in the closet I want every last detail."

Rob smiled, "So not the jealous type?"

"Not in the least, I play well with others and have learned to share my toys. As I told Baker, exclusivity is not really my thing. Honesty, trust, those are the important ones."

"Hmm, and just when did you have this conversation with the formidable Ms. Baker?"

"Last night at Sully's. She inquired about us."

"About whether we were exclusive?"

"Yup, she was three sheets the wind and may have let a few desires slip."

"Oh? Did the pretty detective want me to come out and play?"

"Not you, hot shot. Us."

Rob's jaw dropped. "Seriously?"

"That's the impression I was left with but, as I said, she was three sheets to the wind."

Rob was speechless. What does one say to that? "An interesting thought but let's see what 'us' is first."

Ell smiled and bit her lip. She liked the sound of that.

———————

They managed to beat Virginia to the office so Ell took a few minutes to interview the receptionist. He remembered the event but the details were vague. A white girl with darkish hair came in and picked up the package. She may have been short. He did check her ID but could not remember anything on it aside from the name matching that on the package.

Virginia arrived shortly after and led them through the maze of halls to the security room. The system was decent, but Rob immediately noticed that it was monitored off-site, which meant it was not closed circuit and left it vulnerable to external tampering. Given the finesse of the previous job he was doubtful he'd find much more here, but went to work rolling back through the footage. The receptionist had logged the pickup at two forty-three, seven days prior and as suspected the footage showed nothing. This time, however, the scene did not allow for a loop. With all the movement at the reception desk it would have been too obvious. Instead it was simply seven minutes and twelve seconds of snow. Given that the system was physically monitored twenty-four seven the deletion had to have happened after the fact.

"Does the system record on both ends?"

Virginia shrugged, "You'd have to speak with SecCom, I'll have Trevor place a call right away."

"Thoughts?" asked Ell.

"Some of these systems are recorded on-site as well as at

the monitoring station for backup purposes. The on-site system would have been relatively easy to hack but the SecCom servers will have a far more robust firewall. If there's a copy of the footage, it may not be tampered with. In the meantime, I'm going to run some scans on the system at this end and see if I can find the point, time or location of entry. Give me twenty minutes here and have Trevor route the SecCom call to my cell."

They left him to it and headed down to Virginia's office.

"Can I get you a coffee, Lieutenant?"

"Thanks, that would be nice, and you can call me Ell."

"How do you take it, Ell?"

"Just like my men, hot, strong and sweet."

Virginia giggled and headed over to her sideboard.

Ell was admiring the artwork in the room when Virginia returned and handed her a cup.

"It's quite the collection but there seems to be something missing," she said, motioning to a blank space of wall just above the sitting area."

"I've reserved it for a very special piece in the upcoming auction."

"Anyone I'd know?"

"The artist is an unknown but the piece is quite striking. Perhaps you can stop by for coffee some time and we can discuss it."

"Fairly confident you'll get it, I see."

"I rarely have a problem getting what I desire."

'I'll bet,' thought Ell.

"So tell me, Ell, and I hope this isn't too presumptuous, how is it you can sit there, knowing my interest in Mr. Faeye, and portray no animosity?"

Ell laughed internally, of course Virginia knew Rob's last name, why wouldn't she?

"Animosity? Why should there be any animosity?"

"No need to play coy, Ell, I can sense the chemistry between the two of you. It's not that often I meet a woman who does not see me as a threat."

"I'm sure you are, or at least could be, you are a beautiful woman with much to offer, but I lead a lifestyle that does not include or allow for jealousy."

"I envy that, much of my life is consumed with obtaining what others want. Jealousy and spite tend to be a day to day occurrence."

"You can rest assured you will receive neither from me."

"I must admit, I find you to be a bit of a conundrum, Ell. It intrigues me. Once all this," she waved her hand at the door gracefully, "has passed, I would like to get to know you better."

Ell was amused. This woman was an enigma. She presented herself in a way that seemed a dichotomy to who she truly was. Ell could definitely relate.

"I'd like that."

Virginia pulled a card from her purse and handed it to her.

"My personal contact information, this way you won't need to route through the gauntlet of assistants."

Ell set down her coffee and checked her phone for the time. "I should check on Rob's progress. As much as I'd love to stay and chat I have pesky killers and thieves to catch."

"By all means, go catch them, Lieutenant. We'll chat when you have time."

Ell got the feeling that wasn't a request, though it was doubtful that Virginia Collins had to request much. Slightly confused, yet highly fascinated, Ell headed back through the corridors to the security closet.

"So what's up, hot stuff?"

"Your professionalism never ceases to amaze me."

"File a complaint."

"Noted and filed," he flashed her a nasty grin. "SecCom, on the other hand, is the epitome of professionalism. Highly secure with great redundancy and, at the moment, they're scrambling to explain a mass security breach before word gets out to their clients."

"You're kidding me."

"I'm afraid not, the system not only records and stores on their end but there is a real-time RAID system in place to ensure no data loss. Whoever did this managed to breach their system and destroy not only the original recording but both backups. They are checking their nightly off-site now but I'm less than optimistic."

"Can I assume this would not have been an easy task?"

"A fair assumption. They're not the NSA, but their firewall system is impressive. It took significant skill and finesse. It also took an intimate knowledge of the service provider."

"Lovely, how much longer do you need here?"

"Should have what I need in about five minutes. The SecCom techs are sending me their data as it comes in."

Ell let him finish up, standing back and watching him work. He was like a machine, organized, quick and precise. She found his focus extremely attractive. She wasn't sure why but she stepped forward, placed her hands on his shoulders and began to slowly knead the muscles. He smiled and let out a soft moan.

"As nice as that is, you're not speeding up this process."

"Multitasking not your strong suit?"

"Not when one of those tasks involves my mind drifting to thoughts of tearing your clothes off, strapping your arms behind your back and fucking you till you scream."

Ell lifted her hands slowly, her own mind starting to reel, "Oh my."

"Oh my indeed, Ellison. Trust me when I tell you that it takes all my will to be with you, to see that lust in your eye and not take you. As much as I would love to toss you down and devour you right now I will not. I know your boundaries and I am doing all I can to respect them, but soon, very soon, I intend to make you moan loud and hard."

Her body and mind were whirling. She wanted him now more than ever. She grabbed his head, turned it slightly and kissed him hard and deep. "Soon," she whispered, backing off and letting him continue.

Chapter Twenty-Two

*T*he ride back to the precinct was tense. Both were fighting primal urges and attempting to focus on work… they were failing miserably.

They separated in the lobby and, as much as Ell hated to watch him walk away, she felt a portion of her mind finally relax. 'We really need to fuck,' she thought, the sexual tension building every second they were together. Part of her just wanted to do it, anywhere available, but she knew he was right. He wanted to make their first time together mean something. He had a plan, and she was more than willing to give him whatever he needed.

She bypassed her office and headed straight for the bullpen. Baker and Jones were back from interviews and quickly updated her on the progress. Most of the employees were fairly tight lipped, but two admitted to being approached recently by a young lady in regards to a new opportunity. The money offered was good but the firm had no reputation. Given the risk, they had chosen to pass. Interestingly, it was not Deedrie Bouton that had approached them. Each would have recognized her immediately. Instead, Julie Downs provided the offers.

The most interesting interview was the follow-up with Sebastian. He had spoken with Angel and, given that the client was deceased, she advised him that confidentiality was no longer a concern. He passed on a number of interesting details about their encounters. First, the paid portions of their evening did not revolve around any type of roleplay. Instead, they had a couple drinks and Deedrie continually steered the conversation to his job, what it entailed, what perks were available, his favorite sessions etc. On their second encounter, she asked him about his goals in the business and presented him with a job offer which she promised would help to fulfill them.

He was polite and said he would do some research and consider it, though he had no intention of doing so. The startling portion was that Deedrie quizzed him about his client list. Not who was on it but rather how much of it he controlled and whether or not his clients would follow him elsewhere.

Ell asked them to write it up and ensure it was added to the file. She made a mental note to call and thank Sebastian personally.

Rique on the other hand, had not been so lucky with Rosee Currtin. The name had to be an alias as no data could be found on any local or state databases. The woman simply did not exist.

She wasn't back in her office five minutes when Rob messaged her.

"You were right, no bypass just a log wipe. Found the point of entry and algorithm used. I'm running signature comparisons now. – R"

"Anything on the video? – E"

"May be a two second shadow on day one, attempting to reconfigure and clear it up. – R"

'Day one. Why the two separate entries?' she thought. If you were breaking in to see the painting in order to stage the murder why not take it with you? What is gained by waiting until afterwards and risking a second break-in. It didn't make sense. She needed the timeline.

She headed back to the bullpen, which was finally hustling with detectives, and began painting her own picture of events. Looking at the board she was more convinced that the second break in was redundant. The time frame was also significantly longer. She had attributed it to the need to wipe down the artwork and remove prints but why was this not a concern on the first visit? What was she missing?

Rique joined her at the board, noticing her confused look.

"What's up?"

"The two break-ins don't make sense. If you were breaking in to get the image off the painting in order to setup the crime scene why not take it at that time? Based on the surveillance loop they didn't even take the time to wipe down or cover their tracks on the first visit."

"We're assuming both breaches are related to the murder."

"Makes sense."

"If the murder wasn't planned at the time of the first?"

"Huh?"

"Let's say the killer broke in simply to get a look at the painting, with no plans on removing it or taking any other action. There'd be no concern for prints, nothing is missing, there's no trace of the break-in and there's been no crime so the odds of it coming to light are slim. No need to clean up."

"And the second?"

"Cover up. The painting is now tied to the murder and, odds are, we're going to start looking. The killer needs to cover their tracks which means they need to wipe down the storage unit."

"So why take the painting?"

"Souvenir?" he asked, but neither of them was convinced.

"It plays right up to that point."

"There has to be something else about the painting. A reason the killer wanted it."

"Maybe they just liked it."

"Or didn't," she mused.

They let that hang in the air for a moment, rolling over the possibilities. Rique began flipping through the case files. "We know the painting and the position of the body tie directly back to D.B.E. so who stood to lose from her moving forward with the company?"

"Other agencies, maybe. But it's a grasp, even with all the publicity she was going to have a hard time growing the business from the ground up before she was a real threat."

"You're looking the wrong way," commented Baker from behind them. She had removed the sunglasses but Ell could see that the effects of the night before were not wholly eliminated.

"Pardon?"

"The question isn't who stood to lose from the launch of D.B.E. but rather who stood to gain from having Deedrie out of the picture. The scene, the posing, it's not a cold and clinical hit but it's not just personal either. There's a message in it somewhere."

"Yeah, a giant fuck you, and it's aimed at me," muttered Ell.

Rique kept flipping through the case files, "Ok we know Bouton had about," he paused staring at his notes. "How many zero's is that? Well... a shit ton of assets. According to the estate anything liquid is going to an array of different charitable organizations and her corporate holdings were left to her father, though, without her, they're probably not worth much."

"D.B.E.?" asked Baker.

"It wasn't specifically outlined so it should be included with the other corporate holdings."

"So unless Mr. Bouton was desperate to add another couple percent to his growing financial empire, odds are it's not about financial gain. Fuck, we're going in circles chasing a bloody motive." Ell's frustration was growing. 'Missing piece,' she thought, remembering Rob's advice. "Put it away for now, let's build the rest of the picture and when we get there we'll see it."

"Lieutenant," Jones called from across the room and Ell headed over.

"I just got a call from Danielle Summer, she's one of Angel's escorts that Downs tried to recruit. Says she didn't think much of it at the time but, mulling it over today, she thinks someone may have been tailing Downs that day. The two of them met at Swish, that trendy martini bar on seventh. Downs made her pitch and left some documentation. Ms. Summer said there was a short brunette that appeared to be eyeing her up the entire time. About a half hour after Downs left, the brunette slid into the chair beside her and bought her a drink. Ms. Summer figured the girl was interested in her. She was flirting pretty hard and kept the drinks coming. Apparently, she asked a number of questions about Downs. At the time, Summer figured she was fishing to find out if they were a couple, but in retrospect she thinks it may have been something else."

"When was this?"

"About a week ago. Her description was pretty fuzzy but I've asked her to come down and meet with Scribbler for a sketch."

Ell knew that, fuzzy or not, Denise "Scribbler" Cue would get something relatively close out of her. She was one of the best artists on the force and had a keen ability to lead people back to a specific memory.

"She'll be down first thing tomorrow so I'm touching base with Denise to make sure she's available."

"Good work. Scribbler will get us something close."

Ell checked the time, five-forty. Another shift almost gone and she felt like she was still spinning her wheels. Four days in and she couldn't find the break she needed. The first forty-eight hours are often the most important in solving a case and that time frame had long since disappeared.

She headed back to her private cell and started pouring through the barrage of incoming emails she had been ignoring for the last few days. Lund's report had arrived so she pulled it open and started weeding through it, looking for anything that he may have neglected in their earlier conversation. She hadn't expected anything and thirty minutes later she was reassured of that fact. She filed it with the rest of the case files, sent her daily update to the commander and grabbed her cell. She sat there staring at it for a few minutes. She saw her hands trembling and realized how nervous she was. *'Christ Frost, get it together.'*

"Grabbing dinner, interested in joining? – E"

Her heart was pounding as she waited for a reply.

"Sounds good, meet me at the front doors in ten. I know just the place. – R"

She let out a deep breath and headed back to the bullpen.

"Baker, Jones, finish up what you're on and call it a night. I want to regroup first thing tomorrow with fresh minds so lay off the Bellini's," she added with a smirk. Walking over to Rique, she rested a hand on his shoulder and said in a much quieter voice. "Keep that in mind if you plan on seeing Angel, limpy."

He smirked at her, "Not tonight. Seeing as I've been here since just after five, I've got a date with a bottle of beer and a soft couch."

"Live it up, stud."

"If you only knew, L.T. If you only knew."

Ell let out a groan and headed for the doors.

She had just managed to get her nerves under control when she looked up and saw him waiting for her. Her body temperature rose, her heart fluttered and her mind began to reel. He was smiling, a devilish, beautiful grin, leaning against the wall, his tight T and open black blazer framing his body nicely. She tried not to stare but her mind and body were working on their own. It was then that she realized he had changed and cleaned up for dinner. *Fuck.*

"I hope this perfect place isn't some five star restaurant. Some of us don't have a luxury penthouse with a full wardrobe on-site."

"I'm certain that won't be a problem. Besides, you look ravishing, Lieutenant."

"Have a thing for overworked and dirty?" She saw his eyes light up and added, "Don't answer that."

He smiled grabbed her arm and led her out the doors to his truck.

"Really? The truck? Let's just take the Mercedes.

"As much as I like the shiny trophy, you don't know where we're going so unless you'd like to hand over the keys...?"

She glanced at him, then the car, then him, as if putting a lot of thought into it, "Truck it is."

He laughed and helped her into the passenger side.

"Where are we going, anyway?" she asked as they pulled out of the precinct.

"Just a quiet little spot nearby."

She was relieved and yet nervous at the same time. Quiet and private were good but she was struggling to maintain her composure. She wanted him, more now than ever and spending a quiet evening together, while nice, didn't scratch the itch.

"Relax, Ellison. I promise you'll enjoy it."

Christ how did he do that? She thought she was doing a solid job maintaining a good front yet he saw right through it. Through her. With every word her want grew, her need accentuated with every glance. She took a deep breath to steady herself. His hand came across the console and rested gently on her leg. He squeezed softly and she began to get her nerve back.

"Thanks," she said quietly.

"Just a dinner."

"Yeah"

They rode in silence for the rest of the short trip. When they stopped she was confused. There did not appear to be a restaurant in sight. Rob parked, hopped out and circled the truck to help her down. She wanted to ask but decided to trust him, grabbing his hand and allowing him to lead her across the street. They headed down a narrow, dark alley until they reached and old wooden door. He held it open for her then led her down a set of concrete steps into a beautiful, relaxed Italian diner that could have been straight out of an old mob movie. He held up two fingers to the matre'd who nodded and led them through the dining room to a secluded back corner.

"How in the world did you find this place?" she asked taking a seat and beginning to relax.

"The owner is a friend of the family. My father was one of the original investors back in the late sixties. The food is fantastic but it is very traditional so if you're not a fan of Italian I will apologize in advance."

He smiled, glancing deep into her eyes. Ell was taken by the subtle connection. It was something she could not explain. She had never felt it before and while, on some level, it frightened her she was slowly beginning to appreciate it.

The waitress came over to take their drink order. She was a cute Italian girl in her mid-twenties. Ell quickly gave her a once over and decided she liked what she saw. Rob looked up at Ell with a slight smirk.

"Wine? Or would you prefer scotch?"

"Funny man," she mocked. "Wine would be perfect, thanks."

"A bottle of the Barbaresco please."

The waitress set down two menus and headed to the bar. Ell picked up her menu and realized she was in trouble. It was strictly Italian, not the food, the text.

Rob laughed at the dismayed look. "Would you like me to translate?"

"Just order me something good. We'll use it as a test of your taste. Hopefully it's better than your billiard skills."

"Squid and ice cream it is," he mocked, drawing a dry smirk.

The waitress returned with the wine. Rob ordered for the two of them and poured them each a glass. It was a deep red wine with a distinct oak. Ell was far from a wine connoisseur but she liked it.

"So, Ms. Frost. Tell me a little about yourself." The question caught her off guard. Here he was sipping his wine, treating this like a date and all she wanted was for him to grab her, force her against the wall and tear her clothes off. Dating? This was not what she was used to. 'Shit, you invited him, Frost. You knew what you were doing,' she thought.

"Not much to tell, besides, would a skilled stalker such as yourself really need to ask?"

"Touche, unfortunately my time and resources have been otherwise occupied."

"Ok, I'll give you a little leeway. Born and raised locally, no siblings, my parents passed away about eight years ago. I work, I eat, I sleep and occasionally, when I'm not being told 'soon', I get laid."

"Such a precise and detailed history, Lieutenant," he mocked. "What can't be found in a file? What drives you? What are your passions?"

"Now, where's the fun in telling?" she smiled slyly.

"Indeed, you are a bit of a mystery, Ellison. While I am enjoying the puzzle, there is so much more I want to know."

"And what about you, Mr. Faeye?" Ell took a long slow sip of her wine, Rob's eyes focused on her lips, the passion and want evident.

"I am an open book, what would you like to know?"

"Have you always been dominant?"

"I suppose, though it took me a lot of experimentation to understand what I need and where my desires come from. I've played switch, for curiosity more than anything else and I've gone through periods where I have had to, let's say, suppress my feelings because of who I was with."

"And are you currently?" she paused seeing the confusion across the table. "With someone?"

He thought for a moment. "Yes, I'm with you."

Her heart raced, as cheesy a line as it was, when coupled with the energy in the air, the lust flowing over her and the smooth and simple manner in which he said it, it was perfect.

"Have you ever collared anyone?"

"Only in the traditional sense. I actually don't agree with collaring aside from play, of course. My views on the subject are not reflective of the community but I have an issue with the concept of ownership that a collar typically portrays. While it is a source of pride and even a symbol of love and devotion in its basic premise, it is often viewed as something else. I have no wish to own."

"The traditional sense?" asked Ell, confused.

Rob smiled, "I was married. What is a wedding ring if not just a commonly accepted form of the collar?"

"How long?"

"Pardon?"

"How long were you married?"

"Twelve weeks, three days and sixteen hours. They couldn't tell me the exact minute her heart stopped."

""I'm sorry." Ell could see the sadness in him as he spoke. She reached out and gently took his hand.

"It was a long time ago. Past demons I've dealt with and accepted."

"And what of you, Ellison, have you ever been collared, traditionally or otherwise?"

"No, it's never been an option. My profession does not lend itself to building the relationship necessary. It also requires a rather high level of discretion. What is it about the collar you object to?"

"Primarily the ownership aspect. I have no desire to be in a relationship revolved around ownership and have always felt that the premise goes against the nature of the lifestyle. Where does it fit in to a relationship built on mutual love, trust and honesty? Ownership seems to counteract those values. Symbols are fine but they have an intrinsic meaning that often leads to assumption and misinterpretation. If the emotion being symbolized exists, the symbol itself is not required. Is it something you want, something you fantasize about?"

"No. When I was younger and just beginning to understand the nature of it, I would dream of one day being cared for at that level but I know it's no longer an option."

"But it is, if you want it to be, Ellison. As I said it is just a symbol. The relationship, what it represents, that is possible no matter how much discretion you require."

"Perhaps, but it symbolizes certain things that I'm not sure I want."

"Like what?"

"Pure devotion for one. I'm not really built for monogamy."

"Devotion and monogamy are not necessarily mutually dependent items. You've seen me flirting with others over the last few days. Did you question my devotion to exploring what we may have?"

"No, I suppose I didn't"

The waitress returned and set down a plate of fresh tomato

and basil bruschetta. Ell contemplated his statement while taking a bite. It was glorious. A fresh, mildly sweet concoction.

"Wow, this is amazing." She relaxed back into her chair and realized that for the first time in a while she was content. The stress seemed distant and the built up anxiety had seeped away. Even the sexual desire was slightly dampened. It was there, and given a moment's notice she would devour him as quickly as the food on her plate, but the frustration that accompanied it was gone. How did he do it?

"Stop."

"Stop what?"

"Thinking, analyzing, contemplating. Just enjoy it and take a break from everything."

She stared at him, shook her head and smiled.

"So when did those skills materialize?"

"Skills?"

"The telepathy."

Rob laughed, "It doesn't take a telepath to read you, Ellison. You wear your thoughts, worries and frustrations like a badge of honor."

"I'm a brick," she responded with a sultry glare.

"Right, sorry, you're a brick. My telepathy was a gift from the robot overlords. I try to use it for good."

"In that case, I'm glad I've kept you too busy to pursue that endeavor. I don't trust them."

"You wound them, Lieutenant, they are a peaceful people who wish only to subjugate and enslave the populace for their pleasure."

"Mmmmm, sounds fun," she responded, licking her lips, a wanton look in her eye. Her boot slowly made its way up his leg coming to rest against the bulge of his rapidly hardening cock.

Rob steadied himself, "Ellison, I don't think the establishment would be impressed with me tearing your clothes off and bending you over the table."

"Care to find out?" The want was returning quickly.

"Yes, but I rather enjoy the food here and would hate to think this was my last visit."

"But what better ending could you possibly expect?" She had removed her boot and was now gripping him with her toes, stroking the full length of his erection.

The waitress arrived, as if on a very poorly timed cue, and set down their entrees. Ell discreetly retracted her foot and admired the meal. Blackened lamb with light pasta and parmesan on the side.

"Is there anything else I can get you?"

'Yeah, some rope, a soft leather whip and a little privacy,' thought Ell.

"This will be fine, thank you," replied Rob trying to act naturally.

The waitress smiled and left them to the meal.

"You could have asked her to stay and play," said Ell as she cut into the tender lamb.

"Eat up, Ellison, you'll need that strength... soon."

Chapter Twenty-Three

*T*he remainder of dinner was fun and satisfying. The food was terrific, the energy seductive and Ell was able to embrace the night for what it was. By eight o'clock they were headed back to the precinct and she was ready to attack the case with a renewed vigor.

"Thanks for the invite, Lieutenant, dinner was enjoyable," he said as they pulled to a stop in front of the precinct.

"It could have been more so."

"Yes, but imagine the scandalous headlines. 'Police Lieutenant banned from local restaurant for moaning in pleasure'."

Ell laughed, leaned over and devoured him in a soft, deep kiss. "May have been worth it."

"Undoubtedly."

The two of them hopped out of the truck and headed into the building.

"Where are you going?" she asked. "I figured you over paid consultants would be off long before now."

"Normally, but I've been doing some extra work for this real bitch in homicide."

"Funny man. I heard it was for some 'hot Lieutenant down in homicide'."

"The two are not mutually exclusive traits, Ellison," he quipped, hightailing it into the stairwell before she could reply.

'Point Faeye,' she thought, continuing down the hall to her office. As she headed past the bullpen, Baker stepped out, an uncharacteristic awkwardness surrounding her.

"Lieutenant, do you have a minute?"

"Jesus Baker, didn't I tell you to go home and rest up."

"I... I wanted to talk to you before I headed out."

"Ok, what's up?"

"Umm... could we do this somewhere private?"

"Cell's open but you may want to grab a chair, that thing in there will kill you."

"That's fine this won't take long," she said, following Ell into the office and closing the door. The girl was nervous about something. Twitching, stammering. She wasn't herself.

"So what's up?" asked Ell taking a seat on the corner of the desk.

"I..."

"Christ, out with it Baker."

"Ok, about last night."

Ell held up a hand, "Forget about it. We went out. We had a good time. We all paid for it this morning. End of story."

"I just don't want it to get weird. I said some things that I probably shouldn't have."

"So, for the love of god, stop making it weird. You had a few too many, we all lose perspective when we do."

"It wasn't just the booze talking," she said quietly, "but I know it wasn't appropriate and I'm sorry I put you in that position. It's just... well... I shouldn't have said any..."

Ell interrupted her without thought. Leaning in, she gently placed her hands on the sides of Baker's face, staring into those brilliant green eyes. Unable to resist, she pulled the detective into a passionate lovers kiss.

Baker was startled but could not help but retaliate. Her hands slowly worked around Ell, sliding into her hair and gripping tightly. The built up passion and frustration washed over them both. Baker's grip on her hair tightened and drove Ell's primal urges forward. Their lips parted, each pulling back just slightly, staring deep into each other's eyes with uncontrollable lust. As if possessed, Baker pushed Ell backwards, flat against the desk, and pulled the tight olive sweater over her head. Restraining her arms while baring her braless chest in the process. Her hands grasped Ell's tits as their lips met again. Her touch was soft yet commanding. Ell was overcome by a sense of restraint and freedom. She wanted this, needed this, desperately. Baker pinched her nipple and the pain sent waves of pleasure through her body. Moaning deep, she prayed for more. The redhead ran her lips across Ell's neck and down towards her chest. Her tongue flicked out, circling a nipple and Ell's breath quickened. A soft nibble sent shivers across her skin as she bucked involuntarily.

"Fuck, yes," grunted Ell as the cold feeling of hard steel snapped around her wrist. As if out of nowhere her right arm was cuffed and fastened to the leg of the desk. Baker slid her upwards, swiping the monitors to the floor, pulled the second set of cuffs from Ell's belt and quickly fastened her left wrist in a similar fashion. Ell's body was stretched tight across the desk, her arms pulled back and down by the restraints, her ass barely resting on the edge of her desk.

Baker stood, looking down on her with a forbidden lust. "Is this what you wanted?" Her hand tracing gently across Ell's midsection, beyond her belt and down to the denim covered lips of her pussy. "Is this what your body has been begging for, Lieutenant?" Ell's jeans were soaking through yet Baker continued to tease her. Slowly she pulled each boot from Ell's feet before, finally, releasing the button on the front of her jeans. Ell's body was quaking in anticipation. Yearning for more as she struggled gently against the cuffs. The denim slipped quickly free of her hips and she was exposed, begging for more. Baker's tongue traced its way up from her knee, across her inner thigh. Her legs parted as if by feral instinct and her body stretched with need and want. Her thighs were wet from the anticipation and Baker savored the taste as she worked upwards towards the prize. Ell's eyes clenched shut and her arms pulled hard against the metal cuffs as Baker's tongue brushed lightly against her lips, just inches from her rapidly swelling clit.

"Please... please fuck me," she begged and was immediately penetrated by two fingers. Baker flicked her clit with her tongue, her fingers pushing against Ell's front wall, sliding at a slow rhythm. The anticipation was too much and Ell's body began to erupt covering Baker's face in sweet, wet juices. Her mind blanked and her body convulsed as she came hard.

The beautiful redhead stood, leaned over her to unfasten the cuffs and kissed her deeply. Ell instinctively licked the juices from her lips and chin. Baker looked down at her for a moment, smiled slightly, and flushed a deep red before backing away.

By the time Ell regained her composure enough to sit and

begin dressing, the detective was gone. She took a deep, satisfied breath and stared at the door in confusion.

'What have I done?'

An hour later she was still having a difficult time concentrating on the case. Her computer, having been swiped off the desk, was useless. Her frustration was gone but a whole new level of concerns had surfaced. She decided to call it a night and deal with the computer and the rest of the disaster in the morning. She grabbed her phone and fired Rob a message on her way out the door.

"Shutting down, thanks again for supper – E"

"Tugging a thread on Dunder that appears to be holding. Update you in the morning. Sleepwell, Lieutenant. – R"

Ell thought for a moment and texted him back.

"Team meeting at seven, you available? – E"

"I'll set the alarm. – R"

"Better make it six thirty. I may need some help with my computer. – E"

"What did you do now? – R"

"Wasn't me, I'll explain later. Night, sir. – E"

She'd tell him about Baker in the morning and he'd help put it into perspective. It wasn't a conversation for tonight. Her mind was shot. She needed a hot shower and a soft bed.

Five-thirty a.m. came too quickly. She opted to forgo a run on the treadmill for fifteen minutes of pretend sleep. It was worth it. A quick look at her phone on the way to the precinct did bring one surprise. An email from Sebastian.

"Ell, I think your instincts are good. The redhead yearns

for control but she's unselfish. Given the right education she'd make quite the Domme. If she's interested in exploring it, give her my number. I'm always up for another pupil."

"No, shit," she laughed.

She arrived at the PD at twenty after six, ready to prep for the team meeting and praying that Baker would not make things awkward. Not surprisingly, Rob was leaning on her office door, chai latte in hand. He was unshaven and still in the same clothes she'd last seen him in the night before. He handed her the latte.

"Thanks, did you forget to go to bed?"

"You're welcome. I crashed in the 'penthouse' at about four. The thread turned out to be long and weaving but it held up. I'll bring everyone up to speed in the meeting."

Ell nodded. "Prepare yourself," she said, swinging the office door open. The contents of her desk, including both monitors and all peripherals, were strewn across the floor, just as she'd left them.

"Jesus Christ, Ell. Lose your temper?"

"Right idea, wrong emotion. Baker paid me a visit when we got back from dinner."

"Baker 'paid you a visit'?" he asked raising his eyebrows.

"In her defense she came to make sure things wouldn't be awkward after the conversation at the bar and ... I guess I started it."

"I'd say you solved the awkwardness."

"Hard to be awkward when your three quarters naked, cuffed to your own desk and cumming hard and fast. I have a feeling this mornings meeting may be interesting, though. She was pretty embarrassed when the emotions calmed down and she took off in a hurry."

Rob broke out into laughter. "Sorry but seriously, it's too funny."

Ell glared at him as he started to piece the computer back together.

"Just let it play out. She's not highly experienced but she'll get there. Don't make it a big deal and it should help to smooth things over."

"That's the plan but... shit, I shouldn't have done it, Rob. I'm her supervising officer, this could get messy."

"Come on, we both know it wasn't like that and there is no way Baker will think it was. Talk to her, without the cuffs this time," he winked. "You'll work it out."

"If this gets out..."

"Stop worrying, Ellison. It happened and you can't change or deny it. Deal with it, work it out with her and decide what the two of you want."

He fired up the computer and thankfully both monitors were still working.

"All fixed, Lieutenant."

"My hero," she mocked.

"At your service, my lady. I'm going to grab my notes. I'll meet you in the bullpen. And, Ell..."

She raised her eyebrows.

"Next time I want video."

Chapter Twenty-Four

*F*inally organized and settled, Ell found the team already assembled in the bullpen. Her eyes locked with Baker's for a moment as she approached and the redheaded beauty smiled and then returned her gaze to the timeline Rique had setup. Ell was relieved. At least they could put on a professional guise and muddle through for now.

"I trust you're all well rested and ready to go?" she said and there was a chuckle amongst the team as all eyes focused on Rob.

"The civilian gets a pass. He was up all night running a lead on the case. I vote we also add extra style points for the manly stubble."

Rob flipped her a nonchalant finger and she continued. "Ok, Grumpy, why don't you give us a run down on what you found so you can get some beauty rest."

"Shane Dunder."

"Yes?"

"That's the run down of what I found. Our mystery man is holed up in Melbourne, Australia living under the brilliant pseudonym 'Blane Sunder'. Someone went to a lot of trouble to not only ensure his trail was nearly non-existent, but also allow him to hide in plain site. Mr. Sunder has a full financial, educational and career background recorded in all the right places. He has an Australian birth certificate, passport and T.F.N. He is gainfully employed as a hardware tech with records reflecting eighteen years of exemplary service."

"And you're positive it's him?"

He shot Ell a weary, yet still slightly cocky, look.

"His employer for those eighteen years? The oceanic division of Bouton Holdings. But, there's an issue. As much as the fed's want to believe it, Mr. Sunder is not Ανάσταση,"

Four faces went from optimistic to downtrodden in a matter of seconds.

"As I mentioned yesterday, I was able to pinpoint the algorithm used on the entry logs for the Collins break-in. I was cross-referencing the code looking for a signature and was able to find a near perfect match. The Ανάσταση encryption. The signature is unique so I compared it to my data from the Collins office surveillance and, sure enough, it hit again."

"Ok so we know Ανάσταση was involved but the breach could have been orchestrated from Australia just as easily as two blocks away."

"The Collins' breach, yes, but not the Gallery. That system was closed circuit with no remote access or connection. The wipe and loop had to be done on-site."

"So Dunder bolted to avoid the federal inquisition because there was no way to clear his name." said Baker.

"And Stacey Bouton got him off then, presumably, used her family influence and funds to make him disappear. That's some pretty serious loyalty to a pro bono client. Even for an old college buddy," added Jones.

"Yeah, and it would not have been cheap or easy. The guy's been avoiding the full resources of the federal government." Ell glanced back at Rob. "So how'd you find him, hot shot?"

"Skill, talent, hard work and shit load of pure dumb luck. I gave up on tracking Ανάσταση online pretty quickly. He's been out of the game for a number of years and even before that he was a ghost that could never be pinned down. Hard to track a ghost, so I switched to flesh and blood and focused on Shane Dunder as the man we knew him to be. People have habits, things that are not changed as easily as names and locations. I dug into Dunder's. He has a penchant for the 'finer' things in life such as online porn. The feds found over a terabyte of it on his harddrive when he was arrested. It took a while to track down his accounts, and even longer to get a back trace on recent login activity, but with the help of some 'grey area' friends we were able to nail an IP. From there we cross referenced the mug shot to recent surveillance footage of Blane Sunder in Melborne."

"So you were up all night surfing porn with some online buddies?"

"We must all sacrifice for the good of the case."

"Ok, so where does that leave us. We know this mystery hacker Ανάσταση is involved. Deedrie had his encryption software and the same signature has been found at both security breaches. There must be a link between the two of them somewhere along the line. If it's not Dunder then it's someone else from her past. What else do we have?"

"Scribbler will be here in about an hour to try and nail down a sketch of our mystery woman." said Jones.

"I've got a deeper search running on Currtin and variations of the name but I'm not hopeful at this point," said Rique. "If she and Jones' mystery woman are one in the same, the sketch may help us, but at this point we're just spinning our wheels."

"And, we're still nowhere on motive," said Baker.

Ell stared at the timeline, the puzzle was missing too many pieces to make sense.

"What about Downs?" asked Rique.

"What about her?"

"Right now the suspect pool is pretty much empty and motives don't seem apparent. We haven't been able to corroborate Down's alibi and with Deedrie gone she's the sole director of D.B.E."

"Yeah, but she's not a shareholder," said Baker. "Sole director or not, as soon as the estate is settled she has nothing. Mr. Bouton isn't about to go forward with the business and if he did, he'd replace her."

"We know that, and we understand how things actually work, but Downs was approaching possible escorts as Bouton's 'partner'. Is she smart enough to know her position means nothing with Deedrie gone?"

They all looked dumbstruck. Ell had to admit the theory had teeth, the odds of Downs understanding the difference in a shareholder and director were slim. If she thought she could take over, it could be a valid motive.

"It's slim but it's as good a theory as anything else we have at the moment. Run with it but, given the last two interviews, there's no use pulling her in until we have something solid. Jones, I need you to work with Rob and do a deep search into the victim's past. At some point there is a crossover between her and our mysterious hacker. Find it."

"Baker, you're with me," she said, heading towards her office. Baker looked around, unsure, and then started to follow her out.

"If you have a coat and purse, grab them and meet me out front."

Ell closed her office door and headed towards the parking lot. Baker caught up to her half way there. Ell kept going without looking back, unlocked the car and slid into the soft leather driver's seat. Baker dropped into the passenger side silently and Ell threw the car into drive and peeled out of the parking lot. The ride was quiet and awkward. About ten minutes in Baker finally broke the silence. "Where are we going?"

"Breakfast."

"Umm... I've already eaten."

"Yeah, me too."

They continued in uncomfortable silence for five more minutes before Ell pulled into a small, secluded diner.

She came to a stop and hopped out, Baker following along. The waitress sat them in a quiet back corner at Ell's request and left a couple menus. Ell slid Baker's handcuffs across the table.

"You may need these."

Baker took them, trying not to look as uncomfortable as she felt.

"So we should probably talk."

"Do we have to?" asked Baker, unable to make eye contact.

"Given that we will be working together for the foreseeable future, it's probably a good idea."

"Lieutenant..."

Ell stopped her. "Given the nature of this conversation, let's go with Ell."

"Ell, I'm sorry. God this is awkward. I know we shouldn't have... well... you know, and I should have stopped. I had no right taking it that far."

"What? What the hell are you talking about? Were we in the same room last night because I'm fairly certain you didn't start anything."

"But what I did, forcing you like that..."

"Jesus Christ, Jamie. What force? I wanted that more than you know, I practically begged for it and I got exactly what I wanted. You may have controlled the situation but you were feeding off my need every step of the way."

The waitress returned with a couple coffees and they sat in silence until she was out of earshot.

"I... I... What?" asked Baker.

"I don't know if you realize it, your sexual nature is to take control, but unlike a lot of people, you don't do it for yourself. Hell, you didn't even lose your shirt last night and you damn sure weren't looking to get yourself off. It's the classic traits of a sexual dominant and I'm pretty sure you know my leanings."

Baker was uncomfortable and Ell wasn't sure how to change that.

"Jamie, relax. Look at me."

She did as asked, noticing an unexpected tenderness in Ell's eyes.

"Do I look upset about it? Do I look hurt?"

"No, you look... beautiful."

It was Ell's turn to blush. She smiled, "Thanks. You need to know that there was nothing wrong with what you did last night. Well, with the exception or turning beat red and taking off before I had a chance to thank you. You're right that it shouldn't have happened, but not because of anything you did or how I feel about you or it. I'm your superior and it was inappropriate for me to start something like that."

Baker burst out into laughter. "You have to be kidding right? I'm not some needy secretary pleasing the boss, Ell. I wanted you so bad I could taste it. I still do."

"How's it taste?" Ell asked with a flirtatious grin and Baker tried her best not to blush.

"Sweet."

"Ok, so where do we go from here?" asked Ell.

"I don't know. Is there anyway we can just go back?"

"Is that what you really want?"

"No."

"Me neither, but if we're going to explore this there has to be some ground rules."

"Like?"

"Like, not at work. We need to keep our professional relationship separate as much as possible, and you need to know a few things about me. I'm not monogamous, I never will be, and as much as I'd love to help you learn and grow sexually there is only so much I can do. I don't have the same sexual leanings as you so my understanding is academic at best."

"I'm not looking for monogamy. I don't know what I'm looking for. Hell, I'd never even been with another woman before last night."

"Seriously?" Given how well it went, Ell was surprised.

"Seriously. My history has been sparse and unfulfilling. What I felt when I pushed you onto that desk, the rush of emotion, I've never felt anything even close to that before.

Honestly, I don't know what I want, but I don't want to give up the opportunity to feel that again."

Ell reached across the table and gently cupped her hand. "Let's just play it by ear, at some point we'll figure out what it is."

"I'd like that."

"And, if you are interested in exploring the dominant psyche further I have a friend that can help." She said it without even beginning to think through the ramifications of exposing her relationship with Sebastian.

"Let me think on it. And, thanks for... well... being you."

"No need to thank me for that. No matter how hard I try, that's the one thing I can't change."

Chapter Twenty-Five

*T*hings were moving quickly when they arrived back at the precinct. Rob and Jones were making headway on the search for a link between the hacker Ανάσταση and Deedrie Bouton. Despite being unable to identify the hacker, they had been able to locate a very early copy of the Ανάσταση signature in an unexpected piece of code.

"Twitter," said Rob.

"Twitter?" asked Ell.

"We were brainstorming where Deedrie and Ανάσταση could have met, what would have brought them together. The two of them seemed like an odd pairing. Jones mentioned that there was something in the case files about Deedrie's first business being something 'techie' so we pulled up your notes. Deedrie sold her business to Twitter and they instituted a number of the features she already had in place. It got me thinking. About three years ago a small group of hackers, claiming to be 'Anonymous', released a stolen chunk of the Twitter source code. It was a huge breach and Twitter immediately took action and rewrote a massive section of their security code to protect users. The original source code is still available online so I pulled down a copy and began to analyze it. The Ανάσταση signature can be found in three separate functions."

"So Deedrie's code was written by Ανάσταση and incorporated into Twitter when they bought her out?"

"That's the assumption."

"Jesus, she was what, sixteen when they bought her out? Her sister wouldn't have crossed paths with Dunder until college so that definitely rules him out."

"Which we expected. Jones is running a background check on friends, classmates, everyone she knew, to see if we can locate a link. We figured a quick chat with Mr. Bouton may also help shed some light on who wrote the code."

"I'll get him on the line as soon as possible. In the meantime, keep on it."

Ell headed back to her office and placed the call. James Bouton was not in the office but his secretary promised to have him call as soon as he arrived. Ell left both her office and cell number.

Since she had time, she headed up to the third floor where Scribbler's calm sanctuary was located. The room was like nothing else in the precinct. It was specifically setup to allow for a calm and relaxing atmosphere. Warm wood furnishings, neutral paint tones, plenty of natural light and extremely comfortable, fabric couches. Denise insisted it was the best way to gently coax a solid description from a witness. Ell figured it was just a good excuse for a swanky office, but the woman got results so who was she to argue.

She peeked through a small window and noticed Scribbler hard at work, a beautiful, leggy blond sitting across from her with her eyes closed. Ell chose not to disturb them but made sure that Denise saw her give the universal 'call me' sign, mocking a phone with her thumb and pinky. Scribbler nodded and Ell headed back downstairs.

Rique snagged her just as she came off the elevator. His eyes wide with discovery.

"L.T. you need to see this." She fell into step behind him. "While digging into Downs I decided to run an automated routine on variations of Rosee Currtin just to see what may jump out," he continued heading across the bullpen to the whiteboard timeline.

"Coincidence?"

Ell stared at the board and began to curse.

"Rob," she called, pulling him away from Jones' desk where the two of them were cross-referencing a series of searches on associates of Deedrie Bouton. He walked over and she motioned to the board.

"Start concentrating on women. White, possibly dark hair though it could have been a wig."

"And a size five shoe," called Baker from across the room.

"What she said."

The team dug in and Ell headed back to her office. She wasn't there fifteen minutes when the phone rang.

"Lieutenant Frost."

"Good morning, Lieutenant. This is Keith calling from Commander Nuez's office. The Commander would like a few moments of your time, if you are available."

"Frost, it's Keith. The Commander wants to see you. See how much quicker that would have been."

"Yes, Lieutenant. May I inform the Commander that you are available?"

"Christ," she muttered. "I'll be there in five."

She locked her computer and headed up. Keith greeted her upon arrival and she cut him off. "Heading in, thanks Keith."

"You're welcome, Lieutenant," he said as she closed the door behind her.

"Lieutenant."

"Commander, the cyborg appears to be back at full operational standards. What can I do for you?"

"Stop scaring my assistant for starters. I understand you've agreed to an exclusive interview on the Bouton case."

Shit, it had totally slipped her mind.

"Honestly sir, it was my only option. The reporter was about to go live with rumors about the connection between Bouton and Collins. I should have ran it past you but it was extremely time sensitive."

"Ell, it's fine. I just wanted to know what you plan on telling her. Has there been a break in the case?"

"A break? No, but we do have a few leads that we're beginning to tie together. We are actively tracking an online hacker that goes by Ανάσταση. She's tied to both Bouton and the Collins break-in. We're not sure how involved she may be but her alias keeps popping up."

"Do you plan to go live with any of this?"

"Quite frankly, I don't have a clue. With everything coming down so quickly I haven't had time to even think about the interview. How'd you hear about it?"

"PR received a call from Cindy Shepard with the Chronicle. She was trying to figure out what time she needed to arrive for the interview and what the protocol was. Needless to say, they were confused."

"Shit, sorry."

"No need, Lieutenant. The interview is booked for noon and PR would like you available at eleven-thirty for a briefing. I hope the timeline works but the case takes priority. If something breaks just give us a heads up and we'll take care of re-booking the interview."

"Thanks, it feels like we're turning a corner on this one. Still short on suspects and motives, but the pieces are starting to line up."

"Piece by piece, I know you'll get there. Now, go put a few more together while you can."

"Thanks, Commander."

She headed back to her office, settled into her chair and her phone immediately rang again.

'Oh, come on,' she thought as she picked it up.

"Lieutenant Frost."

"Lieutenant, Denise Cue. You wanted me to call?"

"Thanks Denise, I just wanted to follow up on this mornings sketch. Anything I should know?"

"Just that you don't make this easy. Witness was half cut at the time, and her memory is blurry as hell. We're just taking a break now before starting to revise the details. Should be another hour, maybe two if I need to keep dragging it out of her."

"Ok, fire the sketch down as soon as you have something

workable. Honestly, I have no idea if this woman ties in but, at this point, we can use any lead available."

"You'll have it as soon as I'm done with it."

"Can't ask for much more than that," she said, looking around her private cell and remembering Scribblers luxury villa on the third. She nearly laughed at the irony of the statement.

She waited a moment, half expecting another call, part of her ready to toss the phone against the wall should it ring. After two minutes of silence she relaxed and turned back to her computer. She moved her mouse to remove the screen saver and was greeted with a series of alerts.

"Signature detected, TCP/IP configuration rerouting, Traceroute enabled."

'What the fuck?'

With a deep sigh she pulled herself back out of the chair and headed across the hall. Rob was nowhere to be seen.

"Jones, where's the tech slave?"

"Finally crashed, I think he headed to the bunks."

Ell turned on her heel and headed down to find him. Luckily there was only one bunk in use so she didn't have to search. She was about to open the door, sneak in and wake him gently but she stopped short. Instead, she knocked and waited for a reply. When none came she knocked louder. A groggy voice came from inside.

"Unngngnm, what?"

"No sleep for the brilliant."

He opened the door, shirtless, tired and looking extremely gorgeous. Ell surveyed his half naked body, resisting the urge to run a hand across his chest.

"Sorry," she said in a quiet, dreamy voice.

"I can think of much better ways to wake me up."

"I... oh hell." She leaned in and kissed him softly, nibbling his lip as he pulled back.

"Much better. What can I help you with, Lieutenant?"

"I'm not sure what you did to my computer this morning but it's A.F.U. at the moment."

"A.F.U.?"

"All fucked up."

"Nice," he smiled. "What's it doing?"

"Nothing, it's just giving me some damn alert box about an OP signature being routed or some such gibberish."

His eyes shot to full alert. "Signature detected, traceroute enabled?"

"Something like that. Why?"

He didn't answer, instead he was at a full sprint heading for the stairs and taking them two at a time. She followed quickly, unsure why but suspecting it was something important. Rob slid around the corner to her office, barely keeping his footing, tossed himself into the desk chair and went to work. His fingers were a flurry, eyes in a deep squint. Ell rounded the corner, ready to ask for an explanation but he held up a hand to stop her.

"Not now, five minutes," directing his full concentration back to the machine. Ell leaned against the door jam watching him work and amazed at the transformation.

"Come on you bitch, make a mistake," he muttered.

Frustration and excitement were apparent through his concentration. He paused for a second, as if in thought, then attacked the keyboard again.

"Malaysia? Find a better proxy. Jesus, twelve deep? Who the fuck are you?"

Another flurry of keystrokes were followed by a self-satisfying grin. "Nailed your ass."

He leaned back with a deep, hard sigh and looked up at Ell. She was eyeing him with deep attraction and curiosity.

"Care to explain, Mr. Wizard?"

"After seeing the lengths Ανάσταση went to in order to cover her tracks at Collins, I setup a few extra security procedures on the case files. I figured, in her shoes, if you were getting close I'd make damn sure I knew so I could take measures to wipe data, mislead or run. I setup a hidden script to flag any erroneous access using the Ανάσταση signature as a cross-reference. I figured I could backtrack the connection if she tried to weasel her way in."

"And?"

"And she bit. She used your account because you had the access she needed. Now that the files are encrypted she couldn't simply hack the server, she needed to route through a machine with the decryption software in place and she needed a user account with high enough clearance for full access to the case files. Bitch routed through twelve proxies on four continents to get here, but I hit it in time and was able to hide the backtrack long enough that she didn't know it was happening. She was too busy erasing files and backups to realize I was there."

"Hold on, did you just say 'erasing files and backups'?"

"Had to keep her busy doing something, but I've got a full bit scrape of everything she touched. I'll have you back up in about ten minutes. You're missing the point. I nailed her IP and it's local. Ties back to a Verizon hardline."

"Text me the IP address along with some details on the breach, how it occurred and whatever the hell you just said you did. Verizon's not going to release any data without a warrant so I'll need anything you can give me."

Ell snagged her phone and dialed D.A. Jason Stranik.

"Hello?"

"Stranik, I need a telecom trace warrant in a hurry."

"Prank call?" he asked snidely.

"Close, elite hacker attempting to penetrate the precinct network and delete an active investigation."

"You have an IP address?"

"Yeah, It's a Verizon hardline."

"Not very elite if you were able to trace it."

"I'm wounded, it wasn't me. Apparently the overpaid consultants we hire are occasionally worth it."

Rob gave her the finger, never looking up from the computer as he continued to restore the damage Ανάσταση had done.

"Send me the data you have on the breach, I'll find a friendly judge and hopefully have you something in the next couple hours."

"As fast as you can, this has ties to Bouton, in case that helps."

"Can't hurt."

Ell disconnected and left Rob working on the files so she could go update the team. She did a quick check in with each of them, bringing them up to speed as she did. Nothing new had popped on their end, but they continued to slug through the background information in hopes of finding something that may tie back.

Baker was alone, staring at the timeline, when Ell came over. She gave her a quick rundown on Rob's progress, trying desperately not to get lost in her beautiful eyes. Jamie gave her a knowing smile and she returned it, grasping her hand for a moment and giving it a squeeze. As she pulled it back she slipped her a business card with Sebastian's contact information and a handwritten note.

'In case you're interested.'

Ell headed out of the bullpen and back across the hall. Rob was just finishing up on her computer.

"Back up and running, Lieutenant."

"My hero."

He gave a sarcastic bow. "At your pleasure, ma'am. I see this little endeavor has taken about a half hour. If I was vindictive, I'd take it out of your 'dancing tech monkey' time."

"Oh, I think we can find a much more enjoyable way to use that time," she whispered.

His eyes lit up slightly, though exhaustion was beginning to settle in.

"If you're done here, I think you should get back to the bunks before you pass out."

"Care to join me?"

"More than you know, but I'm afraid this pesky murder investigation keeps getting in the way."

"Soon?"

"Soon"

Rob staggered out of the office and Ell sat back down, trying to center herself and remember what she was doing before all hell broke loose. She pulled up her case files, glad to see them intact, and began reviewing the data. There was something in there. She just needed to find it.

Time drug on and nothing new hit her. Was it possible they were simply chasing dead ends? Her mind was churning through the possibilities and coming up with nothing that made sense. She was getting frustrated with the constant circling back just to come up dry. Closing her eyes in an attempt to focus, she tried visualizing the scene one more time. There was something there, something missing but she couldn't put her finger on it. Her desk phone broke her concentration. With a heavy sigh she gave up on it and answered.

"Lieutenant Frost."

"Ell, I think we have something here. We're dealing with blurry memories but we have something close."

Ell almost laughed, Scribbler's 'close' tended to be damn near dead on. She'd yet to see one of her sketches that didn't have a near perfect resemblance.

"Fire me a digital and file the original. I'll get the team canvassing with the image and see if we can pull an ID."

"On its way. Hope it helps."

"Can't hurt," she said, quietly laughing at the inside joke.

She grabbed her cell and messaged Rique.

"Scribbler has the sketch. I'll fire it through shortly. – E"

"Are we heading out to canvass? – R"

"You'll have to take one of the girls, I'm scheduled for a fucking exclusive in two hours. – E"

"It's good being the queen. – R"

Scribbler's email came in while she was messaging him so she pulled it up and clicked on the image.

"Son of a bitch," she said, nearly under her breath. Looking down at the image it now made sense, the scene, the painting, and most importantly, the motive.

"Cancel the canvas and wake Rob. Round table in five. Nailed the bitch! – E"

Chapter Twenty-Six

She gathered everything she had and headed across to the bullpen. Rique and Rob walked in seconds after.

"Sixty-two minutes sleep. Seriously, Ell? The human body can't run on that."

"Be thankful for the nap because the next few hours are going to be all hands on deck."

The team gathered around the whiteboard.

"So what's up, Lieutenant?" asked Baker.

Scribbler's sketch just came in. Ell slapped it onto the board with a touch of dramatic flair and heard a couple gasps as the pieces began to fall into place. The team stood there, silently staring at the photograph like drawing of Stacey Bouton.

"The sister? This is who was questioning the escort about her meeting with Downs?" asked Rique.

"Yep, which means she knew a hell of a lot more about what Deedrie was up to than she admitted. Ten will get you fifty that Deedrie's 'Twitter' code was written by little sis prior to heading of to get her Com Sci degree. And I'll go double or nothing that Rob's IP trace is going to lead us somewhere in Bouton Holdings."

"She's Ανάσταση," said Rob. "Makes sense. What better way to ensure anonymity than to get Dunder off and then make him disappear? The feds were getting close, pinned down an IP trace that could have easily led to her, but they fixated on Dunder instead. Make him disappear and now they're spinning their wheels focusing on him."

"The description fits with Rosee Currtin but what's the motive?" asked Jones. "Why kill her own sister and leave her in such an embarrassing position?"

"Anger, jealousy, and a seriously deluded sense of obligation. Stacey's bought into the 'Bouton' name and she's done so in a big way. Deedrie hated it. She was about to launch a national escort agency using the name itself. It's one thing to separate yourself from the family name but it's another to drag that name through the dirt. Her father felt that nothing Deedrie did would really hurt his reputation. He was his own man and, quite frankly, Deedrie was his baby girl. So what do you do when daddy won't see that your sister is out to destroy him? You expose her for what she is."

"And the painting?" asked Rique

"Digging, at least originally. She wanted to know what Deedrie was up to. When her mom told her about the painting she went searching. After the murder she realized we'd be digging as well, and she needed to cover up the original break-in and wipe the place down."

"I have to admit, it plays," said Baker. "So how do we prove it? No chance in hell you'll get a confession out of her with what we have and if we're right about her being Ανάσταση she could disappear quick if we start pushing."

"So we need to start looking into her and we need to do it quietly. Lund has a partial from the beak-in that we can use once we have the bitch in a cell, but we need something that ties her to the murder. The story makes sense, but before we drag her ass in here we need something else."

"They never identified the crop," said Baker.

"What?"

"The bruises from the crop didn't match the tools on scene, Lund's team were unable to match it with anything they located."

That was it, thought Ell. The piece that had been nagging at her. Why the hell would she take it with her?

"So we find it, quietly, and use it to tie the bitch down."

Rob let out a brief laugh. Ell shot him a glance and raised her eyebrows.

"Sorry, it's just the wrong implement for the metaphor, figured you'd know that," he added with a wink.

"Leave it to the expert," she shot back and the team disbanded with a renewed focus."

Rob followed her back to her office.

"What can I do?"

"If you're not going to pass out on me, start putting together a file on Ανάσταση. Concentrate on proving the link. I'll let you know when the Verizon warrant comes in and we can put the final nail in that particular coffin. As far as I figure, we have her dead to rights on the Collins' break-in and theft, but if we drag her in on it she'll bail out, rabbit and we'll never find her. I want her ass on the murder before I toss her in a cell."

A thought occurred to her. "What are the odds she'll try to breach the system again?"

"It's risky, she'd only do it if she thought there was something she missed."

"We need to keep everything we have on her out of the files for now, if she does make an attempt I don't want her knowing we're on to her."

"I'll let the others know. It may also be useful to add a couple misdirects, just in case."

"Misdirects?"

"An indication here or there that we are actively pursuing someone else. Make her feel comfortable and she may let her guard down."

"Nice, can you work up something reasonable? It'll have to be subtle."

"Subtle's my middle name."

"Rob Subtle Faeye, I learn something new every day."

———

The next hour was productive, Ell began building her case and laying it out. Everything fit. Every piece of the puzzle worked, but they needed the glue to hold it together. Her phone rang again, for a moment she considered ignoring it but thought better.

"Lieutenant Frost."

"Lieutenant, James Bouton, I had a message to call you. Has there been a break in the case?"

Best to play this one off casually.

"We're following some promising leads but nothing I can really talk about at this point."

"I'm going to take that at face value and assume you're not trying to placate me."

"I wouldn't think of it, sir. You deserve the truth and I intend to find it."

"So, how can I help you?"

"We were going through Deedrie's history, I doubt it's pertinent but you mentioned that she got her business start with an online application. Did she have a background in technology? Nothing we've found suggests that she had a strong aptitude for it."

"Dee wasn't computer illiterate, but no, she didn't have an interest beyond the basics. She was very business minded. Stacey got the geek gene, I suppose."

"Really?"

"Yeah, we still laugh about it in the family. Dee paid her a flat contractor fee for the Twitter code and made her sign full intellectual property release papers. When the buyout came Stacey was unimpressed, but Dee made sure she was taken care of. Bought her sister her first stallion as a thank you."

Ell grinned. *Nail one*

"Thanks, that clears up a few things."

"Not sure how it helps but you're welcome. Please do what you can to keep me in the loop. I know there are aspects of an investigation you can't disclose, but we need to know that her killer will be brought to justice."

"They will, you have my word." Ell felt sorry for him. He didn't realize just how much 'justice' was going to cost him.

She fired Rob a message and let him know that it was confirmed that Stacey wrote the Twitter code. One more piece and it fit perfectly. The alarm on her phone buzzed. Eleven fifteen, time for her prep meeting with PR. She locked her computer and headed out. About three strides out the door, it hit her.

Bought her sister her first stallion as a thank you. Stacey Bouton was an equestrian.

"Rique," she called from the entry to the bullpen. His head snapped up. "I've got this bloody exclusive to get to, see what you can find out about Stacey Bouton owning horses."

"Horses?"

"Yup, and be discreet."

She hightailed it down the hall, headed for Media Relations.

Chapter Twenty-Seven

$\mathcal{I}$nterview prep was useless. The media team wanted to know what she planned on releasing so they could temper and spin it. She had no clue. Given the current status of the case, she wasn't sure what to release. The article wouldn't run until the next day, but who knew where the case would be at that time. She honestly wanted to give this girl something newsworthy, but releasing anything of substance, at this point, could tip their hand. PR gave her the standard run down on making the department look good and then set her up in their conference room where she would be meeting Cindy Shepard.

Ms. Shepard was escorted in five minutes later. Ell stood to greet her.

"Lieutenant, thanks for doing this."

"Hold the thanks till we're done. You may feel differently."

Cindy gave her a quizzical look as the two of them sat.

"Listen, I'll be frank with you. Off the record. The investigation is at a critical point, and there is only so much I can release without tipping our hand and spooking a suspect."

"I appreciate the honesty. I wasn't sure what to expect

here so a little trust and honesty is refreshing. I'll return the favor, I have sources with information that has been verified and I intend to run with it as part of my article. If you agree to give me a straight-forward, honest interview, without divulging anything that will jeopardize your case, I'll tell you what I know. If you can convince me it's necessary to hold any of it back, I'll consider it."

It was a fair deal and more than Ell had any right to request. She was immediately suspicious. "What's the angle?"

"The angle?"

"Yeah, the angle. What do you get out of it Cindy?"

"A good night's sleep, knowing I have done what I could to help a grieving family find some closure."

Ell raised her eyebrows and flashed a skeptical look.

"And a decent rapport with one of the city's top investigators. This job is as much about contacts as it is about news. We use those contacts for information and they use us for their own agendas. Those who make something of themselves need to learn how to balance the two."

Ell liked this girl. No bullshit, no manipulation. An honest approach. It was refreshing.

"Ok, so how do you want to do this?"

"Let's start with the basics."

The interview lasted about forty-five minutes and Ell gave her what she could about the case. She was careful not to allude to anything that may flag back to Stacey Bouton, though she did admit that they were actively pursuing a tie-in between the murder and the Collins break-in. She avoided mentioning D.B.E., but did mention that the victim's recent business activities were a source of interest. Cindy kept things simple and let her circle around questions when needed. Surprisingly, a number of the inquiries had little to do with the case and more to do with Ell and her team.

"Reader's want more than just plot, they need to know the characters involved," said Cindy when questioned.

Ell was not very comfortable with being in the public eye and did the best she could to route her answers to the team. She wasn't a fan of the limelight. The thought of a story focusing on her made her skin crawl.

"Thanks, Lieutenant," said Cindy as she began to wrap up the interview. "How's it feel?"

"How's what feel?"

"To be on the other side of the interrogation," laughed the reporter.

"Unnerving," replied Ell with a grin.

"As promised, here's what I intend to run with. I know that Deedrie posed for the painting that was reported stolen from the Collins' Gallery and I know that this painting was commissioned in relation to a business she was beginning to promote. My sources say the business name is D. B. E. I have full incorporation documentation and have been trying to line up an interview with Julie Downs, who is listed as a secondary director. Unfortunately, she's been ducking my calls."

Ell considered the information. Was there anything there that could hurt the case? 'What the hell,' she thought.

"Off the record. I doubt you'll have much luck with Downs, but consider the nature of the painting as a corporate image and it may lead you down the right path."

"Thanks, all business aside, I hope you nail whoever did this, and not just for the story. I've been digging pretty deep on Deedrie Bouton and despite her wild girl image, she was a good person. She didn't deserve it."

"None of them ever do."

They shook hands briefly and Ell headed back to the bullpen, hoping she didn't give away anything that would hurt her case. 'Easy solution if you did,' she thought. 'Get this bitch in a cage before it runs.'

The bullpen was nearly abandoned. Rique and Jones had caught on to Ell's train of thought, digging into Stacey's horses, and had taken off to visit the Greenview Stables in search of something to tie her to the missing crop. Baker and Rob were huddled around a desk laughing and flirting while reviewing some documentation.

"Stranik came through with the warrant and the Verizon data just arrived," said Baker. "Wish I'd have taking you up on that bet."

Ell's jaw dropped, "Bullshit, the IP doesn't tie back to Bouton Holdings?"

"Nope," replied Rob with a sly grin. "The hardline is installed in a condo on twenty-second belonging to a Stacey Bouton, personally."

"You're fucking kidding me. What elite hacker does this type of shit from her home computer?"

"One that doesn't think she can be caught," he replied. "It's arrogant and sloppy. She was at the top of the game for so long that she forgot the basics of covering her ass."

"Print it, hard file it and wipe it from the email and electronic records, just in case. I'm not letting her slip past us over a bloody email trail. Text me as soon as Rique's back, I'm heading up to talk with the Commander."

Baker slid out of her chair and followed her to the doorway.

"Lieutenant."

Ell stopped, the look in Baker's eye sending a warm pulse through her.

"You can take this back," she said, sliding the business card gently into Ell's hand. "I'm sure he's good, but I think I've found someone else that can teach me."

Ell looked past the redhead at the beautiful smile on Rob's face.

"Jesus Christ," she muttered. "Just don't wear him out on me."

Keith was guarding the Commander's outer office, as usual. He glanced up, surprised, when she entered then immediately checked his calendar.

"Lieutenant, I see you do not have an appointment, is there something I can help you with?"

"Nope," she said heading for the Commander's door.

Keith cut her off at the pass.

"If you wish to speak with Commander Nuez I will need to inform him of your arrival and ensure his schedule is clear."

She stared at him for a moment, side stepped him, and knocked on the door.

"Come in," said the Commander from within.

Ell opened the door, turning to Keith. "See how much time I saved you?"

He glared at her and returned to his desk.

"Do you get some sick satisfaction out of riling him up, Lieutenant."

"With my job, I need to take my joy where I can find it."

Nuez laughed and gestured to a guest chair. "What can I help you with? I trust the interview went well?"

"Peachy," she grinned and Nuez winced.

"I really hope I don't regret that."

"Hold on to that thought. We've had a break in the case and I'm pretty sure you, the mayor and the victim's family are not going to like it."

Nuez steadied himself. "Give it to me straight, what's up."

"Stacey Bouton murdered her sister."

His face dropped, "Since you're in this office, I have to assume this is not just a theory."

"I wish it was. We have solid evidence that she is our mysterious hacker, Ανάσταση. Knowing that, I can tie her conclusively to the Collin's break-in. Lund has a partial from the scene which I have no doubt will match. I have a witness sketch that proves she was investigating her sister's new escort agency and I have a pretty respectable motive."

"Which is?"

"Reputation and jealousy. Deedrie could do no wrong in her father's eyes, and she was about to tie his name to a nationally advertised sex trade. Stacey lives and breathes the Bouton legacy. If this came out it could ruin her family, both personally and professionally."

"Seems about right, but I don't hear anything conclusive in there tying her to the murder."

"If there was, this wouldn't be the office I was in. We're digging, off grid and quietly, and as soon as I have it I'll go see Stranik about an arrest warrant. Given her funds and abilities with a computer, we've been keeping this out of the case files and working it discreetly. We know she made

Shane Dunder disappear, if she does the same for herself we'll never find her."

"Why are you keeping it out of the case files?"

She had forgotten that Commander Nuez was not up to speed on the PD security breach.

"She's already penetrated our systems once, earlier this morning. Rob was able to do some fancy techie shit and track her IP address. I pulled a telecom trace warrant and Verizon confirmed it was her home computer. Luckily, Rob had some trap in place at the time or we'd have never known she was there."

"Since I.T. is not scrambling around the precinct, I assume he contained the breach?"

"Yeah, no data lost. I didn't ask if there were any other issues but I know he was doing scans and shit so I assume he's on it."

"I'm afraid to know how much that's going to cost the taxpayers?"

"I'll do my best to keep his invoice reasonable."

Nuez laughed hard, "I bet you will. If you plan on going after her, you better make sure the case will hold. No one involved is going to like it and you know she'll fight it."

"That... is why I'm in this office. When I drag her ass into the box I want you prepared for the shitstorm that is bound to follow."

"If you can nail this down, we'll ride that storm together. Let me know if and when."

"Will do."

Ell strolled out of the office without so much as a glance at the angry assistant. "He's all yours, Keith."

Chapter Twenty-Eight

"*T*ell me you have something," she said, catching Rique and Jones hustling in the front doors.

"We found four riding crops, all various sizes and all belong to our suspect."

"Tell me you got a warrant."

"Based on the Ανάσταση evidence Judge Driker signed a "sneak and peek" on our way over. We got lucky, the stable boy was too busy to notice us. We were in and out, valid warrant in hand, without anyone knowing we were there. Unless someone notices the crops missing, Ms. Bouton won't have a clue."

"Get them to Lund stat, and tell him to rush it. I want to know if one of them matches the bruising on the body."

A crop match would be good but it still wouldn't be definitive. She'd have a hard time tying it to the murder even if the bruising matched. It wasn't fingerprints or ballistics, there could be hundreds of thousands of crops identical to the one used. They needed something else. A witness. DNA. Something more than conjecture and circumstance. She strode into the bullpen to grab Baker and begin another review. Rob was back in high concentration mode, this time on Baker's computer.

"What's going on?"

"Beats the hell out of me," responded Baker. "I was doing a search on Stacey Bouton, looking for anything I could find online that may tie into the case. Nothing specific just global stuff. Anyway, I got an alert from the virus scanner about a blocked download, figured it was doing its job so I kept going. About five minutes later some weird alert flashed on screen. When Rob saw it he tossed me out of the chair. He's been in some 'Rainman' geek trance for about ten minutes now."

"Son of a bitch," screamed Rob as his fingers flew across the keyboard.

"Good with his fingers," commented Baker, earning an elbow to the ribs.

"Shit... come on bitch the bypass is the easy way, take it."

"Is this normal?" asked Baker. Ell just shrugged and headed over to see what he was doing.

"Come on... come on... that's it, take the easy route." He hit a quick series of keys and leaned back in victory.

"Ok, out with it Mr. Wizard."

He sat there as if trying to find the words to explain what happened.

"Stacey had a dial-back trigger in place on a website she created specifically as a trap for anyone trying to cross-reference her name and her hacker alias. Baker stumbled across the site and it fired off a trojan while notifying Stacey of both the hit and Baker's IP. It was old code and the virus scan nailed the trojan before it could install, but Stacey took it upon herself to dig deeper. Odds are she recognized the IP address so she came snooping. I figured a trace was useless at this point, so I followed her hack and tried to guide her into a trap. She pulled Bakers search history but I had it wiped before she got there. Then she went back at the case files. She must not have expected them to be there. I gave her a few minutes to review them since we've kept out references to her, then I subtly guided her into a special file I'd added. On the surface it was a simple timeline of Deedrie's last few weeks, but while she was busy reading it, I had a fairly robust worm snaking in the back door."

"In non geek speak English?"

"I guided her to a virus of my own. It's now running through her computer gathering data and uploading a copy to my cloud service. Based on the average hard drive size, I should have a decent copy of her computer in about forty minutes unless she detects it."

"Is it legal?" asked Baker.

"Given that she downloaded the file while breaching a restricted system and did so of her own volition as opposed to being hacked? It's a grey area. May hold up, may not. Depends how progressive the judge is."

"Run with it for now and let me know what you find. If it comes down to it, we'll check admissibility later. What did she search on the system?"

"She was checking on the status of the investigation, evidence logs, suspect pool. She took a lot of time on my red herring."

"What did you add?"

"Just some notes that indicated you were focused on Downs, I took Riques theory and expanded it. Tweaked her interview to add a few leading questions and a couple statements that could be incriminating. Made it seem like she was planning to take the business forward with or without Deedrie. If nothing else, it will make her think you're focused elsewhere. The search that triggered it all is bound to tell her something, however. She may not think we're looking at her for murder but she knows we're digging for a connection to Ανάσταση."

"So what's her next move?"

"Who?" asked Jones returning from CSI.

"Bouton knows we were digging into her history, but thinks we're focused on Downs as the killer."

"She has a lot to lose, if she's going to rabbit she'd wait until she was certain it was necessary," commented Rique following her in.

"True, so, she's going to want to make sure we stay focused on Downs, but how?"

"Well, if you really were focused on Downs what would you need?" asked Rob.

"Evidence, something concrete," replied Baker.

"Yeah, but since Downs is innocent we are not likely to find any. Unless..."

"She's gonna plant something," said Jones.

Ell glanced over at Rique. "The plain clothes, are they still on Downs?"

He smiled and nodded. "Two shifts, twenty-four seven."

"Give them a heads up and make sure they call in if they see any trace of her. The rest of you figure out what she may have to plant. If we are missing a piece of evidence, I want to know what it is."

Ell turned with a mission, her stride long and confident as she headed down the hall and hit the staircase. On the second floor she bypassed the collection of alpha geeks crowding the elevator and headed directly for Lund's office.

He stared in awe as she walked in. "Slumming twice in a week. Someone alert Guinness."

"Why? You out of beer?"

"I like you better when you're hungover."

"Yeah me too. When my head's pounding all the annoying people just disappear. What's the verdict on the crops?"

Lund looked at her like she was insane.

"You know I've had them for under ten minutes, right?"

"How long does it take to match a tool to a bruise?"

"About ten minutes and I just finished doing exactly that. One of the crops, graphite handle with a brown leather head, matches the bruises in size and shape, but it's going to take me a while yet to prove whether or not it was used on the victim."

Ell hadn't considered that an option. "Is that possible?"

"If it was used on her, then yes it's possible. Likely is a different story. I'll know more in about an hour and, yes, I'll let you know as soon as I do."

Ell said a quiet prayer to the gods of evidence and headed back to her office. If she could tie the crop to Deedrie's death it would be a big step forward and, in most cases, enough for an arrest warrant. Unfortunately, this was not most cases and Stacey Bouton was not most suspects. Too many loose ends and her arrest would unravel. She needed something definitive.

Baker was waiting for her outside her office door.

"Question."

"Shoot," she said unlocking the door and heading in. She was about to sit on the edge of her desk but the image of the

previous night flooded her mind. After a second of considera-
tion, she chose the chair.

"The nature of the crime keeps creeping up on me. Sanders was certain the body was posed prior to death, the blood
settling etc., which means, if Stacey did this, her and
Deedrie were playing some pretty kinky games before hand. I
know this case is delving into a lot of sexual kink that I don't
understand, but they were sisters."

"As odd and unaccepted as that may be, it wouldn't be
the first time siblings experimented together, and by all accounts they were close growing up."

"But not lately. They'd drifted apart. It doesn't make
sense that they would decide, now, that a little kinky incest
sounds fun."

She had a point. Ell considered the possibilities.

"So what does make sense?" she asked.

"Well, if they had a history, if this wasn't the first time,
then Deedrie wouldn't have been put off by it. It also adds a
subtext to the motive. Here's what I was thinking. The two
of them were close, neither ever married and no serious re-
lationships in the past. Let's assume this wasn't their first
time together. It's possible that relationship meant a lot
more to Stacey, being the younger of the two, than it did to
Deedrie. Then six months ago things change. Deedrie starts
experimenting in kink. It's research for her business but
little sis doesn't know that. All she knows is that her sister
is out there partying and getting laid. She finds out what's
really going on, why her sister abandoned her, and it's the
final straw. Broken heart, family reputation, daddy issues,
they all come into play. She goes to see her sister, says she
wants to patch things up, she misses her, blah blah blah.

'Look I brought a crop because I know you like the kink'."

Ell was impressed.

"Solid theory. Prove it."

"Pardon?"

"Go find me the evidence that backs it up. If these two had a history together, there's something out there that proves it. A letter, a friend in the know, a cum stained dress and a box of cigars, something. Find it."

"On it, and... really Lieutenant? A Clinton reference? Time to update your material."

Ell flipped her the middle finger. A beautiful smile crossed Baker's face and she whispered, "Anytime, Ell," as she turned and headed out.

Ell was surprised by the statement and left speechless, staring at the doorway.

Baker's voice echoed through the hall.

"Oh, how the mighty have fallen."

The next thirty minutes were filled with impatient waiting. They were gaining ground but not quickly enough for Ell. For the first time in days they had a solid suspect and a convincing motive. She hit this point in every case. She had her killer, had the explanation, and was waiting for that final piece of evidence that would slam the cell door shut. She hated the wait.

Rob was the first one to call her. His worm had been successful and he now had a full copy of Stacey Bouton's home computer.

"I'm not sure if I want to know what you found," she said before he could launch into it.

"Why's that, Lieutenant?"

"I'm still not certain on admissibility, and whatever we find on that machine could get tossed as 'fruit of the poisonous tree'."

"I've been thinking about that. The only reason for inadmissibility that I can think of would be stolen evidence law. The cloud service is in my name, the code was written and implemented by me and, as you enjoy pointing out, I am not an officer of the law. I am a private, overpaid consultant. Stolen evidence only applies to law enforcement."

He had a solid argument but, honestly, she didn't know enough about case law to make the call.

"Shit, let me conference in Stranik."

She dialed the D.A. and conferenced him into their call.

"Lieutenant, busy day I see, what can I do for you now."

"Just a little legal expertise. If I have a civilian that is in possession of stolen evidence and they hand it over I'm good, right?"

"Generally, yes. With some exceptions."

"Ok, now let's assume that civilian is under a consulting contract with PD."

"This is where the exceptions begin to materialize. The contract itself doesn't matter. Was said civilian acting under the orders of a law enforcement agent?"

"Yes and no, they were consulting on the crime in question and had been asked to do a number of things through the course of investigation, but the specific act in question, the theft of the evidence, was not done under direct order from any agent."

"And the consultant will swear to this, knowing that it could trigger a personal civil suit."

"Sure," said Rob.

"It's not black and white, Lieutenant, opposing council will fight it. I'd say there's a fifty/fifty chance it could be tossed. How pivotal is the evidence to the final case?"

As she hadn't seen the evidence, Ell didn't have a clue.

"It's pretty damning," replied Rob.

Ell's heart picked up pace at those words.

"If it's tossed do I have a case to pursue?"

Ell considered the question. With any other suspect she would already have them in a cell.

"Yes, but this is a high profile suspect with the funds to back a fight."

"Suspect aside, with what you have now would I get an arrest?"

"Yes."

"Then take the evidence and we'll roll the dice. Worst case scenario I can argue inevitable discovery based on the path of the investigation thus far."

A wave of relief washed over her, as much as she feared losing this in court, the decision was not hers and it had been made.

"Can I assume you need an arrest warrant?"

"Give me five minutes and I'll let you know."

Stranik disconnected and Ell waited a moment.

"What did you find?"

"Four digital photos of the crime scene and a handful of other erotic images of Deedrie and Stacey taken over the last five years."

Baker had called it.

"The crime scene photos, anyway to determine when they were taken?"

"Not an exact time but only one is post mortem. The bitch did it Ell, and she took photos as a bloody keepsake."

"Send me copies. I've got some calls to make."

Chapter Twenty-Nine

*E*ll notified the Commander to prepare for the storm and got Stranik back on the line for an arrest warrant. She emailed him the information he required and he assured her she would have what she needed within the hour. She used the time to gather the troops and formulate a plan.

They were not dealing with an overtly dangerous suspect, but precautions were still required. You never knew how someone would react when confronted, and Stacey Bouton had the money and knowledge to disappear if she knew they were coming. Their first issue was locating her. They knew the hack that morning had come from her personal residence, but hours had passed since then. Ell considered placing a call to Bouton Holdings to see if she was at the office, but, given the events of the day, a call from the investigating team could spook her.

"Let me handle it," said Rob pulling out his cell and dialing before she could stop him.

"Bouton Holdings, how may I help you?"

"Yes this is Robin with Sherwood Florist, I have a delivery for Ms. Stacey Bouton and the sender has provided us with both a business and home address. Would Ms. Bouton be in the office today?"

"Yes, she is, would you like me to transfer you?"

"No, I wouldn't want her to know she's getting flowers and ruin the surprise. There's nothing quite like the look in someone's eyes when you hand them an unexpected bouquet."

"Of course, Ms. Bouton is scheduled to be in the office all afternoon."

"Thank you so much."

Rob disconnected. "Location confirmed."

"Robin with Sherwood Florist?" asked Ell.

He shrugged. "I was going to go with Adam from The Garden of Weedin but it felt too obvious."

Ell shook her head but couldn't hold back a smile.

"Ok, we need the layout for Bouton Holdings. The place is a maze, and there's no telling where she'll be, so our best option will be sending a small team inside while simultaneously securing all exits."

"On it," replied Rique heading for a computer.

They attacked the minutia of the plan. Positioning, coordination, team allocations and a list of every contingency they could think of. In the end, Ell was satisfied that they were as prepared as possible. D. A. Stranik was good to his word and an arrest warrant was received just under an hour after her call.

The team was suiting up in vests and weapons so Ell pulled Rob aside. "It's not standard procedure, but if you want in on this I can make it happen."

Rob gazed deep into her eyes. "I believe I've seen enough of the field this week. There is a soft couch in my office calling my name. Take care of yourself, Ellison."

He leaned down, not caring who else was in the room, and placed a soft, gentle kiss on her forehead.

"Go get some rest," she replied. "You'll need your energy for the upcoming dancing tech monkey session."

"Soon," he whispered.

"Soon."

⸻

They approached in silence, keeping the black and whites a couple blocks from the scene. Jones and Baker circled through an alley and secured the rear fire exit of the fourteen storey building. Ell and Rique moved in quietly from the front. She pulled the S550 to the curb and was about to get out when something caught her eye. Half a block down, Stacey Bouton was sliding into the driver side of a silver BMW Z4 Roadster.

"Son of a bitch."

Rique grabbed the radio as Ell found a break in traffic and pulled out in pursuit.

"Suspect on the move. Silver BMW heading south on 4th. Plate number Bravo Hotel India Three. Repeat, that is Bravo Hotel India Three. Monitor and maintain, we don't need to push this."

Bouton had a lead foot and a three-block lead in downtown traffic. Ell downshifted, cut across three lanes, barely missing a four by four, and accelerated.

"Fuck Frost, what happened to monitor and maintain?"

"I'm maintaining, monitoring is on you."

"If you push it she's going to spot us and bolt."

"In that piece of shit?" laughed Ell. "Let her try."

"Keep your distance, Ell, but don't look like you're trying to keep your distance."

Ell flashed him a grin, catching the reference. "Yeah, fly casual."

Bouton took a right onto eighth and headed for the freeway. Ell barely saw it happen and had to slam on the brakes to cut back across and make the turn. The move had her dropping further behind so she floored it while merging onto the freeway heading west.

"Home is east, figure out where she's heading so I don't have to run the bitch off the road."

She let off, maintaining five car lengths between them and trying not to attract attention. Stacey was moving but she didn't appear evasive. It took some restraint but Ell managed to stay back far enough to remain unnoticed. Rique was scrolling through case notes on his cell.

"Shit, there's nothing out here that remotely ties to her. The only record we have of anything west of twelfth is Downs' apartment."

"That's it. Jones called it. She's going to plant something on Downs to draw our focus. Relay the destination and get the plain clothes officers on the line in case we lose her. Whatever she's going to plant ties her to the murder. I want her in cuffs before she has a chance to ditch it."

He coordinated with the teams, both on-site and in pursuit. Ell's phone chirped indicating an incoming text. She pulled up the message on her window display and grinned.

"Crop contains traces of the same lotion as the murder weapon. Skin cells located and sent for analysis. – L"

Ell noticed Jones approaching in her rear view. "Tell Jones to keep on my tail and when we get to Downs' I want her blocking the front of that car. We'll take the rear and if the bitch tries to run for it we do whatever's necessary."

Stacey exited the freeway and took a right on sixty seventh, Ell maintained her distance until they were a couple blocks from Down's apartment. She tapped her brakes twice as a signal and Jones accelerated past both of them and cut in front of Bouton. Ell hit the siren and Jones came to a halt. Stacey was taken off guard and slammed her brakes sliding to a stop. Ell threw the S550 into park and both she and Rique jumped out, weapons drawn.

"Stacey Bouton, I have a warrant for your arrest. Open the window and slide your hands out."

There was no reaction but Ell could see movement within the car. A flicker of flame flashed in the rear window and it took her only a second to realize what was happening.

"The evidence," she screamed and, without thinking of the possible consequences, she rushed the driver's side door. She could see Bouton taking a small torch style lighter to a stack of papers within. She reached for the handle and the door slammed open catching her in the chest and sending her reeling back a couple of steps. Bouton scrambled out of the car and made a break for it. Ell regained her footing, ready to pursue, just as Baker joined the fray and connected with a spinning heel kick to Stacey's temple. She went down for the count and Ell stood back and watched as the gorgeous redhead snapped the cuffs on her quick and easy.

'Man, she's good at that,' thought Ell with a sly smile.

Rique had busted open the passenger window of Bouton's car and extinguished the flames. The papers, eight by ten printouts of the four crime scene images Rob had found, were partially burnt but easily recognizable.

Ell stood back and watched as her team went to work securing the suspect, evidence and scene.

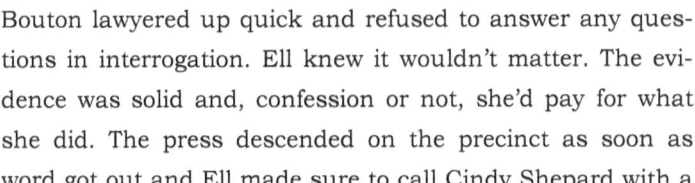

Bouton lawyered up quick and refused to answer any questions in interrogation. Ell knew it wouldn't matter. The evidence was solid and, confession or not, she'd pay for what she did. The press descended on the precinct as soon as word got out and Ell made sure to call Cindy Shepard with a quick quote for her story. May as well make the exclusive matter. The team returned to the precinct, wrote up the remainder of the case files, avoided the press and began sorting through and reassigning the other active cases that had come in that week.

Ell stood in the doorway of the bullpen reflecting on the situation. No fanfare, no glory, just cops doing what they do. Each would celebrate the arrest in their own way. A drink to the deccased, a night out away from it all or maybe some time with someone important. Come morning they'd all be back in here earning a paycheck and doing what they could to solve the next one. It's why she loved the job.

Epilogue

The knock on the door was unexpected, he was early again. Ell raced down the stairs and found him already standing in her foyer. His black jeans hugging his hips and hanging perfectly. The tight white T displaying his biceps and chest. Her heart beat faster and her skin began to warm and flush. He glanced over at her, wrapped in a silk robe, her hair dripping, and grinned.

"Did I catch you in the shower again?"

He did it on purpose and she knew it.

"You're timing is impeccable."

"So what can I help you with today, Lieutenant."

"Bloody computer is acting up, figured I'd cash in some of that tech monkey time."

"Define acting up?"

"It won't do a damn thing. I don't know what the hell's wrong. That's why I called you."

"Always worth the visit," he said glancing over her wet, silk wrapped body, his eyes quickly filling with lust. "Lead the way." He gestured to the stairs, his eyes admiring her ass as she walked in front of him.

She lead him into her office, he took one look around and raised an eyebrow in her direction. The computer was in pieces, each component laid out, neatly on her desk.

"I don't know what happened but I really need to get some work done."

He saw the look in her eye, the mischievous gleam. She bit her bottom lip, not quite meeting his gaze.

"This is not going to be a cheap repair, Lieutenant."

"Oh," she said, surprised. "Things are a little tight right now," her eyes glanced briefly at the bulge in his jeans. "How much will it cost?"

He took a step forward, she retreated. He looked deep into her eyes and stepped forward again. She was going to retreat but his hand caught her arm and pulled her close. "I think, perhaps, you can work it off," he whispered. She was about to answer when he slammed her hard against the wall, his lips attacking hers. Her body melting in passion as he held her arms pinned above her head.

He released her lips, twisted her arms behind her back and rolled her so she was facing the wall, panting with excitement. He used his body to hold her in place as he removed the belt from her robe. The silk slid off her shoulders and he released her arms momentarily, allowing it to cascade to the ground. Her skin soft and warm as his lips began to nibble the back of her neck. She moaned deeply.

Using the silk belt he quickly secured her wrists behind her back, pulled her off the wall and began walking her beautiful naked body across the hall to the bedroom.

She had been prepared. The bed had cuffs and restraints running to each corner. A selection of plugs, dildos, lube, whips and a long thin cane were laid out neatly on the dresser. He noticed she had chosen not to include a crop. So many choices. He walked her to the edge of the bed, her naked body tingling with anticipation. She stood facing the edge and he wrapped his arm around her from behind, cupping her breast. She tipped her head to the side, her hair flowing over her shoulder as his lips began to trace their way down the side of her throat.

"Kneel," he whispered and she did so immediately. He stepped back and began slowly removing his own clothes. "You look absolutely beautiful, Ellison."

Her body flushed in a mixture of excitement and embarrassment. "Thank you, sir."

He shivered, his excitement evident as his cock, now free, twitched.

"Turn," he requested, and she spun to face him, still on her knees.

She licked her lips as her body began to react to the sight of him, naked, before her. Her heart rate continuing to rise, her skin tingling and her pussy growing wetter at the sight.

She looked up at him, begging with her eyes, and he nodded with his own. She licked her lips once more then ran her tongue slowly down the length of his erect cock. She opened her mouth and began to suck him with a slow, deep rhythm. He moaned lightly, her lips devouring him to the base as she took him deeper into her throat with each stroke. She could feel his response, hear his increased breathing. She pulled back running her tongue across his head. His body was beginning to react, he was close. She continued to attack his cock, begging for him to cum, but he stepped back, quickly separating the two of them.

"Not yet, Ellison. You cannot pay that easily."

He pulled her to her feet, his lips caressing hers. Nibbling on her lower lip as he pulled back just a fraction."

She gazed up at him, her face full of want, need and lust. He smiled, released the silk belt from her wrists and gently laid her back on the bed. He lifted her body, setting her down just shy of the headboard, his body pressed against her, his hands sliding up her arms slowly, raising them outwards and gently slipping her wrists into the soft leather cuffs. His lips traced across her eyes as he pulled the restraints tight. She gasped in ecstasy, the slight pain from her arms being stretched rolling over her as she began to pant. He slowly ran his lips down her neck, his hands gently cupping her beautiful tits. He pinched her nipples lightly and she moaned. His mouth followed quickly, his tongue circling her nipple, her back arching in pleasure.

His hand dropped to her soft, bare pussy. She was wet and yearning. He let his fingers gently brush across her lips as he continued to nibble on her nipple and caress her breast. His fingers dipped inside her but she refused to spread her legs. He tried again and heard a slight giggle. She was playing him and would pay for it. He removed his lips from her breast, grabbed each ankle and wrapped them in the other two leather cuffs. He stood, looking down at her beautiful body laid out before him, and pulled the restraints tight. Her legs parted quickly, being pulled to each corner of the bed. She was spread eagle, panting, wanting more. He strode over to the dresser and perused his options. So many roads to pleasure, but first a little pain. She had teased him relentlessly, after all. He pickup up a soft suede flogger, twirled it in his hand, and then flicked it down hard against the dresser, listening to the smack of the strands. With a nod he returned to the bed. Ell was breathing heavy, her body tingling in anticipation.

He let the soft suede rest gently against her chest, pulling it down and brushing it across her skin. The touch of leather caused her to shiver and shift in her restraints. He smiled and let the strands brush across her clit before raising it. He twirled it in his hand, watching the anticipation in her eyes, and then gently set it back against her chest, dragging it across her tits in a slow tease. Ell closed her eyes, concentrating on the sensation, and he quickly snapped the handle in a full circle whipping the straps against her midsection. The pain was faint but perfect. Her body bucked as she gasped, bringing a grin to his face. He twirled the flogger again, this time allowing the straps to snap down across her breast and nipples. She began to pant as the pleasure erupted through her body. She wanted more, she needed more, and he could sense it. The third snap of suede was lighter, the soft leather landing squarely on her clit.

"Please, please take me, sir."

He needed no encouragement. He set the toy aside knowing there would be plenty of time for toys another night. Tonight they needed each other. Lowering his body onto hers he kissed her deeply and gently slid inside. Savoring the moment as bliss overtook them both.

About The Author

R. C. Butler is a software developer, graphic artist, freelance writer, and poet. Born in Edmonton Alberta, the need to create has been a running theme throughout his life. As a teen, Butler found his outlet in poetry, short stories and architecture, which eventually led to an educational background in software development and graphic arts. The mix of right-brain creativity and left-brain logic are the drawing factor in his love of the software industry.

As an author, he has completed numerous freelance short stories and poems as well as developed and hosted an online writing community. His first full length novel, The Order, was released in 2012.

Ellison Frost will return in 'Honor Bound'.

www.ingramcontent.com/pod-product-compliance
Lightning Source LLC
Chambersburg PA
CBHW030424180626
46812CB00005B/2166